FORTY NIGHTS

FORTY NIGHTS

PIROOZ JAFARI

Published in 2022 by Ultimo Press,
an imprint of Hardie Grant Publishing

Ultimo Press   Ultimo Press (London)
Gadigal Country   5th & 6th Floors
7, 45 Jones Street   52–54 Southwark Street
Ultimo, NSW 2007   London SE1 1UN
ultimopress.com.au

A catalogue record for this
book is available from the
National Library of Australia

Forty Nights
ISBN 978 1 76115 058 6 (paperback)

10 9 8 7 6 5 4 3 2 1

Cover design George Saad
Text design Simon Paterson, Bookhouse
Typesetting Bookhouse, Sydney | 12/17 pt Adobe Caslon Pro
Copyeditor Ali Lavau
Proofreader Ronnie Scott

Printed in Australia by Griffin Press, part of Ovato, an Accredited ISO AS/NZS 14001 Environmental Management System printer.

The paper this book is printed on is certified against the Forest Stewardship Council® Standards. Griffin Press holds chain of custody certification SGSHK-COC-005088. FSC® promotes environmentally responsible, socially beneficial and economically viable management of the world's forests.

Ultimo Press acknowledges the Traditional Owners of the country on which we work, the Gadigal people of the Eora nation and the Wurundjeri people of the Kulin nation, and recognises their continuing connection to the land, waters and culture. We pay our respects to their Elders past and present.

For my beloved Maman, for giving me the gift of literature and the courage to write.

ACKNOWLEDGEMENT OF COUNTRY

I acknowledge the Wadawurrung and Wurundjeri People of the Kulin Nation, the sole custodians of the lands and waters that have nurtured me throughout the life of this novel. I honour their culture as the oldest living culture in the world and thank them for yarning with me about their stories.

My heart aches for you I said, your pain shall pass she replied

Be the moon in my darkest night I pleaded, if it comes to pass, she said

Learn the art of loyalty and compassion from lovers, I said

That shall not be possible, she said dismissively

I shall not let your vision enter my mind, I said

I am a night farer and will find a way, she replied

The scent of your hair has led me astray in the world, I cried

That too shall be your guiding light, if you open your mind, she replied.

HAFEZ, DIVAN-E HAFEZ

I dream this endless dream
Walking on frozen cobblestones in forgotten lands
Where ancient stories have fallen captive to darkness
Where spirits have been taken away

Shadows build a wall around me
Tall and distant, unwavering and unforgiving
Their talons dig deep into my heart
Their coldness inescapable

I reach out to the fire; it reduces me to ashes
I turn to the moon for solace; she weeps behind her vale
I look to the stars for hope; they have abandoned the sky
I surrender myself to the sea; she will carry my tale

A small flame flickers in the faraway land
Nestled deep in the timelessness of time
A heartbeat, impossible to reach
Forty nights lie between us

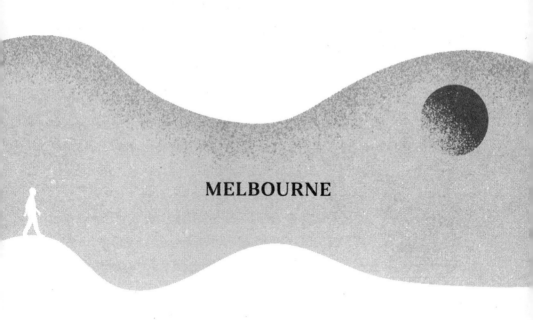

MELBOURNE

I'ᴛ's ᴀ ʜᴜᴍɪᴅ Dᴇᴄᴇᴍʙᴇʀ day and rain clouds are crowding the Melbourne sky. I haven't been able to get Maman's voice out of my head all day. Don't forget to celebrate Shab-e Chelleh, she is saying. You must keep the tradition alive.

On my way to the station after work, I stop at Roshan Supermarket & Halal Meats, the Afghan grocery store in Sunshine, to gather a few things.

Walking around the aisles when your stomach is empty is never a good idea; before long, my basket is overflowing with items I don't need. But I manage to find pomegranates, watermelon and nuts, the customary foods for the winter solstice in Iran. Of course, here in Australia tonight is the summer solstice, but my body and soul are still in sync with the northern hemisphere and its changing seasons.

All day I've been recalling how Maman taught me about Shab-e Chelleh, also known as Yalda. 'It marks the start of forty nights of winter. Christmas and Shab-e Chelleh in fact belong to the same tradition,' she said, explaining that Christmas celebrates the birth of Christ, of light and kindness, while Shab-e Chelleh, the longest night of the year, heralds the birth of the sun and the end of long winter nights. Sometimes she would go even further and say that Christ was only a myth, much to the horror of my aunty Tangerine. According to Maman, the similarity between the two customs illustrated how old traditions were preserved and passed down through the generations, being absorbed into new rituals in order to ensure their survival.

I keep piling things into my basket, so that I end up walking to the station carrying two heavy bags stuffed to maximum capacity; I have to fight off the summer flies by shaking my head from left to right like a cat. When the train pulls up to the platform, I'm relieved to spot two vacant seats. I place my shopping bag on one of the seats to ensure no one will decide to join me and slump into the other seat. The threatened rain has started and I watch the raindrops roll down the windows that separate me from the darkness outside, keeping the outer world at bay and enabling me to dwell a little longer in my thoughts of Maman. After the long day at the office, my stomach is rumbling, and I recall the meals she would make in the colder months: Fesenjan, ash reshteh and ash-e jo. My mother was an amazing cook, so it's hard to choose a favourite dish, but the one I crave most would have to be her Fesenjan, a hearty chicken dish that warms you even when it is

2

achingly cold outside. Even now, in the middle of summer, the thought of it evokes Tehran in the depths of winter.

I have vivid memories of arriving home from school at lunchtime to find the house filled with the aroma of smoked rice and pomegranate molasses. I would kick off my shoes, throw down my schoolbag and run into the kitchen with my mouth watering in anticipation of the gravy so rich and sweet and tangy that it seemed capable of melting the snow outside.

I followed Maman around the kitchen from a young age so I know her recipe for Fesenjan by heart; now, on the train, I decide that this will be my dinner tonight.

My head against the window, I drift into sleep dreaming about Maman's cooking, and wake when the conductor taps me on the shoulder at South Geelong station. 'Train terminates here, mate,' he says.

I drive home through heavy rain that angrily lashes my small car. Despite the poor visibility there is a pleasant scent in the air, a mix of paddocks and the salty smell of the bay. Seeing the cows and the sheep grazing is delightful, though I know that before long the trucks will arrive to take them to their unhappy end.

My house is on a street filled with holiday homes, meaning it is sleepy for most of the year, waking up only for the summer months. My neighbour on the left is a quiet man who tinkers with vintage cars, several of which he parks outside my house (just as well I never have any visitors). He has a dog, a German shepherd, so old that she only barks occasionally and rarely moves; it's painful to watch her back legs give way when she tries to walk. Between our two houses is an old lemon-scented gum tree that is host to a variety of birds: crows and magpies open the day, while currawongs make the sunset call with a sadness beyond measure. To my right is a pensioner who likes a chat, or a complaint, depending on his mood. For a long time he complained about not having teeth to eat 'proper food', but now he has been fitted with false teeth and he hates them. Come to think of it, his conversation mostly consists of complaints. I guess that's what loneliness does to people. Other than him, the neighbours keep to themselves, which suits me.

When I pull up in front of my house, I see Mr Cat standing behind the sliding glass door, waiting for me. His mouth opens and shuts continuously but I can't hear anything through the door. As I enter, he winds himself around my legs, almost tripping me on my way to the kitchen.

After I feed him, he turns his back on me and goes to the backyard for his night-time stroll. 'Fine! Be like that!' I call out and set about preparing my own dinner.

As I tip the walnuts into the food processor, I remember how Maman would use the grinder attached to our black-and-white Laminex kitchen table. It was a laborious task—something I didn't appreciate at the time. She made everything look so easy, so effortless.

Once the walnuts have been reduced to a soft and creamy paste, I scrape them into a pot with chopped onions, spices and pomegranate molasses.

Where is the chicken? I can hear Maman asking.

I'm a vegetarian, I would reply.

A little bit of chicken won't hurt, she'd insist.

Maman! I'm a vegetarian! It's not about eating a little bit or a lot.

I picture her scrunching her face in dismay. *But without chicken, it's not a proper Fesenjan!*

While the stew bubbles on the stove I sit on the sofa with my phone. I'd received a text message before I left the office that I hadn't yet replied to. It's from Habiba, who has a shop on the ground floor of my building.

Tishtar, please can I see you first thing in the morning?

I reply: *Yes, of course. See you tomorrow.*

I bet it's about that social enterprise idea that she was considering, I say to myself.

I put my phone on the coffee table, turn on the news and stare at the TV. The newsreader's lips move, her facial expression changes, but I don't take in anything except the moving images: footage of people caught in floods in south Asia; bushfires in California; ice melting in Sweden; the last-minute Christmas shopping rush; the stock market report; and the weather—the latter arguably the most interesting part of the program.

I go to the kitchen to check on the stew. The walnuts have released a layer of oil, meaning the dish is ready to serve. I spoon a mound of fluffy basmati rice onto a plate and then ladle two scoops of juicy Fesenjan on top.

I pour a glass of shiraz and sit at the table, but I've lost my appetite. I play with the grains of rice on my plate, pushing them back and forth like chess pieces. My head is saturated with the humanitarian cases I have taken on, people's stories, the tragedies they have lived through. My clients' hopes and dreams rest on my shoulders and I'm worried about letting them down.

My reverie is broken by the ringing of my phone. I look at the caller ID and see that it's my older brother, Satyar, who is in Tehran visiting our parents. Satyar has been living in Austria for decades now. I left Iran more than a decade after Satyar.

Whenever he visits our parents, he makes a video call so that we can all see one another; my parents don't know how to use modern technology.

I accept the call and Satyar's kind face appears on the screen. He has aged so much; his hair is completely grey now and there are wrinkles in the corners of his eyes.

Baba is sitting next to him, and he waves at me. In the background candles are burning, and I can see Maman moving around the room.

'How are you, brother?' Satyar asks.

'I'm okay, merci! What a nice surprise!'

'Well, I thought we'd give you a call so that you can join us on Yalda Night,' he says. 'Surprised you are still up! You haven't forgotten, have you?'

'No, of course not!' I say, trying to sound enthusiastic.

'It's Shab-e Chelleh! You can't go to bed early! It's only five o'clock!' Maman calls out, and she shuffles closer. She has a bowl of mixed nuts in her hands and offers me some. 'Are you all set for the longest night of winter?' she asks with a grin.

'It's actually close to midnight here, the shortest night of summer! Four days before Christmas, in fact,' I say.

'Oh, that doesn't matter,' Maman says. 'Regardless of where you are, you must still celebrate this night. It has a special place

6

in our culture.' She peers at the screen. 'What's the weather like over there?'

'Been raining all evening.'

'Oh, I love the rain,' Maman enthuses. 'Did you know that I named you Tishtar after the god of rain in Persian mythology? He fought Ahriman tirelessly to break the drought and bring rain to dry lands.'

'Yes, Maman, I did know that.' Since I was young, Maman has reminded me of the story every time it rained. 'What's the weather like there?' I ask.

'Ah, you will love this—hold on,' Satyar says, and he gets up and takes the phone to the window. He opens the curtains and shows me the view. Everything is blanketed in snow.

'Oh! I miss the snow so much!' I say.

'The Alborz mountains are covered in white,' Satyar says. 'I will send you a photo later.'

My heart yearns for a sight of the tall mountains that overlook both Tehran and the Caspian Sea region.

He then spins the camera around and shows me the lounge room. Small flames are flickering in all corners of the room. The coffee tables are laden with plates and bowls containing sweets, pomegranate seeds, nuts and watermelon, all the essential elements of Yalda Night, and music is playing softly. Maman's copy of *Divan-e Hafez*, the collected works of the revered fourteenth-century Persian poet, is sitting on a side table, together with her glasses.

'What do you think?' Satyar asks.

'It's magical!' I say. 'I miss seeing Madar and Aunty Tangerine at the gathering though.'

'May they rest in peace, both of them, both aunty and your grandma would have been proud to see you succeed on foreign soil,' Baba says. He was the youngest of seven siblings. Aunty Tangerine passed away a few years back, and now Baba is the only one left.

'Yes, amen. Now, show us how you are celebrating Shab-e Chelleh,' Maman says.

I flip my phone camera and show them my small coffee table furnished with one candle, a small bowl of pomegranate seeds on one side and plate of mixed nuts on the other.

'And Hafez?' Maman asks.

I point the camera at the small copy she sent me a few years back.

Now that she has approved my arrangement, we can get to the rituals.

Maman holds her *Divan-e Hafez* close to her heart and asks who wants to seek wisdom from the poet. I tell her I want to know what he has to say about all that has been on my mind.

Maman says a prayer for Hafez's soul then opens the book at random and reads out the verse:

Last night I dreamed that the angels knocked on the cellar's door.
They made the human clay and sipped on wine.
The heavens could not bear the burden of the trusted gift.
My wandering soul was chosen to fulfil the task.

'Wow! Very powerful!' Maman says.

'Hmm, what do you think it means?' I ask.

'You know, I've always believed that you are very special, even before you were born,' Maman reminds me. 'And only the chosen ones are trusted with important tasks in life.'

'And what is his task?' Satyar interjects.

'That's a matter for him to find out,' Maman says as she kisses the cover of the book and places it gently on the coffee table.

After a cup of tea, Maman repeats the ritual for Satyar, who smirks and plays with his moustache. This annoys her—she takes Hafez very seriously.

We eat pomegranates together and raise our cups of tea, wishing for peace and health.

Soon it is close to midnight and I have to get some sleep, so I say goodbye to my parents and brother and end the call.

I need to silence the thoughts; so much is going on in my head. I look at the dirty dishes piled in the sink. I will deal with them tomorrow, I decide.

I have a hot shower to relax my body, but my muscles have turned into iron. I crawl into my bed.

By 1.30 am, when deep breathing hasn't achieved much, I get up and fix myself a glass of warm milk with some honey, sure that this will put me to sleep—but no. Around 3 am it occurs to me that fresh air is the solution. The air is very stale in my bedroom; it smells of rice and the burned-out candles. I open the window and the wind rushes in, flattening the lace curtain against my face. It is really dark outside, and I can hear the waves. My house is only two hundred metres or so from Port Phillip Bay. When it storms it is churned up and restless, and tonight is one of those nights; it is not dissimilar to how I feel. The cool change has arrived after a humid day and the cold westerly wind howls through the cracks of the house, rattling doors and windows. The air outside is so cold the tip of my nose goes numb from standing near the window. It never ceases to amaze me how the temperature can drop by twenty degrees here, and so quickly.

I put my beanie on and go back to bed. I curl up into a ball and shut my eyes. At some point I fall into the land of dreaming, and I hear a familiar voice. 'Are you coming?' it says, brushing past my ear like a feather. It is so gentle it seeps into my soul, and a warm feeling washes over me.

Then something touches my face. I lift my head and see the outline of Mr Cat standing next to my pillow, his ears two small triangles sharply set above his head. He looks like a mini Batman, on a mission to fend off the darkness. He is tapping my face with his paw, his pads spongy and cold. Behind him, the gum tree casts shapes and patterns on the curtain; the shadows grow wide and slim, tall and short, as the lace moves around with the wind.

'Five more minutes,' I groan. 'Just five more minutes. Surely it is too early to get up—it must still be the middle of the night!' I pull the doona over my head, hoping he will leave me alone for a little longer.

A few minutes pass in silence, then Mr Cat plops down next to me and starts purring; I can feel the vibration through the covers. 'Peace at last,' I whisper. I reposition myself in the bed and hug my pillow, squeezing it to me.

I'm thinking about the gentle voice that called me earlier; her voice still hangs in the air. I'm thinking about my dream— the recurring dream in which I am running through the dark on the wet cobblestone streets of an ancient town. I enter a building, the giant door moaning as I push it open. I go from room to room. I am certain that Gretel is there, but wherever I turn another door slams in my face. I can feel her presence but cannot reach her. Then a glimpse of her rushes past. I try to call her but have no voice. And then I wake.

Revisiting the dream unleashes familiar images in my mind, all tangled up and interwoven like tree roots in a forest a thousand years old. It is like a movie reel unravelling before my eyes: glimpses from a distant past, a lifetime ago, many lives ago even.

Mr Cat starts kneading the sheet with his claws, disturbing my moment of contemplation. I flick the doona and he jumps down. I turn the light on and sit in the bed for a few minutes, propped up against a mountain of pillows. 'You just don't give up, do you, Mr Cat?' I say. He is sitting next to the bed, staring at me with his big green eyes.

My phone beeps, and a text message flashes across my screen. *Tishtar! I need to see you today. Will you be at your office? It's urgent. God bless, Habiba.*

It must be important for Habiba to be texting again.

I should get in by about 8, I reply. *See you then.*

Mr Cat has gone ahead to the kitchen, his meows getting louder and louder. 'Alright, alright, I'm coming!' I call.

In the kitchen, I open the cupboard and rummage around desperately. 'Shit, we have no tins left,' I say aloud. I pour some dry food into his bowl and he walks off in disgust. 'Sorry, Mr Cat! I'll buy some more food for you tonight after work, I promise! But, for now, you'll just have to settle for crunchies.' He ignores me and goes to the bedroom with his tail erect like a placard in a protest march.

I turn on the stereo and start my morning playlist, a selection of tracks I have put together for the start of each day. First up is Samuel Barber's 'Adagio for Strings', a choral rendition.

I stand in front of the wardrobe in a daze, staring at my clothes, overcome by a sense of weariness. Finally, I choose a shirt and a pair of pants and pull them on; they don't really match but I can't be bothered to change them. Everything feels like an enormous effort today. In the bathroom I examine my face in the mirror. I probably need to trim my stubble but decide against it. Who cares what I look like anyway?

At 6 am I grab my backpack and start the drive to South Geelong station to catch my usual train to Sunshine. The sky is pink and the outline of cows and sheep in the paddocks on either side of the road melt like soft marshmallows against the horizon, which is obscured by a thick layer of fog hanging just above the ground. The air is fresh after the overnight westerly wind and heavy rain.

Thirty minutes later I arrive at the station and park my car in the same spot as always: the last bay under the lonely tree next to the railway tracks.

An assortment of passengers waits on the platform, wearing everything from puffer jackets to business suits. The scents of aftershave and perfume mingle in the air. Faces are illuminated by devices they hold in their hands; almost everyone is looking down, their eyes glued to their screens as though looking for answers or waiting for commands from some unknown sender. I put my headphones on and continue with my playlist. Track five, Bach: the 'St Matthew Passion'.

When the train pulls in everyone rushes to board. I hurry to my seat: the same seat in the same carriage as the day before, and the day before that.

As the train clatters along the cold tracks the sun peers over the horizon and licks the You Yangs, leaving a tinge of orange on their faces. At their feet, cows are grazing, steam rising from their nostrils. The You Yangs are not as tall as the Alborz mountains, but they have a presence about them, untold stories tucked away in their rocks from thousands of years ago. If only those rocks could talk, what tales they would tell. Gazing at them, I wonder if they separate the lands on either side or protect them. Maman used to say that the Alborz mountains kept the Caspian Sea region lush and green by capturing the humidity inside their apron while Tehran suffocated in the heat during dry summer months.

As we get closer to Sunshine, the farms and paddocks are replaced with rows and rows of mass-produced houses. It makes me wonder how people identify their homes when they all have the same design and are made of similar materials and are even uniform in colour. My stop is approaching, so I make my way to the exit, through bodies all pressed against one another like sardines. This carriage is the third of three; the service is running at a reduced capacity today. On days like this, no allowance is made for personal space or claustrophobia.

As I make my way down the aisle, I scan the faces of the other passengers. Some are deeply asleep, others are staring at their screens, and a handful are reading a book or staring dreamily out the window. A woman is frantically applying make-up; she keeps rummaging in her handbag—for the right shade of lipstick, eyeliner, mascara. My eyes dart to the far end of the carriage, where Gretel sits most days. I crane my neck, hoping to see her, but she isn't there. My heart sinks.

I step out of the carriage at Sunshine, inhaling fresh air before the train releases a big puff of diesel smoke. I walk up the stairs, across the bridge and down another set of stairs, swept along in a sea of people. At the bottom of the stairs, we disperse in all directions. I make a beeline for the cafe on the corner to buy a strong coffee before continuing on to my office.

I have been running my legal practice from a rented room on the top floor of an old two-storey office building shared by a couple of tax agents and a handful of small businesses. On the ground floor is Happy Sunshine, Mrs Nga Chu's small Vietnamese bakery. Her rolls are very popular among the local office workers. I too get my lunch from her a few times a week. Every day, on my way to the office, I see Mrs Nga Chu taking her grandson to the primary school nearby. Early in the afternoon, she leaves the shop in the care of her sister while she goes to collect the little boy.

Next to Happy Sunshine is Sunflower, a mixed business run by Habiba, who had texted me last night and this morning. Habiba sells imported fabric, while a few women she supports also make dresses which she sells to the local Somali community. She calls it the Women's Circle; a community development officer from one of the local NGOs insists that this is a social enterprise and Habiba gets annoyed by her interference and jargon. The women giggle under their hijabs when the NGO worker comes in with offers of help; Habiba says they don't need to be saved.

I arrive at the building just after eight. I can see Habiba at her desk in the back corner of her shop. As soon as she spots me walking past her window, she waves at me and signals that she will come up in a moment. I go upstairs and find my office is cold, so I put the split system on. It's an old building and never gets any sun. The room smells of old timber and damp. It is just big enough to accommodate a small desk and two worn-out leather chairs for clients to sit on. I have a small window overlooking the Sunshine train station, with very little sun coming in. I turn on my laptop and Habiba appears at the door.

'Habiba! Come in! How are you, sister?' I ask.

'*Alhamdulillah*,' she says. 'I need your help, Tishtar.' She sits down in one of the leather chairs. Her round face is neatly framed inside her brown silk scarf; its shade matches her kind brown eyes.

'It's about my nieces—they have no one to protect them. The situation in Somalia is no good, and I need to bring them to Australia.' She is speaking quickly, her voice trembling, and her bangles jingle as she waves her hands in the air.

'Okay, Habiba, slow down,' I say. 'You know I will do what I can, but I need you to give me some information so I understand the case a bit better.'

'Okay, sorry, sorry, Tishtar,' she says. 'I'm just really worried. They are two innocent girls who could at any moment be abducted or killed by al-Shabaab or some other extremist group. I cannot bear to think what could happen to them. The oldest, Fowziah, is seventeen and the little one, Fatimah, is only twelve.' Tears are streaming down her face.

'I cannot even begin to imagine your fear, Habiba, but let's start at the beginning so I can work out what we need to do to help them,' I say. 'Can you tell me a bit about what happened to their parents? Where are the girls now?'

'My sister, she died a few years back, and her husband was killed by the militia three years ago,' Habiba explains. 'The girls have been moving from village to village, staying with various relatives. But you see, everyone is in the same situation. All the villages are full of orphans and widows and no one can afford to feed an extra mouth. Everyone is just trying to stay alive and they cannot really protect someone else's children. I have been sending money to our relatives, begging them to look after Fowziah and Fatimah, but often the money goes missing in transfer. Or when it gets there, the middleman takes a portion and passes on only a little bit of what I have sent. I am trying to find a way for them to get to Kenya. We have a relative in Nairobi who might be able to look after them for a few months, but after that they will have to leave again—he has nine children of his own.'

I have opened a new file on my laptop and am taking notes as she speaks. 'Habiba, tell me, do they have documents to show who they are and that their parents are dead?'

Habiba's shoulders droop as she slumps in her seat. 'They have nothing,' she says. 'Like I told you, they have been moving from village to village, from one shack to another, trying to stay alive and avoid the militia groups.' Her head hangs low, and she starts playing with the corner of her hijab.

Looking at the despair and desperation on her face, I feel helpless. There is no question that her nieces' circumstances are dire, yet without supporting documentation they can't meet the Australian government's rigid eligibility criteria for refugees. Still, I have promised I will do my best, and that is what I mean to do.

'Okay, Habiba, we must try to gather some evidence. It is not compulsory to produce birth certificates, but it is helpful. Meanwhile, can you talk to your relative in Nairobi and see if he can approach the UN office there and get them an appointment as soon as possible?'

Her brown eyes light up with a glimmer of hope. Wiping away her tears, she apologises for burdening me with her troubles.

'There's no need to apologise,' I assure her. 'You are worried, and rightly so. But we will find a way to help Fowziah and Fatimah.'

'Inshallah!' says Habiba, and she asks how my evening was; I had told her I would be celebrating Shab-e Chelleh.

'It was nice, thank you.'

'Did you have family over?'

'Well, not really. We had a video call, though, which was better than nothing.'

'Ah, the tale of us migrants! You must come to our place for iftar. And don't even think about saying no—I will not accept any excuses!'

I recall the first time I met Habiba, a few years earlier. I was rostered on as a pro bono lawyer at the local community legal centre. She had come with two other women from her community, the same ones who are now active in the Women's Circle. They had started a business and had received a notice from the tax office for breaching the law.

'The laws in this country are so confusing,' one of the women complained. 'They tell us not to rely on government money, but when we try to be independent, they punish us!'

'Back in our village, we would just start a business on the side of the road or at the local market. Why is everything so hard here?' another one wanted to know.

It was a good question.

I tell Habiba that I will start looking for a solution to her nieces' dilemma immediately, and when she returns to her shop I bury myself in case law. Not for the first time, it is clear to me that the textbooks have been written by people with no under-standing of the horrific circumstances many of my clients face. But I am determined to find a way.

When I next check the time, it is nearly two in the afternoon. I go downstairs to get a tofu roll from Mrs Nga Chu, who has just walked into the shop with her grandson.

'Hello, Henry!' I say to the little boy.

He looks down shyly.

'Say hello, boy!' Mrs Nga Chu commands.

'Hello,' says Henry softly.

'Go now—sit and do homework!' His grandmother steers him towards the red plastic chair in the corner, next to the tall fridge.

'He is lucky to have you, Mrs Nga Chu,' I say. 'My best child-hood memories are from the times I spent with my dear grandma.'

'I look after the little boy before and after school,' says Mrs Nga Chu. 'My daughter works in the city, comes home late. His dad works in Ballarat, comes home only weekends.' She goes behind the counter to yell at her sister Anh. She hands a bag of groceries to her and returns to the counter with a bundle of coriander and carrots. She starts chopping a hunk of roast pork on the bench and continues conversing with her sister. I am amazed that the pair can hear each other over the thwack of the knife and how much shouting it involves.

Mrs Nga Chu appears to be in her fifties and I assume that she came to Australia as a refugee. I wonder about her experiences of the Vietnam War, her own personal story. Her weary eyes, sunk deep in their sockets, hint of horror and loss.

'Tofu, no chilli, no butter, no soy sauce?' she asks without looking at me.

'Yes, please. You have a good memory,' I say.

'Ayyy, I know my customer, I know what you like.' She grins.

'Mrs Nga Chu, can I ask how old you were during the Vietnam War?'

'Ayyy, I was young girl,' she says. 'Maybe fifteen when war in Vietnam. I can hear guns and bombs. My family, all dead. Bang bang, they were killed in front of me. I watched everyone die. I come to Australia with my aunt and my little sister here, Anh.' She keeps her head down as she stuffs shredded carrot and coriander inside a crunchy roll for me.

Before I can respond, she hands me the roll. 'Five dollar.' She snatches the money from me, then continues yelling at her sister without engaging in any further dialogue with me. It's clear she's not interested in talking about the past any more than she already has, and I don't blame her. There is a sadness in her eyes and I wonder if perhaps she had lost the love of her life during the war. If only I could ask her. If only we could sit down and talk about her past.

As I sit at the desk eating my roll, I think to myself how easily humans become statistical information in official archives, with very little mention of what young people like the then-teenage Mrs Nga Chu and hundreds of Fowziahs and Fatimahs have experienced because of war and conflict. Where are the more detailed statistics? How many broken hearts? How many lovers who never held hands again? How many children who grew up without their parents? History has failed to record these, and will continue to do so.

Mrs Nga Chu's story reminds me of my own early years and experience of the Islamic Revolution in 1979, and the war between Iran and Iraq in the 1980s, and the impact both events had on my family and on thousands of families across the country. Horrific human tragedies that are seldom referred to nowadays. It feels as though our wounds are considered old and irrelevant. A sense of injustice washes over me. I feel outraged at the cruelty of history.

I imagine historical records related to Iran collecting dust on the shelves of libraries and in damp, dark historical archives. We are just like actors; we stand on stage and play our roles and then, before we know it, the curtains come down. When they rise again there is a whole new cast of characters, and we are forgotten.

Memories from that time go around and around in my head, like wooden horses on a carousel in an amusement park.

I reach for my phone to check the time and see a message on my screen. It is my parents' number.

I spoke to them only last night; it is unusual to hear from them again so soon. I wonder why they have rung. I check the voicemail, and Maman's message plays: '*Allo? Tishtar? Darling, call us when you can. Love you.*'

My heart is racing as I dial the number; I am sure something is wrong.

'Allo?' says Baba.

'Baba, it's me,' I say.

'Hello, my good boy, how are you? How lovely to hear your voice! I miss you a lot. Hang on, I put your maman on, she wants to speak with you. I kiss you a thousand times.'

My mother comes on the line. 'Hello again, my darling. How's your day at the office? How's your practice going?'

'It's going well. I am getting more and more referrals now, so my practice is slowly building up.'

'That is wonderful, darling,' Maman says. She sighs. 'It has now been two decades since you've left Iran! It's not easy to move to a foreign country where you know no one and achieve what you have. You have shown great determination. I'm happy that you have pursued law—but don't forget your photography! It's very important that you continue with that, even as a hobby. Your photos are very good. We were so proud of you when you presented your collection at the completion of your degree. The panel of judges were very impressed.'

I can't understand why she has called to ask about my work and to talk about photography. Surely there would have been a better time to discuss my career path.

'You know the Hafez poem last night?' Maman asks.

Ah—now she is coming to the point, I think. 'Yes, what about it?'

'I was up all night thinking about the verse, about Madar, about you and your journey.'

At the mention of Madar, my dream from the night before is suddenly vivid in my mind.

'Now, my love,' Maman continues, 'when we talked last night, you said you had something on your mind. What is bothering you? I sense you are carrying a burden.'

'Don't worry about it,' I say, swallowing the lump of sorrow in my throat. 'We'll talk about it another day.'

'But I can't shake this feeling I have that you are carrying something heavy,' Maman protests.

'Maman, I'm busy now—I will talk to you another time.'

'Well, okay, darling,' Maman says reluctantly. 'I'll let you go. We'll talk soon.'

We end the call, and I try to focus on my work. For the most part I succeed, but going on the train home that evening, my mind is like a congested freeway—there is just no way out of my tangled thoughts. I am thinking about Habiba's nieces, about Madar, about my childhood in Iran. And I am thinking about the path that led me to Australia. I came here to rebuild and restart my life. I wonder if I have accomplished that. In so many ways, I know I have—completing my university studies and practising

22

law. Yet a few pieces of this puzzle are still blank; they keep slipping through my fingers. I wonder what my life would be like now if I had migrated elsewhere—or if I had never left Iran. When you leave your country, a slender thread still connects you to your roots. The longer you live in your new country, the more the thread stretches, until finally it breaks. When you visit your old home you realise that you don't belong there anymore; when you return to your new home, you realise that you have never fitted in. With no thread to tie you to your past, you become a rootless plant. That's not a life rebuilt, surely.

I am still dwelling on this, the train gliding along the steel tracks, when the sky lights up and I hear a huge boom. I jump out of my skin. A bomb has exploded! I am about to duck for cover when I glance out of the window and see the You Yangs standing tall and strong in the distance. I realise that there was no bomb, just a powerful lightning strike. Years have passed since my experience of the Iran–Iraq war, but loud noises still make me jump.

As people get on at the next station, I hear someone complaining about the cold weather: 'It's crazy—it was sunny all day and now look at the sky! I'm sick of the cold, I'm truly over it,' says a woman to the person beside her.

I sink into my seat, put my headphones on and think about Madar. I picture her small face above her shrunken body. I imagine her cloudy eyes gazing out of the window, staring into nothingness, wondering why I had not gone to visit her in the nursing home. Memories of her leap out of the archives of my soul one by one.

TEHRAN
AUGUST 1978

SHE WAS VERY SMALL, my Madar. Barely five feet tall, with a hunched back that carried a collection of her life stories and a bony chest that held her brave and generous heart safe. Madar's house was about forty-five minutes from ours. She lived in Shahpour, a suburb located in the south of Tehran, Iran's capital. She had lived there ever since she was a young woman and married Baba Bozorg. It was a busy suburb, polluted and choking with traffic.

The rest of Tehran wasn't much different: most pockets of the city were quite dry and filled with a jumble of apartment buildings and houses of all shapes and sizes. We lived in a modest house in the central part of the city, and slept and awoke to the sounds of cars, trucks, buses and motorcycles on our busy street. Maman complained about the fumes and pollution every day as she dusted the shiny wooden surfaces of the furniture and polished them with oil. 'Oh my God, I already cleaned everything yesterday,' she would complain to Baba. 'I wish you had listened to me when I suggested that we buy a house in the northern suburbs. Now the value of those properties is through the roof.'

She used to have a go at poor Baba at every opportunity, though dust and property values were two separate issues, I thought. Baba never argued back; he only stared at the ceiling and looked like he was calling to the heavens to defend him. Maman would eventually run out of steam and settle down, or focus on a new source of irritation. There was always something.

In the house to our right lived a couple who kept to themselves and only greeted us for Nowruz, the Persian New Year. To our left was an elderly couple who moved quietly about in their small garden. They were as silent as two old mice. My room, the smallest of the three bedrooms, overlooked the houses at the back. Directly across from my window, two elderly sisters lived with their chickens, plus a tortoiseshell cat and a fat white cat. Next to them there was a young family with three kids. They also had a few chickens, as well as a rooster that woke up the whole neighbourhood every day at the crack of dawn. There was nothing more annoying than being woken up by him early on a summer morning. We only ever greeted that family with nods, as we didn't really know them.

In the front yard there was a small garden where Maman took pleasure in planting flowers and herbs—mint, basil, tarragon, spring onion, radishes and rocket—in spring and summer. Pink, red, yellow and white roses were scattered across the lush green lawn. A grapevine climbed the red-brick wall that separated us from our neighbours. It provided us with an abundance of grapes in summer, and Maman used the vine leaves to make her signature dolmades and juiced the unripe grapes. 'The sour juice from these grapes is better than lime or lemon juice,' she used to say. She was right. Her chicken stew, and her Shirazi salad made with olive oil, fresh lime, red onions, cucumber and tomatoes, was always ten times tangier when she used the sour grape juice.

Maman was famous for her hospitality. She would spend hours in the kitchen preparing a variety of dishes, and relatives and close friends gathered at our house for dinner on most weekends in the summer months.

Aunty Tangerine was a regular no matter what. She knew almost everybody and was universally adored for her vibrant presence. Most people could only stand her in small quantities, though—she was a handful. She always arrived early, to Maman's horror. She would be wearing a bright red dress, the latest design from Italy, matched with her signature Revlon red lipstick. Her Yves St Laurent perfume always preceded her into the house. She would spend a long time in front of the mirror fixing her ash-blonde hair while putting her order in for a *hot* cup of tea. When the tea was served, she would press her long white fingers to the glass to test its heat. She would either give a nod of approval or would request that the tea be hotter. 'Tea must be served straight from the samovar to one's mouth,' she used to say.

Aunty Tangerine's loud laughter rang through the house when Baba and his brothers told tales from the past. The sound of Aunty Tangerine's high-pitched screech made everyone else laugh too.

☾

In contrast to the crowded, busy streets of central Tehran, the northern suburbs, sitting on the skirts of the Alborz mountain range, were home to the more well-to-do families who lived in big mansions in wide tree-lined streets. The air was fresher and cleaner there, and the temperature cooler. Madar didn't like being on her own so she would often come and stay with us. There were two yards on either side of Madar's residence, and each side of the house had its own entrance from the street. Madar resided in the northern half, and her distant relatives occupied the southern. Madar told me that after Baba Bozorg passed away, she had very little money to support her three small children, so she started renting out the other half of the house. Sometimes she would host relatives there between tenants.

It was as though the building had two faces. One was old, lonely and worn out, while the other was painted with the colours of life, redolent with the smell of herbs and spices, an old persimmon tree always laden with fruit in autumn, the banging of pots and pans, the laughter and squeals of children running around.

On Madar's side there was a small fishpond, and to its left a dilapidated kitchen with cracked walls blackened by wood smoke. Old cookware layered in dust and spider webs was stacked on wooden racks above a wall oven. Next to the old kitchen there was a small storage room, where Madar kept bags of smoked rice, legumes, beans and flour, and jams and pickled garlic in massive brown jars. Outside the kitchen, an overgrown jasmine bush was decorated in hundreds of small flowers during spring and summer.

Opposite the kitchen, on the other side of the yard, there stood an outdoor toilet which I was scared of using, as it was dark and the floor creaked and moaned when you walked on it. I always felt as though ghosts were hanging from the ceiling like bats, though I was too scared to look up and confirm this.

Madar's bedroom overlooked the small fishpond. Underneath her window was a rosebush. In one corner of the room there was a large bed with a massive brass bedhead and a hand-knitted quilt. Madar had placed a framed picture of Baba Bozorg on the mantelpiece: a sepia photograph taken on the steps of the house next to the rosebush. In the photo he was wearing round glasses and had a well-trimmed beard. He was holding a book in his hand. I never got to meet him—he died very young. Madar used to tell me that I was just like him, in the way that I worried about people and felt compassion for those who experienced hardship. Baba Bozorg would regularly visit prisoners who had no family and would give them his own clothes, returning home in their ripped and rotten garments. Beside the photo, Madar's old Bakelite Blaupunkt radio sat with a doily on top and one underneath. The radio was always on, from dawn to dusk.

Next to Madar's bedroom was a spare room where she kept linen in a tall wardrobe near the window, and a rocking chair where she would sit mending or knitting while we played in the yard. Baba Bozorg's books were arranged neatly on a timber bookshelf, and there was an old chest atop a red Persian carpet in the far corner of the room. I was enchanted by the ancient smell of the spare room and intrigued by the chest. I often followed

Madar when she went into the spare room to fetch something from the chest or fresh linen from the wardrobe. Whenever she opened the chest and rummaged around it I would try to get a glimpse inside before she closed and locked it again. I longed to explore its contents.

☾

From the time I was little, I spent a fair bit of time at Madar's place during the summer holidays. It was like going on an adventure, always full of mystery and stories, and Madar spoiled me and cooked me beautiful food. It was the only time she made an effort in the kitchen. When she was alone she would usually eat something simple, often just a glass of warm milk and a piece of bread with feta, but when I stayed with her she would prepare feasts. I would keep her company in the kitchen as she pottered about. Sometimes she would ask me to go and get some rice from the storage room. The cast-iron door had a huge handle that was hard to reach when I was small. I would have to jump, and it would sometimes take a few attempts before I could open it. Inside, the room smelled like wood smoke and vinegar combined with dust and old timber. A mouse would occasionally dart from one dark corner to another. I thought of them as the guardians of the stores, but Madar would say, 'Vermin.'

Sacks of smoked rice were piled up in one corner. In the other corner jars of pickled garlic and sour cherry jam sat on the cold dusty floor. Every year Madar pickled a new batch of garlic and only she knew which ones had aged enough and were ready to be eaten. She had an invisible system; she never labelled her jars but she knew exactly how old each jar was. She would hold a jar of jam up to the light and know when it was made purely by the colour.

Some of Madar's relatives lived in the southern part of the house, and they spent much of the day with us. I played with their kids, who were all older than me, while Madar chatted away with Seyed Khanum, their mother. She and Madar were from the north of Iran: the Gilan Province, which lay along the Caspian Sea. Madar and Seyed Khanum spoke Gilaki, the dialect of the region. Because Baba was from the same region, I had learned the language from an early age and understood everything they said, even when they tried to speak in code.

Together, Madar and Seyed Khanum always prepared a meal big enough to feed a family of twenty. 'Seyed Khanum! Come over, my dear girl!' Madar would call through the door that divided the two sides of the house. 'Let us cook up a storm.'

'Oh, we are always there, we don't want to impose again,' the shy and modest Seyed Khanum would respond.

'None of that rubbish is accepted on this side of the house! Plus, I am a lonely old woman and would like to have company. Now that the children are gone, I miss having family around. Food always tastes nicer when you share it with people. Besides, my grandson is here, and it would be nice for him to hang out with your kids.'

Madar was caring and thoughtful. Whenever she cooked, she used to say to me: 'You can't eat alone when you know there is a family next door who doesn't have enough. It's a sin to eat a big feast when children nearby munch on stale bread.' Seyed Khanum was a homemaker and her husband earned a very small wage from fixing sewing machines in a small kiosk shared with another man in the Grand Bazaar of Tehran. Madar had invited them to live in the southern part of the house rent-free and she helped the kids with their homework. 'It is important that these kids have the same privileges as you and your siblings: to have education, to be able to complete school,' Madar told me as she flicked through their textbooks to refresh her knowledge of the subjects.

One summer, when I was about eight, Seyed Khanum and her family returned from visiting their relatives in Gilan. She and Madar put the kaka mix in the wall oven while exchanging the latest gossip from their town back in Gilan. Maman had come over too—she had brought shopping for Madar. 'When is kaka going to be ready, Madar?' I asked impatiently. The aroma of cardamom and saffron had enticed me back into the kitchen halfway through a game of football.

'Let's have a look and see where it is at, shall we?' Seyed Khanum suggested.

Together we peered into the oven.

'Oh, it's done! Lucky you came. We were too busy talking and lost track of time,' Seyed Khanum said as she pulled the hot golden-brown kaka out of the oven.

'Go and fetch the others, while I pour the coffee,' Maman told me.

When we came in, she was pouring the dark and silky Turkish coffee into small cups as Seyed Khanum flipped the kaka out of the baking tin and sprinkled it with a mixture of caster sugar and ground cardamom.

I loved Madar's baking. She made the best kaka. Eating it was only half of the joy, though—I also enjoyed the stories that went with it.

'Madar, why is this dessert called kaka?' I asked.

'Kaka means cake in some of the northern European countries near the Baltic Sea,' Madar explained.

'Which countries?' I asked. At school we had learned about the mountains, rivers and seas in the Asian continent and parts of Russia, but had not gone as far as the rest of Europe.

'Oh, like the Scandinavian countries—Sweden, for example. This recipe has travelled across many bodies of water and has made its way into our small northern coastal towns and villages over the past few centuries. Merchants from Persia used to travel to Baku and other Rus' states for trade. Baku was an important port connecting the east to the west. My father, like his father and many generations before him, was a merchant and travelled frequently to Baku and beyond. He took Persian silk, gold and silver and returned with exquisite wares.' Madar took a sip of her coffee and scooped the crumbs off her plate with a small fork.

'Baku was a part of Persia before the damn treaty!' Maman interjected in her usual patriotic way. 'Thanks to the Turkmenchay Treaty and the wisdom of our then rulers, we lost Baku to the Russians!' She waved her handmade straw fan in front of her face.

After a long pause, Madar frowned dissatisfied with Maman interrupting her and continued. 'My father used to make a lot of money before he lost everything due to his fatal illness.' She folded the corner of the tablecloth and narrowed her eyes.

'Tell me more, Madar,' I begged. 'What did he say about life on the other side of the Caspian Sea? What else is in Russieh?'

'Well, I have never been to Baku myself,' Madar told me. 'But my father and grandfather did trade there for many years. They used to say that many merchants from the Baltic Sea region sailed through Russieh and came as far as Baku on their boats. Merchants from Scandinavia travelled eastwards for centuries. It was like a meeting point where merchants from the east and the west met and exchanged goods. They would bring fur and wax. Legend has it that some of them even ventured down as far as our side of the Caspian Sea,' Madar said.

'What else did he say?' I asked.

'He told me that they had been involved in trade in this region for centuries. My fourth grandfather told tales of meeting traders from Scandinavia. He described the men as tall, strong, and skilled both at sea and in building large wooden ships. They were often accompanied by their families. They camped by the rivers along the trade route, where recipes and traditions were exchanged along with the goods. That's how cultures mix, how traditions travel in various ways. My father heard from his grandfather that the Scandinavians had ink drawings on their skin, and that some wore strange silver jewellery and lived a communal life. He said that some of them didn't have religion!' Madar's eyes grew wide and she took another sip from her small coffee cup.

'Who determines what religion is?' Maman demanded. 'Who is to say what religion is or is not?'

'Well, what I am saying is that back in those days, hundreds of years ago, some of them were not Christian, despite the fact that

Christianity had spread throughout Europe,' Madar elaborated. 'They didn't wear a cross around their necks, unlike merchants from most other parts of Europe. They wore something that looked like a hammer.'

'There! That's my point!' Maman's voice was raised and she spoke passionately. 'Just because they didn't wear a cross did not make them less worthy to be on Earth than the rest! In fact, I guarantee you that they would have been the keepers of old traditions and practices in the face of the tyranny of the invaders. Throughout history, humans have committed atrocities under the guise of religion, and had it not been for brave people, nothing would have survived from such rich practices, some of them thousands of years old. Now we have to visit museums to see remnants of those ancient cultures. Humans are the worst creatures!'

'Go now—go and finish that game of football,' Madar said to me. 'Tonight, I will tell you more tales, I promise.' As the older children fled back to the yard, Madar, Maman and Seyed Khanum turned their cups upside down.

'But I want you to read my cup too, Madar! Can we do mine?' I pleaded.

Madar narrowed her eyes and said: 'Fine, go on—do it gently, though. Put the saucer on top and flip it towards your heart and then put it down. Once we are done with ours, I will call you over.' Obediently, I left the room. Perhaps they didn't want me to hear the adult conversation, I speculated, or perhaps it was a discussion only for women.

I returned to the backyard for another round of ball games, then raced back to the kitchen. My little cup was still sitting on the coffee table.

Madar came over and sat next to me. 'Now, now, let's see what is happening in your world,' she said and then lifted my cup delicately from the saucer. I watched her cloudy eyes as she tilted her head this way and that way, turned the cup around a few times and raised an eyebrow.

'What do you see, Madar?' I asked.

'Hmm. You have lots of adventures ahead,' she said. 'Your path will take you to faraway lands. I can see the back of a person standing on top of what looks like a cliff or a rock. Then there is a big gap, like a vast valley or body of water. Actually, I think it's a body of water, because I see a small boat. See? There? In the distance, I see a figure with long hair.' Madar grew pensive. She turned the cup around again, held it at various angles, and finally turned it towards me and pointed at the figure with the end of her teaspoon. 'Oh! And there is your big nose!' she said, laughing. She kissed my forehead. 'Come on, enough now! This is women's talk! Take your cup to the kitchen and wash it—properly, though, not a man wash!'

I picked up the cup and took it to the sink.

The afternoon sun was streaming through the window, painting the kitchen walls with a warm glow. Before I turned the tap on, I looked into the cup once more. I stared at the person on top of the cliff and, on the far side of the body of water, the person with long hair looking on. *What does all of this mean?* I wondered.

I didn't want to wash away the images, but I knew that Madar would not like to see dirty dishes later on. Reluctantly I turned the tap on and watched the figures soften under the running water until they were completely dissolved. Within seconds the figures had disappeared down the drain as though they never existed.

When Maman left later that day, Madar took me to get bastani sonnati, Persian ice cream. The temperature had reached forty degrees that afternoon, and even late in the day it was still very hot. As we meandered along narrow streets, we could still feel the heat emanating from the brick walls of the buildings; they were so hot they could have baked me like a loaf of bread. Despite the heat, the local boys were playing football with a plastic ball within the boundaries of their makeshift goal posts, comprising two bricks stacked one on top of the other on either side of a field marked out with crooked chalk lines. Every time a vehicle approached they had to move all their equipment to allow it to pass before the game could resume again. We walked for nearly ten minutes—which in that heat felt like ten hours—to the bastani shop owned by Agha Mansour and his brother Agha Reza. When we entered, Agha Reza was busy stirring frozen pieces of clotted cream into the gooey bastani mix. Each time he pulled the large wooden spoon out of the big pot it released a strong aroma of rosewater and saffron into the air. My face was burning from the heat and I would have dived into the bastani pot to cool down if I could.

Agha Mansour rose to his feet as soon as he saw Madar and pulled out a chair for her and a stool for me. He ordered his brother to prepare us a bastani each and poured icy cold water into glasses for us. I had my bastani sandwiched between two wafers and Madar asked for hers in a little cup. 'Hot day, Khanum Bozorg!' said Agha Mansour as he wiped sweat from his forehead with his handkerchief.

'Yes, but today is the fortieth day of summer,' said Madar. 'From tomorrow the heat will break, and the air will start getting cooler.' She scooped the last bit of bastani from her cup and opened her purse to pay.

'No way, Khanum Bozorg, be our guest today.' Agha Mansour refused to take money from Madar.

'No, Agha Mansour, please,' Madar protested. 'I won't come back if you don't take money.'

'No, no, Khanum Bozorg. This Agha Kuchulu is like my nephew—I wanted to give him bastani. Please!' Agha Mansour insisted and the matter was finally settled.

We thanked him and headed back home. I thought how exhausting it would be to argue over payment each time you bought something from someone you knew. At that moment, I imagined growing up being quite complicated.

At nightfall, Madar decided that we would sleep in the yard under the stars. She erected a large mosquito net and arranged fold-out beds beneath it for us. Madar's house was near Tehran's airport, and every fifteen minutes or so a passenger plane would soar across the sky. Staring up, I followed the lights of the planes until they blended in among the twinkling stars. Sometimes I stared so long that I mistook a star for a plane. A gentle breeze picked up and brushed against the mosquito net every now and then, and the smell of jasmine wafted through the air.

The air was growing cooler.

'See?' Madar said. 'I told you that after the fortieth day of summer, the heat would break!'

She was exhausted from the day and within minutes she was asleep, but I was wide awake. As my grandmother snored beside me, my mind wandered to the spare room. This was the perfect opportunity to go and investigate the chest, I realised. I waited until I was sure that she was sleeping deeply, then I slowly crawled out of the mosquito net.

I crept inside. Drawing close to the spare room, I heard a rustling. I held my breath and slowly opened the old door. It was rusty, and its hinges squealed. The light from the full moon lit up the room and I saw that the iron chest was wide open. I couldn't believe my luck; usually Madar locked it with a key. My heart was pounding with excitement and the fear that I would be caught. I tiptoed to the chest, kneeled in front of it and peered inside. On the right side was a small compartment containing a trinket box made of silver, with precious stones embedded in its lid. Next to it there was a rectangular tin tied shut with a strip of fabric. Madar kept greeting cards in that tin, I knew—I had seen her taking cards from it to write to relatives for Nowruz. Beside it were a few blocks of lavender and olive soap. There were some folded lengths of fine-quality fabric, too, brought from Russieh. This was meant to be made into suits for Baba Bozorg, but he hadn't lived long enough. Beneath the fabric, I spied a battered yellow tin with small blue flowers on it. I was sure I hadn't seen it before.

The air felt so heavy in the room and the rustling was more pronounced now. There was an unmistakable presence nearby, but

I was too nervous to look around. I was reaching for the yellow tin when I heard Madar's voice. 'Tishtar? What do you think you are doing in there?' Madar flicked the light on. 'Back to bed with you,' she ordered.

'I heard rustling,' I said as I followed my grandmother outside. 'What could it be?'

'You ate too much tonight, you are hallucinating,' she told me. 'More to the point, what were you doing in there without permission?'

'But I did hear rustling,' I insisted.

'It must have been mice. I'll have to get Seyed Khanum to help me clean that room tomorrow. Now, now, it's past midnight. Go back to sleep! If you have a headache tomorrow your maman will kill us both!'

I crawled back into bed and hugged my pillow. Madar closed the mosquito net and took a sip of water.

'Madar?' I called out.

'Shhhhh,' she said as she sat on the edge of her bed, not looking at me.

'I think someone was in the room. Maybe someone was trying to take things out of the chest?' I whispered.

'Don't be ridiculous now! Not one more word!'

Madar slipped under her sheet with her back to me. She was sounding annoyed now, so I kept silent.

I couldn't sleep for hours that night. My eyes were wide open, glued to the stars, as I plotted to investigate the chest further.

The following evening, when Madar and Seyed Khanum went to the shops to buy a few things for dinner, I stayed home with Seyed Khanum's children. When they were occupied playing a game in the yard, I returned to the spare room. Once again, I was both nervous and excited—I felt as though I was a spy on a mission. But as I reached for the latch on the chest I saw that there was a big padlock on it. I'd failed for the second time.

I was sitting on the floor staring at the chest, trying to think of a way to get inside it, when I heard a big sigh and then something shuffling in the corner of the room. There was definitely someone there! Alarmed, I raced outside and joined Seyed Khanum's children in the yard.

As scared as I was by the presence in the room, I was more determined than ever to see what was in the chest. That night, when Madar was asleep, I crawled out of the bed and headed back to the spare room. Once again, the room was illuminated by the full moon. This time, though, it was silent. I looked around cautiously, but I couldn't see anything or anyone.

Earlier that evening, when Seyed Khanum's son was fixing his bicycle, I had pinched his screwdriver. Kneeling by the chest, I put it in the lock and wiggled it around. After a few seconds, I heard the lock click open. I felt my ears burn with anxiety as I lifted the heavy lid, releasing the strong scent of mothballs. Madar had stuffed them between the bundles of fabric. I spotted the old tin and pulled it out carefully. I touched its surface; its corners were dented and the lid was loose. I was about to open it when I sensed that someone was watching me. I heard a rustling and glimpsed the corner of a white dress near the wardrobe by the window.

'You just don't listen, do you?!' Madar's voice behind me made me jump. I knew I was in trouble but I couldn't help myself: 'Madar, there's someone next to the wardrobe!'

'Oh, the wardrobe is talking to you, is it?' she said dismissively.

'It's true!' I protested. 'I saw someone there!'

'Ha! You think I'm old and stupid, but I have raised children—I know all the tricks,' my grandmother told me.

'What are you keeping locked away here?' I asked. 'What's in this tin? Why don't you want me to come to this room?'

'Ay ay ay. So many questions!' But seeing that I was not going to let the subject drop, Madar sighed, pulled over a cushion and sat beside me on the floor. 'This a precious tin that my father gave me after his last trip to Baku,' she explained.

'But what's in it? What's so special about it?'

She stroked the flowers on the surface of the tin with her wrinkly hands. 'He gave me a necklace in this tin,' she said.

I stared at her—she looked so nostalgic. 'Madar, can you show me the necklace?'

'Oh, Tishtar, I'm not sure.'

I didn't know why she was so reluctant. 'Why don't you want me to see it?'

Madar squeezed my hand and opened the tin to reveal a black velvet pouch.

Inside was a long silver chain and a pendant. The pendant was round; it looked like the sun inside a wheel. 'Oh—it looks old!' I exclaimed.

Madar had become teary; I couldn't understand what was upsetting her.

'It's an antique,' Madar began. 'A few hundred years old. It was given to my father by his great-grandmother Katarina, who had inherited it from her grandmother. My great-great-grandfather had married her in Russieh. My grandmother used to say that Katarina was the most beautiful woman she had ever seen. She had steel-blue eyes and light brown hair and her face had a glow like she was from the heavens. Her ancestors were from the Kievan Rus' going back to the medieval times.'

'How come you don't have blue eyes, Madar?' I asked.

'I must take after my mother's side of the family.'

'Do you have a photo of Katarina?'

'No, but I have an image of her in my heart.'

'And this pendant was hers?'

'Yes, the pendant had been passed down through her family for generations. It is a symbol of eternal light.'

'What is eternal light?'

'You see, the sun here is the source of light.' Madar pointed at the sun symbol on the pendant and continued: 'In the old times, people believed that the sun was the source of life and paid respect to it. Some even worshipped it.' She rubbed her fingers on the pendant and took a deep breath. 'Alas, it didn't bring me any eternal light,' she said. 'First my father died, and then the following year I lost the love of my life. I was only a young woman, with two small children and a third on the way.'

I took the pendant from her and held it tight. I felt a warm sensation in the palm of my hand as I stared at it, mesmerised.

'Ah, this necklace carries a sad tale,' Madar said and turned her face away.

'What do you mean?' I asked. 'What tale, Madar?'

'The tale of a broken heart. An unfinished love story in a land ravaged by the cruelty of men. A tale of losing your home to the enemy. A tale of the heroines who fought the invaders with their bare hands; brave women who died to keep their families and culture alive.'

'What's an unfinished love story?' I asked.

Madar wrapped her arms around me. 'Ah, my darling, you are too young to understand—that's why I didn't want you to come in here. You are not ready yet. There is a reason you were drawn to this room, though. When you are older, you will make sense of it for yourself. For now, though, I want you to promise not to do anything sneaky behind my back again.'

I watched as she put the necklace back into the velvet pouch and placed it back inside the tin. She closed the lid and tucked the tin deep inside the old chest.

'Let's go back to bed, it's late.' She groaned as she slowly got up from the floor.

I felt bad that I had upset Madar, but at the same time I was eager to know more about the necklace. As we were leaving the room I took one last look at the wardrobe—I could still see the edge of the white dress.

I closed the door gently behind me and followed Madar back to the yard. I crawled into my bed under the mosquito net and stared at the stars flickering in the sky.

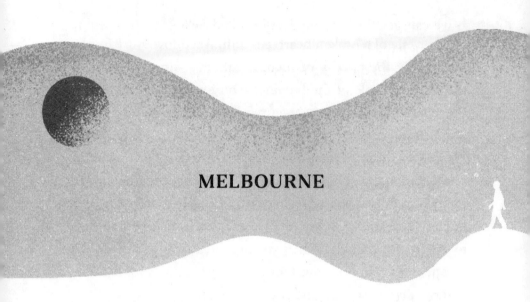

MELBOURNE

IT HAS BEEN NEARLY a month since Habiba talked to me about her nieces, and I haven't seen her around the store much, so I decide to send her a text.

Habiba, I haven't heard from you, I hope all is well with you and your family.

I am drowning in paperwork when my phone rings. 'Hello, Tishtar? It's me, Habiba. Sorry I haven't been in touch. My husband's relatives are here from New Zealand, so I have been very busy with them. But I have some good news. I spoke to a relative who my nieces are staying with at the moment, and he said they might be able to get birth certificates for them from the birth registry office in Mogadishu.'

'That's fantastic, Habiba! Now, tell me: when can you come

so we can get the visa application filled out? That in itself is a job and a half,' I say.

We agree to meet the following day.

☾

When Habiba enters my office the next morning, she is carrying a plate of muffins.

My eyes widen with pleasure.

'I figured you probably needed a sugar hit this morning!' she says as she puts the plate in front of me.

I breathe in the scent of cinnamon appreciatively.

'How's business going, Habiba?' I ask.

'It's okay. I am trying to source donations of fabric so the women can make more garments to sell. We are hoping to get a stall at Flemington Markets, but we need a good supply of fabric before we can do that. One lady, Maryama, wants to teach others how to do alterations so they can earn a bit of money for themselves.'

'So you *are* setting up a social enterprise then!' I tease.

'Oh, don't you start! That community worker was here again last week. She was telling me I can get some money from the council, but I didn't believe her. Nothing is easy in this country.'

'Too true,' I say ruefully. 'Speaking of which, let's get that paperwork started.'

'Do you think they'll be here by next Christmas?' she asks, her face glowing with excitement.

While I don't want to disappoint her, I have to sound a note of caution. 'By the time we gather the documentation we need and get it ready to submit, it will be March at best. I'm afraid there is no way that their visa application will be processed so fast. I have looked into it, and it seems that the only option available is the Orphan Relative visa.'

'Oh, but I am an Australian citizen—can't I just sponsor them as their aunt?'

'No, it's not that straightforward, I'm afraid. The Orphan Relative visa is the only way. The average processing time for this type of visa, all going well, is at least nine months,' I explain.

'Nine months?!'

'Yes, and that is the best-case scenario. It could be longer, up to two years even. I have to be upfront with you, Habiba—I don't want to give you false hope.'

'But anything could happen to them in that time,' she cries.

She is right; the longer Fowziah and Fatimah remain in Somalia, the more they are at risk. Another option occurs to me. 'Come to think of it, there is another way: you could sponsor them to come as refugees. That is possible, but the outcome is less likely to be favourable.'

Habiba is staring at the floor; her enthusiasm of moments before has vanished.

'Habiba?' I say.

She draws herself up. 'Okay, what do I need to do? Where do we start?'

'Well, first I need you to confirm that the oldest girl is under eighteen?'

'Yes, she will turn eighteen in April.'

'Good, because she cannot be over eighteen at the time of application. I need to take your statement and we'll need to provide the details of all your family members as well as your financial situation—bank statements, tax assessment notices, anything that will prove you are able to support your nieces.'

'We are building a five-bedroom house, so that we can all live comfortably. My children can't wait to see their cousins.' She is beaming at the thought.

'Lovely! Now, let's get started.'

I start taking her details and those of her family members. With the exception of her own children, who were born in Australia, everyone else has the same date and month of birth: 1 January. Only their year of birth differs. I double-check with her to make sure there is no mistake.

'Many of us don't know when we were born,' Habiba explains. 'When they filled out our applications to come here as refugees, they just put the first of January for all our birthdays.'

I have seen this date on people's paperwork before, and I always struggle with it. I was doing pro bono work with a group of community lawyers who took on refugee cases when I first saw it. I had been assigned to review files and follow up with clients, and I noticed the birthdate 1 January on the majority of files. I asked the supervising solicitor about it and he explained the reason for it.

'So, people are like cars, we just give them a number plate?' I said. 'Is this the start of the "assimilation" for refugees? To fit into the system, they must have a date of birth, so we just make up one and stick it on their paperwork?'

He looked at me for a moment, then rushed off to his next appointment without responding.

I remember my indignation now as Habiba and I fill out form after form. When they are finally completed, and Habiba is signing them, she says: 'Tishtar, why do you do this? You could be earning lots of money working in the city for big law firms.'

I shake my head. 'Oh, Habiba, I have no interest in making big money from corporations. I didn't study law to make money. If I manage to help you to provide the girls with a secure future, then I have achieved my purpose. But that's enough about me—let's take a break and then get on with the statement you must provide. That's a very important part of the application. Are you up for it?'

She looks at her watch. 'I need to get back to the shop. Could we do the statement tomorrow?'

'Yes, sure, let's do it tomorrow morning. And you should start gathering the other documentation I mentioned, too.'

Habiba frowns. 'But it will take ages to get statements issued by the bank and so on—I want to send the application as soon as possible.'

'I know it's time-consuming,' I say. 'It's important that the application is thorough and comprehensive, though. That's the best way to make a good impression.'

I see that Habiba is looking frustrated.

'What is it?' I say.

'I'm just thinking about the girls. We spoke to them last night on Skype. I wanted to leap through the screen and embrace them. I cried so much after the phone call. It's so hard to support them from so far away.' She swallowed. 'I am just lucky I have my mum here with me. She is such a tower of strength. And she would really like to meet you, Tishtar—please promise you will come to iftar this week,' she says.

Habiba's shoulders are sagging as she leaves my office. I can almost see the weight of her concern for Fowziah and Fatimah on her back. I think how incredibly lucky I have been to grow up with two loving parents who protected me from everything.

After Habiba leaves I call my mother. 'Allo? Maman? It's me.'

'Oh, my darling, we were just talking about you!' Maman says. 'We have been sorting out Madar's belongings. It was her wish to donate all her personal possessions to a family she knew. They came and collected everything with a truck this morning. But she has left something special for you: her Blaupunkt radio. We will post it to you as soon as we can.'

'Wow! I love that radio!' I say. 'It will look good in my study. But why are you only doing this now? She has been gone for some years.'

'Yes, I know,' Maman says. 'We didn't want to sell the house immediately, but it's been sitting vacant for a few years and the developers are eager to buy it. We decided there was no point in hanging on to it any longer; it was falling down.'

'Ah, life is strange,' I say.

'What do you mean?'

'Madar's house reminds me of my dream.'

'Your dream?'

'I have been having a recurring dream for a long time in which I am always trying to get somewhere but never succeed, am always searching, but never find what I am seeking.'

'I see.' Maman sounds distant, as if she is lost in thought. 'Dreams are reflections of your soul, my darling.'

'Maman? There's more ...'

'Tell me, darling—you know you can tell me anything,' she says softly.

'I have been seeing her on the train travelling to work. It's been a few months now.' My voice quivers.

'You have been seeing Gretel in Melbourne?! No, it can't be. I had hoped that the passage of time would erase her from your life!' Maman sounds concerned—anxious even.

'She has never left me,' I say sadly. 'I never stopped thinking about her.'

'How I have prayed to God that she would be gone,' Maman says, distressed. 'I could never offer you any explanation and I secretly hoped that you would never see her again, that you would start a new life and you would have closure. Instead, you travel to the other side of the world and the story continues. Now, tell me, how did it all unfold?'

'I've been travelling to work by train for a while now—I got sick of driving and the traffic. One day, I was standing near the door when a crowd of people entered the carriage. And there she was, after all these years: close enough to touch. I felt light-headed; it was as if my soul collapsed inside my body and I disintegrated into nothingness.'

'And then what happened?' Maman asks.

'I looked at her, hoping to catch her attention, but a few people were blocking her view of me. I slipped away unseen. Soon the edges of my existence softened, and I blended into the thin air.'

'I see,' Maman says.

'Since then, I have seen her often,' I continue. *'Why are you here?* I scream in my head. The more I see her, the more I am thrown about by the forceful currents her presence generates. She is always in her own world and does not seem to be interested in what goes on around her. She often stands near the door or is curled up on the luggage shelf, reading her book. Sometimes she is sleeping peacefully, as if she has not a care in the world.'

'So, she hasn't seen you?' Maman says.

'Oh, Maman, if only I knew. There have been days when I've come so close to reaching out to her, but there is always this wall between us, always something or someone in the way.'

'Oh, darling. I guess Madar was right: follow your heart and the answers will be revealed,' Maman says.

'But when and how, Maman? It's been a lifetime.'

'This is a long road, my love. Remember Hafez's poem? *Everywhere I turned, my fear grew / Oh, the dread of this endless desert . . . this endless path.* Now can you understand why I always worried where this tale was going to take you?'

'Maman?'

'Yes, my love?'

'Will I ever know?'

'Hmm, I think you need to give yourself some time.'

'From the beginning, right from the start, I yearned to know the whole story,' I say.

'I still think you have a bit of a journey to reach the end,' Maman says. 'Promise me you will think about this a bit more—don't jump to conclusions.'

☾

On the train home that evening I am deep in thought when I hear the conductor say something. His voice is muffled. I have sunk to the depths of the ocean of my mind. I struggle to the surface.

'Your Myki card, please.' The conductor is warm and friendly, always pausing for a chat, leaving passengers with a smile on their faces.

I spot Gretel curled up on the luggage shelf near me.

Oh my, you have not changed one bit, I say to her in my head.

Her gaze is locked on the You Yangs, her reflection soft in the window.

I feel as though my body is floating above the train like a small feather. In her presence, it is as though an invisible wave is vibrating through my soul, a powerful current pulling me in. *This is the time, this is the time*, says the voice inside my head.

She tilts her head to the left and glances at the carriage full of people then immediately looks away.

I freeze. My internal organs fold in like an accordion, and all I can hear is my heart pounding in my ears. I wonder why she doesn't seem to feel anything; she just looks around as though indifferent, uninterested. How could she ignore me like this? Maybe she has given up; maybe she has forgotten me. I have no way of knowing.

I put my headphones on and play my music, lose myself in the scenery rushing past outside the window. I feel as invisible to everyone else as I am to her. I need the support of the wall to hold myself upright.

☾

The following day I drive my car to work instead of catching the train, and that evening I drive to Habiba's house.

Her family's home is in the heart of West Footscray, in a narrow street with houses all crammed together. Some are older Edwardian cottages, some are a bit newer and tidier, and there are a few rundown terraces nestled in between. I manage to squeeze my car into a tight parking spot then get out and walk towards number 38. On the street, a few young boys are kicking a ball. A woman comes out of her front gate and puts a bucket of lemons next to her letterbox with a handwritten sign balanced on it: $3 FOR 5, it reads.

Habiba's neighbour, an old Vietnamese man wearing a traditional straw hat, is weeding his garden. He greets me with a wave as I pass his front gate. On the other side, a woman is sitting on her verandah on her scooter, smoking a cigarette. An overgrown pink geranium is covering her front fence and a small black-and-white cat is standing guard and runs inside as soon as I get close.

Habiba's front yard is bare; the only green thing is a small native bush, almost on its last legs.

There are many shoes outside the door and my heart sinks, thinking they must have a lot of guests. I remember how Maman used to drag me out of my room whenever we had guests I didn't know well. I ring the doorbell and a tall man comes to the screen door. I can smell his aftershave through the screen.

He opens the door and offers me his hand to shake. 'Welcome, brother. I am Abi Suleyman, Habiba's husband.'

He is a good-looking man, with short hair and a thin beard framing his strong face. His beard is so meticulously trimmed it is as though someone has drawn a line on his jaw with a whiteboard marker. I glance at the pumped-up biceps visible beneath the sleeves of his Adidas T-shirt; Habiba has told me that he goes to the gym all the time.

'Come in, come in,' he says, ushering me to the living room and gesturing for me to sit on their sofa. There is no one else in the living room and I heave a sigh of relief.

Inside the house it's nice and cool; they have their aircon on. It got to forty degrees at midday, and though it is nearly dusk, the heat is still stuck to the pavement and the houses.

I can hear the clanging of pots from the kitchen and Habiba's voice screaming at her kids every now and then. 'Welcome, Tishtar—talk to my husband and I will bring out dinner soon,' she yells.

I look around, admiring the red floral-patterned rug and lounge suite covered in dark green velvet. On the wall is a photo of Mecca in a gold frame. The TV is on, tuned to a football match.

'You like football, brother?' Abi Suleyman asks.

'Yes—and I am glad you call it football too. Soccer is such a foreign word,' I reply. I'm glad that he is not watching cricket, a game I don't understand.

'Argh, soccer! This is real football! Do you play?'

'I did when I was young. Just with the local boys, nothing professional.'

He pulls up a chair and sits near me. 'So, Habiba tells me that you are the finest lawyer,' he says, gazing at me earnestly with his large brown eyes.

'I wouldn't go that far, but I do my best for my clients,' I reply.

'Here is the thing: I am looking for my nephew, who is fourteen. He was last seen in a village near the border of Kenya and Somalia. I want to bring him here. Can you help?'

'I can try, but as I told Habiba, it is a very difficult process and you need lots of supporting documents.'

He takes his phone out of his pocket and shows me a photo of a teenage version of himself. Tall, big brown eyes and a determined face. He is standing next to a lonely tree, endless desert in the background.

'Abdullah—his name is Abdullah. Both his parents were killed in front of him, and his sisters were taken away,' Abi Suleyman says.

I am still speechless at the thought of the atrocities his family has suffered when he looks at his watch then turns on his radio. 'We'll break our fast soon, brother,' he says as he turns up the volume. A man is reading from the Qur'an.

Habiba emerges from the kitchen carrying a large tray. She is beaming and her face is shiny with sweat.

'Ah, I can't believe you actually came!' she says. Little does she know that I almost didn't. I always find a last minute excuse to convince myself why I can't go to a social gathering.

She places the tray on the floor then spreads a cloth over the rug. On it she sets down the plates, glasses, and bowls of herbs and dates before hurrying back to the kitchen.

The smell of spices coming from the kitchen is mouth-watering, but I am worried that Habiba might have prepared a lot of meat dishes, and I don't know how to excuse myself without sounding rude. I hadn't thought to mention to her that I am a vegetarian.

Abi Suleyman turns up the volume of the radio again, and the sound of the man reading the Qur'an reminds me of life in Iran following the Islamic Revolution, and how readings from the Qur'an were broadcast daily at midday and dusk. I am becoming uncomfortable.

Habiba returns with another tray and this time another woman follows. I rise to my feet, guessing that this must be her mum, Sumaya.

I look for a resemblance between the two women but I cannot spot any. Sumaya is taller than Habiba, has high cheekbones, whereas Habiba's face is round. They have the same eyes though, deep brown, the kind that tell you a thousand and one stories.

Sumaya nods at me and says something in Somali.

'Mum welcomes you and asks you to please sit down,' Habiba says, then she orders Abi Suleyman to call the boys to come in.

Despite the instructions, I wait for Sumaya to sit before I too sit on the floor cross-legged.

The older woman glances at me and says something to her daughter and son-in-law.

'She is impressed that you know how to sit on the floor!' Abi Suleyman translates.

'Our cultures are very close, Aunty,' I reply.

She smiles warmly.

The boys run in, all sweaty: three of them, looking just like Habiba. Their round faces are red and they are still arguing about a goal one of them may or may not have scored.

'Nah nah nah! Go and wash your hands first!' Habiba sends them off to the bathroom before they sit down.

Habiba pours tea and I take a sip; the blend of cinnamon and cardamom awakens all my senses. Despite the heat of the day, there is something refreshing about hot tea.

The boys return and, with a bit of shuffling and shoving, sit down. They are still bickering about the game. One blames the quality of the ball for a bad kick.

Their father scowls. 'You are lucky you have a ball to play with! Growing up in the refugee camp, we did not even dream of having a ball!'

The boys fall silent and lower their eyes.

As Sumaya wraps her fingers around her cup, I am captivated by the henna patterns on her hands, though I know it is rude to stare.

She has a majestic aura. She speaks softly with a gravelly voice, almost whisper-like. Her dark brown eyes are deep like the desert at night; the wrinkles at the corner of her eyes are like pathways to eternity. Before she takes her first sip of tea, she whispers a prayer in Arabic.

Something in me stirs again, and I hear Maman's voice. Had she been here, she would have said that the Arabs invaded the east and north of Africa and that's why these nations practise Islam now. I wonder what their customs would have been if not for the invasions that eradicated their old culture.

'Tishtar? Here is your plate!' Habiba says as she hands me a dish of vegetables and pasta.

'Wow, sister, how did you know I don't eat meat?' I ask.

'Women notice everything! Baasto iyo Suugo Suqaar, pasta and beef stir fry, is an old family recipe. Obviously, I left the beef out of yours!'

'Pasta? That's interesting!'

'Yes, from the time we were an Italian colony,' Habiba says casually. 'Mum has told us many stories about how life was for her in those days.'

'It is fascinating how invasion has influenced cultures time and time again,' I say.

'Change in our way of cooking is nothing when our people have been running for safety for decades.'

TEHRAN
AUGUST 1978

Maman came to pick me up from Madar's house. She arrived all flustered and went straight to the fridge and poured herself a glass of cold water and started fanning herself. Her face was as red as a beetroot.

'Hurry and pack your bag,' she commanded. 'The traffic was shocking. The later we leave, the worse it gets, and I don't wish to be sitting behind the wheel for hours. I'll wait for you in the car.'

I went to the bedroom to gather my things. As I entered the room I saw Madar folding my clothes neatly. I had never known anyone to fold things so meticulously.

'Madar?' I said.

'Yes, my love?'

'Please come with us.'

'Oh, I have a few things to do and I don't want to hold your maman up when she is in a rush!'

'She won't mind!' I said.

She didn't offer any further resistance; she was always glad to come to our house as she didn't like to be on her own. 'Okay, go and make sure that I turned the stove off,' Madar said.

On my way to the kitchen I passed the spare room and noticed that the door was ajar. Glancing inside, I was startled to see a young woman sitting in Madar's rocking chair, looking out the window. She had long blonde hair that looked almost white in the bright afternoon sun. She was wearing a white dress and black shoes.

Madar touched me on the shoulder and I turned and buried my head in her skirt to muffle my scream.

'It's alright, my love, it's alright,' my grandmother said. 'Don't be afraid.' She held me against her warm belly.

'Who is it, Madar?' I cried.

'Oh, my darling boy. She is a visitor—she comes here every now and then.'

'But who is she? What is her name?'

Maman appeared at the door. 'What's the hold-up? It's boiling hot in the car!'

'Your mother is right—we should go,' Madar said, hurrying me away.

I tried to look back but Madar kept pushing me forwards.

I crawled onto the back seat of the car and buried my head between my knees. I didn't say a word all the way home.

We were held up by the traffic in several spots, the last because of the demonstrations near Tehran University, a few blocks away from our house. For months there had been unrest across the country—people were demanding change and wanted to overthrow the monarchy, a pro-west government. As we approached the streets near the university, we could see cars on fire. Students were throwing Molotov cocktails at soldiers who answered with gunfire. Ambulances were rushing past carrying the wounded. It was frightening to see all that blood and carnage.

Maman turned down a side street and went the long way around the block to Nosrat Street, where our house was.

When we pulled up, Baba was waiting in the driveway, his face as white as a sheet. 'Where have you been?' he demanded. 'I've been worried sick!' He grabbed the keys from Maman to reverse the car in. 'Go inside now! It's crazy out there!' I had never seen him so agitated.

I ran inside with Madar's travel bag, intending to put it in my room. I wanted her to sleep with me.

Satyar was busy in his own room setting up his latest railway set, a sophisticated model with a real steam locomotive, metal tracks, tunnels, trees, people, even a stationmaster.

'Don't even think about coming in!' he warned when he noticed me lingering in the doorway.

'Don't worry! I don't even want to come into your room!' I yelled back.

'Silence, the pair of you!' Maman shouted from downstairs. 'Tishtar has been home for five seconds and already you two are annoying each other! It is so much more peaceful when you are apart.'

'That's an idea—send him to live with Madar! Then there will be peace and quiet permanently!' Satyar said cheerfully.

'I'll be glad to be away from you!' I retorted.

'Enough now!' Maman called. 'Good God!'

Satyar is nine years older than me, and aside from the typical sibling rivalry and minor quarrels, we generally got along. He would sometimes let me watch as he worked on his train set, though I was under strict instructions not to touch anything. (Little did he know that I snuck into his room and played with his trains whenever he went out with his mates.) In the evenings, we watched *Star Trek*, *The Pink Panther* and *The Flintstones* together, and we both collected action hero rub-on transfers. Satyar kept his collection in an A5 notebook with a brown vinyl cover, and mine were stuck all over my schoolbooks. He would also record some of his music collection onto cassettes for me. One compilation of seventies disco hits—'I Will Survive', 'One Way Ticket'—is still vivid in my memory.

Satyar used to wake me up when he left for school. He would bang on my window, which overlooked the first-floor landing, as he went past. The smell of his Brut aftershave trailed behind him and lingered in the air for hours. When I was annoyed with him I hated that scent. When he left Iran I missed it.

He and Baba used to leave the house early, as they had farther to travel. Satyar went to the same high school where Baba taught physics to year twelve students. Maman dropped me off at my school every day. She taught literature at a local all-girls high school not that far from my primary school.

I continued on to my room and threw my pack and Madar's on my bed. I was still overwhelmed and confused by the stranger I had seen in Madar's spare room. I wanted Madar to explain to me what I had seen.

I rearranged my room and made up Madar's bed, then opened the windows to let some fresh air in. The chickens were roaming in the neighbour's yard while the rooster was curled up under a small bush, blinking peacefully every now and then. The elderly sisters were sitting on their verandah peeling onions, their two cats sprawled out among the clutter around them. I waved at them and they waved back.

☾

At bedtime, when Maman went to make up the bed in the guest room for Madar, I announced that Madar's bed was already set up in my room.

I waited until the lights were out then whispered, 'Madar?'

'Yes?'

'Tell me about the stranger, please.'

'Ah, not tonight, not now,' she said wearily. She rolled onto her side and pulled the sheet over her shoulder.

I tossed and turned; my bedsprings squeaked each time. I had kept the window open for air and I could still hear the sound of gunshots in the distance.

'Stop fidgeting, will you?' my grandmother growled at me.

'Sorry, Madar, but I just can't stop thinking about her. Why do you have a visitor? How come you just left her there in the house? Who is she?'

Madar sighed. 'She comes from a faraway land,' she explained. 'There is a reason for her visit and now is not the right time to talk about that or she will be upset.'

None of what she said made sense.

'A faraway land? Like the ones from across the water? What's her name?'

'Oh, you drain me!' Madar said, and she sat up in bed. She opened her travel bag, pulled out a small bottle of valerian and took a sip.

'Eww,' I said, covering my nose at the smell.

'I have heart palpitations. It helps to calm the nerves.'

I jumped off my bed and flicked the lamp on.

'Oh, your maman will kill us both for being up so late!'

I sat cross-legged in front of her on the floor, hugging my pillow, looking at her with my eyes wide. 'Please tell me about the stranger,' I said.

'Very well, since I can see I will get no sleep if I refuse. Her name is Gretel, and she comes from a distant time and place.'

'What place?'

'A small island, far away from here.'

'Where is it?'

'In the Baltic Sea, off the coast of Sweden.'

'But why is she in your house? I don't understand!'

'Sometimes we just have to accept how things are,' she said. 'Gretel has been on a quest for something for a long, long time.'

'What kind of quest?' I felt hot, and remembered the night I was in Madar's spare room: the shuffling in the corner, the deep sigh, the contents of the chest, and the tin.

The sound of a single gunshot echoed in the darkness outside. It was very close this time, and sirens followed. Madar drew me close and switched off the lamp. I fell asleep listening to her breathing, deep and reassuring.

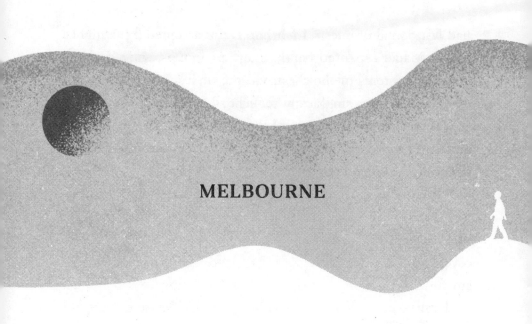

MELBOURNE

WHEN I GET TO work in the morning, Habiba is waiting at the door of my office with two takeaway cups in her hands. 'I got us two strong coffees and brought homemade cake.'

'Thanks. Just what I needed. Let's go in.' I unlock the door and we take our respective spots on either side of the desk.

'Now, Habiba,' I say, 'I want you to describe your experience as a young woman fleeing Somalia and how you made your way to Australia, as well as everything you know about your nieces' situation. Just tell me your story as though you are talking to a friend. I'll stop you and ask you to elaborate if I need more information.'

She looks at me with her warm brown eyes and takes a deep breath. 'Okay. I was thirteen when I migrated to Australia in 2009. I came with my mum and my three older sisters, my father died of ill health when I was only a few months old. We had left Somalia three years before being accepted by Australia. Tensions had escalated between militia groups, and when the unrest was getting close to our village, we just ran for our lives. There was no time to pack anything.

'We walked together with other family groups, hunting for food and water in the villages we passed, but there was very little to spare. We travelled at night for safety, and to avoid the scorching heat. During the day we hid in the bushes. After several weeks, we arrived at the refugee camp in Dadaab in Kenya. The temperature had reached thirty-nine degrees that day and our feet were covered in blisters. I don't think we would have been able to walk any further. Looking back, I don't even know how we did it at all.

'I still remember our first day in the camp. We were so thirsty and hungry. After hours of waiting in the heat, we were given some water and food. I threw up straight away. My stomach could not handle food after being hungry for so long.

'Our days didn't get any better after that. We had to wait for hours for medical attention, for food, water and everything else. There was only so much that the UN officers could offer to hundreds of thousands of displaced people who needed help.

'When we first arrived in Dadaab, we thought that we would only be there for a short time. But when Mum started talking to other families at the camp, we realised that we could be there for months, if not years. Everyone was trying to register with the UN office as a refugee. But the camp was overcrowded and there were not enough hours in the day to process everyone. You could line up all day without reaching the head of the queue, and then have to go through the same wait the next day with no guarantees.

'After months of queueing, finally we got an appointment. We all went in together. It was so crowded in the office—people were sitting on top of one another or on the floor. The air was rancid, with the smell of bodies that hadn't been washed for months, sick children crying and vomiting everywhere, flies buzzing about—ooof, ooof, when I think about it . . .

'So, after spending the whole day at the UN office, we walked out with a piece of paper that showed we were registered. It had our names listed in English. They took our photos and told us that we could pick up our ID cards in a few weeks. I still have those cards, just so that I can tell my own children one day how lucky we are. Looking at those photos, we all look miserable, malnourished and battered by life at such a young age.

'A few weeks later, we queued up again for hours under the scorching sun to collect our UN cards. They also gave us food ration cards and coupons for blankets and warm clothes. Autumn was approaching, and it was going to get really cold at night.

'Queuing up for food rations, water, sanitary products and clothing became a daily affair. We soon developed a system, assigning tasks to family members for collection of goods. I queued up for clothing and sanitary products. With all the girls in our family, we were always in need of such items.

'My mum learned that we, like thousands of others, were in a queue to be considered for settlement into a third country. But because of the sheer number of people it would be several years before we had a chance to be accepted somewhere. She was very resourceful, my mother. She kept going to the UN office every day to see what other options were available to us, until one day someone told her that if we were sponsored by someone in Australia, we might have a better chance. Mum knew that a distant relative had come to Melbourne. She contacted her cousin Abdi Rahman in Nairobi and pleaded with him to find this relative. Abdi Rahman managed to track down that man, who in turn found an organisation that was willing to sponsor us.

'After numerous delays with the paperwork, our application was accepted, and three years after we arrived in the camp we flew out to Melbourne. I'll never forget the day we went to the airport. The lady who checked us in asked us to put our suitcases on the scale, but all we had was one small sack between us. Every time I travel now, I remember that day. Now we have too much luggage!

'In Melbourne, we settled into the western suburb of Footscray. For months we just walked around wide-eyed, looking at the shops and at all the people who looked so different from us. We had never seen people from Asian countries. All we knew were Africans and the white people who worked at the refugee camp. We had no TV back in our village, so our knowledge of the world was very limited.

'We received lots of English language lessons and our mother enrolled me and my sisters in a high school. Because we had missed several years of school, and our English still wasn't very fluent, we were put in classes with girls much younger than us. We were given school uniforms and backpacks, and we ate breakfast at school. We couldn't believe that we didn't have to stand in long queues to get rations.

When I finished high school, my mum told me something that I found very hard to accept: she was actually my aunt. She said that her sister, my mother, had died when I was little and so she took me in. I had so many questions that I didn't even know where to start. *So my sisters are really my cousins?* I asked. She confirmed that, yes, they were my cousins, but she reassured me that this changed nothing. *But do I have sisters of my own? Brothers? Anyone?* I asked desperately. She grabbed a jar of sugar and said: *You see these sugar grains? Can you see where one family starts and ends? No, they are together. Nothing separates them, no demarcation. You have all of us, my child: we are your family. But as for biological siblings, I cannot be sure. We lived in a different village, far away from your mother. The old lady who brought you to me didn't say anything about other kids. You had been passed to her by another elder, who had also cared for you for a time. But even though I didn't give birth to you, I love you like my own daughter. You are a part of me.*

'You see, that's normal. In my culture, everyone steps in to look after you when you are in need. Since that conversation, I asked every Somali person I met if they knew anything about my family, but no one did.

'I met my husband's family when they moved from New Zealand to Melbourne two years ago. They asked my mother to give permission for me to marry Abi Suleyman. They were from the region where I was born, and my husband's aunt said she knew my family. She said that I had a brother and a sister. I became restless—I needed to find them. With the help of my husband's family and their contacts on Facebook, I found my brother. He had fled to South Africa and was living there. He told me that our sister had died and that her children had become orphans. He had heard that they were being looked after temporarily by various villagers. That was it for me: I had to find them. I had to make sure that they were safe. Now that I am a grown woman and have children of my own, I know why my aunt looked after me as though I was her own child. It is not a choice; it is that maternal instinct.

'Earlier this year I was able to make contact with my two nieces for the first time. We all just cried over the phone. They told me about how they are living, moving from place to place, always in danger. They need me. I live a comfortable life here with my husband and want to give them all they deserve: a good education, a loving home, and safety. I cannot bear to think that they might end up in that refugee camp! It's hell! Forgive me, Allah.

'Mum has already made so many dresses for them. They are her sister's grandchildren, and so she sees them as her grandchildren. She sings folk songs from our village to them over the phone, just like she does with my kids. *It is important that your boys don't forget their culture*, my mother says. *This may be home now, but Somalia will be always be where your roots are, where the soil wraps you in its embrace when you close your eyes at night.*'

Habiba falls silent. I look up—her eyes are red and puffy. I was so busy typing that I didn't notice she was crying silently while telling her story.

'Habiba, thank you for sharing these painful memories with me. I am so terribly sorry that you have to revisit all the trauma,' I say.

'The story runs through my veins, Tishtar.' She waves her hand in the air as though flicking a fly away. 'I will not rest in peace until my nieces are safe under my wing. Not a moment goes past when I don't think about the risks they are facing. What if they are kidnapped by al-Shabaab like the men of Boko Haram kidnapped all those Nigerian girls? Oh, the thought of it makes me ill in my stomach.'

I nod my understanding. 'Do you think your mum would be willing to give her statement also?'

'Yes, of course—anything to help Fowziah and Fatimah. I will bring her in.'

C

I am so drained after taking Habiba's statement that I decide to head home early. There, I find am too exhausted to cook or even get takeaway; I have some toast and cheese for dinner. After Mr Cat and I have both eaten, I sit on the couch and Mr Cat takes his usual spot beside me.

I breathe a sigh of relief to be in my quiet, peaceful home. Habiba's description of the unrest in Somalia had transported my mind to my own past.

I pull out my family photo albums and leaf through the pages, recalling snippets of my early years. There are birthday photos, lots of them. A photo of me blowing out candles with Baba clapping in the background, his sideburns quite impressive, and my uncle's tight floral shirt and big collar even more interesting. In another photo, Maman is sitting at the table with her hands clasped under her chin. She looks deep in thought, pale and sad. She had fallen into depression and we didn't know how to support her. Madar is there too, her curly hair a bit unruly. She used to cut her own hair—she would get a pair of scissors and just cut the ends in one straight line. She made quite a contrast to Aunty Tangerine, who is also in the photos, her hair always coiffed, wearing full make-up and brightly coloured dresses.

It is hard to believe, looking at these photos, that our lives would soon be turned upside down as Iran erupted into violence.

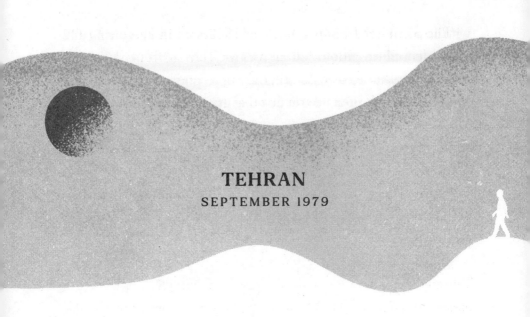

TEHRAN
SEPTEMBER 1979

THE POLITICAL DISTURBANCE IN the country had intensified in late 1978. Students continued to hold demonstrations at major universities, socialist parties ramped up their activities, and Islamic ideology was gaining a mysterious strength. Maman used to say that people did not appreciate the modern, progressive, free country Iran had become in the 1960s and 70s under the Shah's rule. He was the king of Iran, the second in the Pahlavi dynasty that had reigned for more than fifty years. When the Shah was forced to leave, it threw the country into chaos. The Americans had backed the Shah, while the Russians were backing the socialists and communists, and the power of the religious clerics was on the rise. At night, people would turn off their lights and chant 'Allahu Akbar' from windows and rooftops—it was quite eerie.

The Shah left Iran in December 1978, and in February 1979 the exiled cleric Khomeini arrived in Tehran from Paris. He had the grand title of Ayatollah, the highest rank among the Shia Muslims, though how he attained that status was never explained. Most people had never heard of him until the demonstrations began, then suddenly he was being referred to as the saviour of the country. Posters of him were distributed among the community, and soon every store had a framed portrait of him on their wall. 'When did he have a chance to sit for this portrait?' Maman wanted to know.

On the day Ayatollah Khomeini was driven into the city from Tehran's airport, a sea of people lined the streets to see his car pass—the same people who used to line up to wave at the Shah's processions. People change colours very easily and conveniently, it turns out.

Before we knew it, Khomeini had become the Supreme Leader and he renamed the country the Islamic Republic of Iran.

My memories of Iran before the revolution are very scattered and faint, as I was very young when all of this unfolded; I could barely recall the 'good times' that Maman would refer to. She used to say that for my generation and those born after me, the great Iran was only a description, only word of mouth, rather than a lived experience. She would say how sorry she was for the next generation not to know any better, to grow up under the reign of the clergy. 'Politics and religion should not mix!' she used to say.

I recall adults talking about how our prosperous country came to a standstill when the Shah was forced to leave Iran and the autocratic regime took over. It was like a total eclipse; the whole country fell into darkness. Schools were shut down and no one knew when or if they would ever reopen. Everyone was in shock. Thousands of young far-left activists were arrested and executed without trial. The regime turned on every major political party that had helped it come to power. It was ironic that the very activists who had helped topple the Shah's regime were the first to be punished. Mass graves were dug, and families were told months later that their child had been buried with hundreds of others in some unknown place in the middle of nowhere. Some parents never found out what happened to their sons and daughters—chapters of their lives simply ripped out as though they had never existed.

Musicians, artists, intellectuals, and writers were hanged in public spaces, where large crowds would see what happened to those who spoke out and learn the lesson. They even used cranes to lift the dead bodies high into the air for maximum visibility. If we happened to be in the vicinity of one of these executions, Maman would quickly change our route, ensuring that I wasn't exposed to the gruesome sight.

Books, musical instruments and precious compositions written by Iran's talented musicians were burned to ashes. The homes of artists were raided, and their possessions confiscated. Palaces and museums were looted, works of art vandalised.

The entire ministry of the Shah's government was executed by firing squads. I'll never forget coming home every day and seeing the front cover of the newspaper filled with images of the dead ex-ministers. Once upon a time these men had dressed meticulously and sat in the parliament running the country—now they were blindfolded and naked with bullets in their chests. This was the new regime's way of demonstrating power and control. Seeing the photographs was disturbing. I would seek refuge in my room, trying to find a way to make sense of the horrors. It was impossible to get those images out of my head. I still remember them, vividly.

The opposition established radio stations overseas and broadcast analyses and reports predicting that the end of the Islamic regime was near. Maman listened to several radio stations from early evening until late at night. She would start with Radio Iran at 5.30 pm, then move on to Radio Israel, followed by the BBC, and finally Voice of America at 10.30. She drowned herself in the news and became more and more depressed as year followed year with no end to Iran's suffering in sight.

She and Baba also read the daily newspaper and looked at each other in horror at the regime's brutality.

'Oh no—not Mrs Parsa. It can't be! Dear God, dear God ...' Maman cried out one day. She read aloud a report that Mrs Farrokhroo Parsa, the first-ever female senior minister in the Shah's parliament, had been executed that morning. 'This is how the country looks after its progressive women!' she said in disgust. 'Mrs Parsa worked hard to ensure that women have voting rights. She stood for gender equality. Oh no, we can't have that, can we? Women's rights? What a joke ... Apparently women belong behind closed doors and under layers of hijab where no man can see or hear them. An educated woman deserves no better than bullets in her chest.' Maman began to weep bitterly.

Baba went and sat next to her. He rubbed her back and she rested her head on his shoulder, scrunching the newspaper in her hands.

☾

I was lucky to be able to escape much of the horror. Throughout the summer of 1979, I spent more and more time at Madar's house.

Madar used to rise very early in the morning, well before sunrise. She would perform her prayers and then water the plants. I'd wake up to the sound of water running and the smell of wet soil.

Madar spent the morning pottering around the garden before the temperature soared, and I followed her like a shadow. To pass time in the heat of the afternoons, she'd crochet, or talk to Seyed Khanum over endless cups of tea, while I practised English. Maman had bought me several small books in English and set me tasks to improve my fluency.

It was on one of these hot afternoons, when Madar had fallen asleep, that I went into the spare room and spoke with Gretel for the first time.

When I entered, she looked over her shoulder at me and then turned away to gaze out the window. I moved forwards to sit on the carpet near her, then clasped my hands in my lap and waited.

She didn't say a word. We must have sat in silence for quite a while, as the sun changed its position in the sky so that it was shining on Gretel's face. It was the first time I had seen her face in daylight, and she looked like an angel, her hair shimmering like gold, her lips very pink. She was so beautiful.

I finally summoned the courage to break the silence and, in a trembling voice, asked her why she was visiting Madar's house.

She turned around and gave me a cold look. It felt as though an ice cube was running down my spine. She didn't answer my question.

Minutes passed and the silence grew thicker between us. The air was stale, so I got up and opened the window. She flinched and moved her chair back.

'It's okay, I just needed some air,' I said, and she gave me a pale smile. Encouraged, I said, 'Madar tells me you come from an island?'

'Yes,' she replied. Her voice had a faraway quality, as if from another world.

'I would love to know more about your island home.'

'Home? I don't know where home is.'

'What is this island then, if it is not your home?' I asked, quite confused. 'Can you tell me what it's called?'

'Gotland.'

'What is it like?'

'It is breathtakingly beautiful. Long beaches covered in pebbles and limestone, farmlands stretching from east to west, with Visby shining in the middle.'

'Ah, we have pebbled beaches along the Caspian Sea,' I said.

A fraction of warmth lit up her face.

'Why are you here?' I asked.

'You like asking questions, don't you, little boy?' she said, and turned away.

I felt humiliated.

Madar had woken up by now, and was calling me. 'I'm coming!' I yelled back.

'Can I talk to you again?' I asked.

Gretel didn't reply.

I left her and returned to Madar's room.

'So?' Madar said as I entered.

I looked at her, puzzled.

'You have finally spoken to her?' Madar prompted.

'Yes.'

'Hmm. She gave you the cold shoulder, I gather?'

I shrugged. 'Maybe.'

'You are rushing this—you'll push her away,' she warned.

My heart sank when I heard that. I didn't want her to leave—I wanted to know her story.

I visited the spare room every day for the rest of that summer, but I never saw her again.

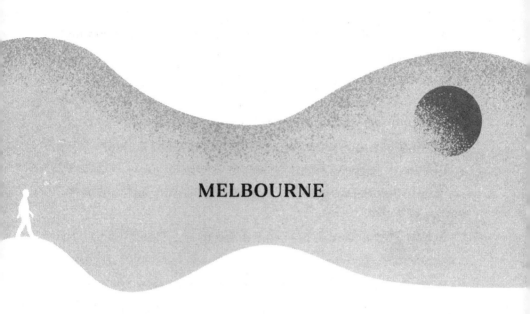

MELBOURNE

A FEW WEEKS HAVE passed since Habiba gave me her statement and we filled out the forms, but we are still missing much of the documentation we need and I am yet to take a statement from Habiba's mother. I am starting to get worried about the time that has elapsed. But one morning, I receive a text from Habiba asking me if I have time to come downstairs and see her later that day. Sumaya is with her, and she has agreed to talk to me.

That afternoon I walk downstairs and duck my head into Habiba's shop. A few of the women are gathered around her desk talking, and in the adjacent area another group of young women is busily sewing. Habiba is on the phone. I wave at her from the doorway and her face lights up. She signals for me to come inside. The women surrounding her rearrange their hijabs and move away.

'Sit, sit,' Habiba says to me as I approach.

She finishes her phone call then stands to pull a folder from her filing cabinet.

'I have good news, Tishtar!' she exclaims. 'My relatives have managed to get birth certificates for the girls, as well as death certificates for their parents. I have their passport photos here, too. We now have everything, right?'

'That's awesome, Habiba! I can't believe you have managed to do all of this!'

'It hasn't been easy. I had to find someone in Mogadishu to go to government authorities to get the certificates. He had to go several times and keep paying the officials bribes so that they would cooperate. Finally, he succeeded.'

'It must have cost you a fortune,' I observed.

'Can you put a price on the safety of your flesh and blood? The girls have been moved from the village they were in. The elder who was looking after them has fallen ill and now there is no one to protect them from the attacks. Many of the men have been killed, leaving the women vulnerable, so they have to move to safer territories. The girls are so frightened. In the last village, al-Shabaab raided the huts and dragged women and girls from them, screaming. They raped them in front of everyone. The elder hid my girls under a pile of rubbish and hay, but they saw every-thing. Those images will never be erased from their memories. Afterwards, the men took all the young women they could find and seized people's goats and the little food they had.

'When I heard this story, I sent some money to my relative and asked him to get the girls out of there as quickly as possible.

They have been on the road for nearly a week, and just this morning our time they left Somalia and entered Kenya. I have had a text from my relative to say that they are only a few hours from Nairobi. They should get there tonight, inshallah.'

'I can't even begin to imagine the terror they must have felt,' I said sombrely. 'But thanks to your efforts to get their birth certificates, we can now complete their visa applications. But as soon as they arrive in Nairobi, they must present to the UN office and register there. The Australian embassy will no doubt request their UN paperwork.'

'Yes, yes, it is all taken care of—they have an appointment in three weeks,' Habiba says.

I am congratulating her on her efficiency when Sumaya appears beside me with Habiba's youngest son.

I quickly stand up and pull a chair over to the desk for the older woman while Habiba fetches her a glass of water and says something to her in Somali.

'Could you take her statement here?' Habiba asks. 'She would feel more comfortable in a place that is familiar.'

'Of course,' I say.

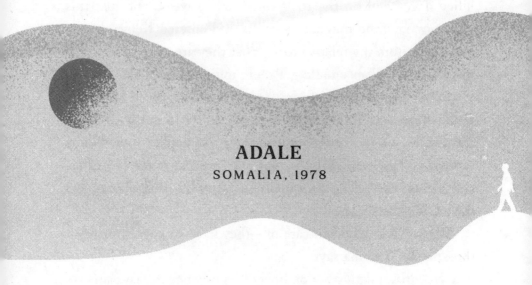

ADALE

SOMALIA, 1978

WE LIVED IN ADALE, a small village in the north of the country. Ours was a small village. We lived in clay huts, which kept us cool in the heat and sheltered us from strong winds. Every year, after the rain season was over, we would replace the hay on the roof. Those days are a distant memory now, though; we no longer have rain.

We had a herd of goats, our only source of income. My mother and us girls would sell the milk and meat at the local market while my father took the herd to the nearby fields for a good feed and a drink of water from the small dam in the next village, where farmers grew vegetables. My father often had to trade a few goats in exchange for access to water for the animals.

The women cooked for the family every day. My mother was very resourceful; she never wasted anything. When we killed a goat for meat, she would use the scraps to make oil and stew. Sometimes she would trade the goatskin for grains and spices at the market and make us a nice stew. The scent of cumin and chilli filled the hut when she cooked; you could smell the aroma from the centre of the village. It drew small children to our hut.

She also baked the best bread in her ground oven. I used to watch her separating the grains delicately with her hands and then grinding them with a rock we had found together in the desert. She would grind the grain into a soft powder then mix it with water. The way she kneaded the dough was the talk of the village. Women used to say that she had hands from the heavens. She sometimes traded her bread in the market for a bag of rice or pasta. We had very little, but we felt rich in our spirit.

In the centre of the village were a few Garbi trees, and people would sit in their shade. This was where older women gathered to make bracelets that younger ones sold at the market or traded for grains, and where older men discussed village politics and the changing landscape. From resolving disputes between villagers to marriage proposals, it all happened under those trees.

The boys would climb the trees and spot travellers in the distance. Sometimes we heard them scream with excitement if they spotted someone on a camel. Only people who had money could travel on camels; everyone else had to walk, often walking for hours or even days to reach their destination. More often than not, though, the movement the boys saw would turn out to be a mirage.

'It's just the heat shimmering above the sand, not travellers,' my mother used to say to them without even looking; she just knew her land like the back of her hand.

Aside from the Garbi trees and a few thorny bushes here and there, the land around us was dry and barren. It was a hard life, but we had each other; ours was a close-knit community.

One day the elders had a discussion and agreed that I would marry Nasir. He was the son of a farmer from a village further north.

Not long after, Nasir and his father came to take me. Two goats and a woollen blanket were my dowry. It was a hot day when I left my village. My husband and his father walked ahead with the goats and I followed behind carrying the blanket and a bracelet my mother had made for me. I held the bracelet close to my heart; it held her kind and reassuring voice, her life lessons and her love. I kept turning back to look at my mother standing under our beloved Garbi trees until she was lost from sight. I never saw my mother again—I later heard that she had fallen ill and died not long after I left.

My husband and I lived a modest life. I helped on the farm and he traded vegetables at the local market, and we had three children. But everything changed when the unrest in the country broke out. My husband started attending secret meetings and then one night he never came home. To this day I don't know what happened to him. I presume he was killed.

I was left with three hungry mouths to feed. His family could not afford to take care of us, so I had to return to my village. The journey took days, for my children were too small to walk far in the scorching heat. When at last we reached the village, it was barely recognisable. It had been burned to the ground, and animal carcasses were scattered here and there. The only thing left were the Garbi trees; even the thorny bushes had been destroyed. I didn't know what had happened to my father and sisters.

I sat under the trees to try to think of what to do. Moving on was the only option, I realised. In the cool of the night, we started walking again until we came to another village, where there was still life. An old woman who had known my mother took us in, Allah bless her soul. She lived in a makeshift hut made of tree branches wrapped in worn-out blankets. She told me that my father had been killed and that my two sisters were married. She only knew where one of them had gone: to Kismayo, a port city near the Jubba River.

We stayed with the old woman for a while, until there was another wave of attacks in the surrounding area. We decided to move further south towards Kismayo, hoping to find my sister.

We reached the city's outskirts in the middle of the night and slept under some bushes. In the pale light of the morning, I got up and prayed to Allah for safety and peace. The children were hungry, and I was exhausted.

We camped there for the next month or so, and I spent the days walking all over the city looking for my sister. I finally found an old relative who gave us the sad news that my sister and her husband had both been killed years back. Since then, she had been looking after my young niece, Habiba and said that she was planning to leave Somalia to seek refuge in Kenya. She wasn't sure if my sister's other children had survived the war, but she had heard that they were taken away to safety by other villagers.

When I saw my niece for the first time, my heart was filled with joy. She looked just like my beloved sister. I promised the girl that I would not let anything happen to her as long as I was alive.

A few days later, we set out for the refugee camp in Kenya, where the next chapter of our lives began.

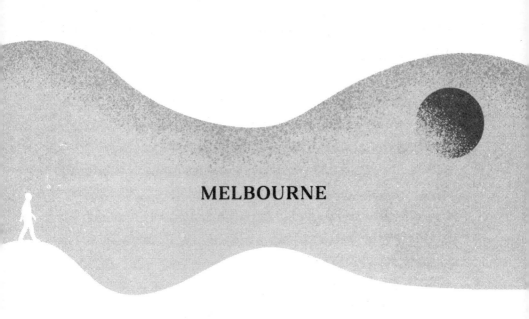

MELBOURNE

WHEN I CHECK IN with Habiba three weeks later, on the day her nieces were due to go to their UN appointment, she tells me that her relative has fallen ill and was unable to take them. They have had to reschedule the appointment, but the earliest date they could get was not for another month.

'Habiba, I have confirmation that the application has been received,' I tell her. 'As I predicted, the case officer has asked for the UN paperwork, and I have informed them that Fowziah and Fatimah have an appointment. I understand your relative's situation, but it is very important that they keep the new appointment.'

'Yes, yes, I will call him again to make sure that nothing gets in the way this time. Each time he takes time off work to take the girls to appointments, he loses money. His employer doesn't pay him. I will send him some more money to cover his expenses.'

'Good. Well, I must go now, or I'll miss my train.'

'Tishtar?' Habiba calls after me.

'Yes?'

'You seem on edge. Is everything alright?'

'Yes, I just don't want to miss the train.' I don't want to miss Gretel, I almost add but I start walking instead.

'Okay, safe travels, brother. Eat a proper dinner!' She waves goodbye.

I run to the station—I only have three minutes to get there if I am to catch the 4.02 pm train. I make it just in time; the doors are already starting to close as I board.

As we approach the next stop, my heart quickens, and begins to beat so loudly that I can barely hear the music through my headphones. I scan the platform, and there she is, her golden hair glowing in the afternoon sun. Gretel enters the carriage through the other entrance, and climbs onto the luggage shelf. The door hisses and closes. I crane my neck, trying to catch her attention. But she pulls her hood up and falls asleep.

TEHRAN
SEPTEMBER 1979

SCHOOL RESUMED IN MID-SEPTEMBER and I had mixed feelings about it. A lot had changed, and not all of the students had returned. Ours had been a coeducational school—the majority of primary schools were—but the Islamic regime had converted it to a boys' school. The girls now went to different primary schools in the area, and friendships were severed. Maman kept reminding me to focus on schoolwork and not on who was or wasn't there anymore. But I was no longer interested in the subjects—with the exception of history, which offered me an opportunity to learn about Gretel's country; I had learned that Gotland was part of Sweden. Maman's good friend and colleague Mrs Bozorgy was a history teacher at her school. I loved it when she visited our house. She was very fond of me and would always ask me about my studies. Now I was always asking her questions about Scandinavia.

The start of school also coincided with my ninth birthday. When I left the school building on the day of my birthday, I saw Aunty Tangerine standing by her car and waving at me. She lived in a two-bedroom apartment four doors down from our house, so she occasionally drove me home.

'Hellooooo, darling!' she said as she kissed me hard. 'Your maman will be a bit late today, so I've come to get you. Let's go to the charcoal chicken shop and pick up a bird for lunch. Madar is waiting for you at home too.'

I climbed into the passenger seat of her green Passat.

'How was school, my love?' she asked as she slipped behind the wheel.

'Aunty?' I said.

'Yes, my love?'

'When will I go to university?'

She shrieked with laughter then ruffled my hair and said: 'You have a few years to go yet, my love. First you have to finish primary school! But don't worry—it will be over before you know it.' Her voice was loving and reassuring.

☾

When Maman arrived home she baked a chocolate cake, which she decorated with cream and birthday candles. Next to the cake sat a pile of presents. I was drawn to one in particular: it was round, and I was certain that it was a football, as I had been carrying on about wanting a black-and-white football, just like the ones I had seen on TV.

That afternoon, guests arrived for my birthday party. After blowing out the candles, I opened the presents.

Aunty Tangerine gave me an envelope with crisp banknotes. My aunt worked at the central branch of the National Bank and always gave us freshly printed banknotes for birthdays and Nowruz.

Next, Baba handed me a small rectangular gift. I couldn't believe it: it was a camera! I always played with Maman's medium-format camera, but I was not allowed to take pictures with it. Occasionally I was allowed to use Baba's Polaroid. 'Now you can take photos with your own camera,' said Baba with pride. 'There are two rolls of film in there, too, just to get you going.'

'Baba got sick of you wasting all his Polaroid film!' said Satyar with a smirk on his face.

Mrs Bozorgy and her family had come too. Her son Ali was two years older than me and her daughter Sarve was sixteen. Sarve was stunning—tall, with curly brown hair and dark green eyes. Ali and Sarve handed me the present they had got me: a comprehensive guide to Scandinavia. I was thrilled. Everyone laughed, and I was embarrassed, for though I was much younger than her I wanted to look cool in front of Sarve.

Mrs Bozorgy knew that I liked her daughter. 'Maybe one day, when you are old enough, you could ask for my daughter's hand!' she told me once. 'But let me warn you: she is her father's precious princess, so you need to work hard to win his heart!'

Last of all, I opened the round present. As soon as I touched it I knew it wasn't a football. It was a world globe, and it was from Madar. 'With this globe you can go on lots of adventures and learn about different countries in the world without needing to travel,' she said with a smile.

'Now you and Sara can go and play,' Maman told me.

Sara was a couple of years younger than me. She was the daughter of Baba's best friend, Bahman. Baba and Bahman were from the same township on the outskirts of Rasht, in Gilan Province. They had come to Tehran together and attended the same university, and now they taught at the same high school. Bahman would come to our house at least once a week, and he and Baba talked for hours over endless rounds of hot tea.

Bahman had married his sweetheart a few years after Baba married Maman. After their first daughter they had a number of stillborn babies, but never gave up hope of having more children, until at last they had Sara, who they called 'the lucky one'. Sara was very smart and was top of her class. Bahman and his wife had three more children after Sara, all of whom were born with profound disabilities. But Bahman and his wife never complained—they were always smiling and they gave their children all the love in the world.

That afternoon Sara and I played with the globe for hours and tested each other's knowledge of the location of various countries. 'I want to become a historian when I grow up,' I said, 'and be wise and knowledgeable like Mrs Bozorgy. I want to learn about the history of the world!'

'I want to become a scientist, like Marie Curie,' said Sara. 'I want to find a cure for children who are born with disabilities.'

When I think about the perfect and ambitious world that we as children had created for ourselves, how little did we know that it was all going to shatter. Perhaps our innocence protected us from the horrors to come.

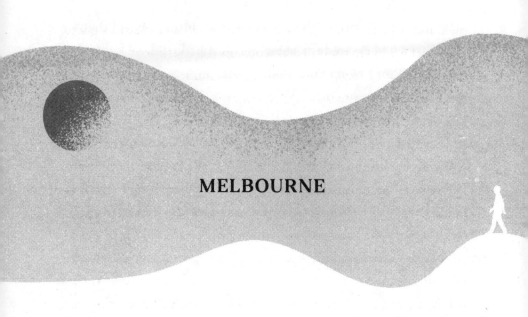

MELBOURNE

IT IS MARCH BY the time Habiba's relative emails me the girls' UN paperwork. I immediately send it off to the case officer at the Australian embassy in Nairobi. About a month later, I receive a request for more information: the embassy wanted the girls to produce UNHCR ration cards and also evidence of their schooling in Somalia and Nairobi. I pass on these requests to Habiba.

'Oh, I don't know about ration cards,' she says. 'I don't think they were given any, but I will check. As far as schooling is concerned, the girls haven't been able to go to school in Somalia for a number of years now because of the conflict, and they cannot enrol in schools in Nairobi as they are illegal residents until they are granted some sort of visa.

'And there is another problem, Tishtar: my relative is unable to look after the girls for much longer. He has nine children of his own and they all live in a small apartment. His landlord is giving him grief for having too many people in the apartment; they are at risk of being evicted. They are treated unfairly because they are refugees. Is there any way you can ask the case officer to fast-track this application?' Habiba asked.

'I will do my best, Habiba, but I have to tell you that these case officers are not usually amenable to these types of requests. If we push the point, they might say that the girls can go to the refugee camp in Dadaab and wait there until their application is processed.'

'No, they can't send them there! The Kenyan government is planning to shut down the camp, and the refugees fear that they will be forced to return to Somalia. Over my dead body they will go to that camp! I will not let that happen!'

☾

I email the case officer at the embassy explaining why Habiba's nieces are unable to produce evidence of schooling and ration cards, and then we wait anxiously. Before long another request comes through from Nairobi.

I text Habiba straight away. *Habiba, we need to talk—can you please come to my office as soon as you can?*

When she arrives I tell her the bad news: 'Habiba, the case officer is questioning the validity of your claims. She is expressing doubt that you are related to the girls and has requested that DNA testing be carried out on all of you. They are saying that the birth certificates may not be authentic, as bogus identification documents can easily be obtained in Somalia.'

Habiba doesn't even flinch. 'Sure,' she says. 'Where and when?'

I'm surprised that she is so pragmatic about it and doesn't seem annoyed or frustrated.

She just shrugs. 'We have nothing to lie about. I will do any test they require. And they may ask any question under the sun, and Allah be my witness, I will respond truthfully. You tell them that.'

'Okay, I will arrange with a local lab for you to have a DNA test and make an appointment for the girls to have theirs done in Nairobi. Once again, your relative needs to take them, as their guardian.'

'Sure, just give me the details and I will organise the rest.'

'I also need to tell you that this will cost a fair bit. I think about five thousand dollars all up.'

Habiba fishes in her bag and pulls out a credit card. She puts it on the desk. 'Here, use this.'

'No, no, you need to make the payment when you go to the lab here, and your relative will pay at the nominated clinic in Nairobi.'

'Fine, I will send him the money he needs,' Habiba says.

She is clearly willing to jump through any hoop in order to save her nieces.

'Habiba, can I ask how Abi Suleyman feels about all of this?' I ask nervously.

Her eyes fill with tears, and for a moment she is silent. I regret bringing up such a personal question.

'Abi Suleyman understands. He has taken extra shifts at the meatworks so we can finish building our house. Some days he is working eighteen hours, but he never complains. We will do anything for family.'

'He mentioned that he is looking for his nephew Abdullah. Has he been able to find him?'

Habiba looks down. 'Abdullah was kidnapped by al-Shabaab. Some villagers saw him being put on a truck with lots of other boys. The militia prey on the young ones. They take the girls for reasons it makes me ill to repeat, and they take the boys to turn them into soldiers. We will never see Abdullah again.'

And with that, Habiba stands and leaves my office.

TEHRAN
DECEMBER 1979

WE HAD GATHERED AT Madar's house for Yalda Night. We alternated hosting the celebration of Shab-e Chelleh each year: one year it would be at our house, the next at Madar's. When we arrived, Madar and Seyed Khanum were already in the kitchen preparing the dinner.

We joined them, each of us doing something to help. I was given the task of seeding the pomegranates. They were huge—one of our family friends had brought them from his hometown of Saveh, where the best pomegranates were grown.

Madar was busy at the stove—she had her apron on and was cooking her signature Khoresh Aloo, a plum and chicken stew. There was something about the way she cooked that dish: the plums melted in your mouth, and the juice of sour grapes added a tangy flavour. Also on the stove was a big pot of rice. I couldn't wait to eat the crunchy tahdeeg, that golden, crispy layer of rice from the bottom of the pot.

It was a cold night in Tehran, and fresh snow had fallen. Every year it would snow on Yalda Night, without exception. I thought it was magical; Maman thought it was a message from the heavens.

Satyar and Khanum's son Seyed grabbed snow shovels and started clearing the path between the kitchen and the main building. Through the kitchen window I could see them piling the snow in one corner. Occasionally they would stop and throw snowballs at each other.

'If you break any of my windows, I will make you stand in the freezing cold all night!' Madar screamed at them through the kitchen door when one of their snowballs hit the glass.

Once we'd prepared everything, we started carrying the dishes of fruit, nuts and sweets to the dining room. As I was about to go inside, I heard Satyar calling me from behind a tree: 'Psst! Meet me in the yard. Quick!'

I followed him cautiously, as I suspected he was up to no good.

'What are you doing?' I called.

'Shush, you idiot! Come closer!'

Then he opened his jacket and I heard the faint mew of a tiny kitten. He had found the kitten when he was clearing the snow off the verandah earlier that evening, he told me, but didn't bring it inside because he knew Maman would not allow animals inside the house.

The kitten was cold and hungry. We snuck him inside and quickly took him to Madar's bedroom. Satyar fetched some milk from the kitchen without anyone seeing and smuggled it into Madar's room.

As the kitten warmed up, it grew playful, and began to chase its own tail.

'I will call him Snow Pea,' I said.

Satyar raised his eyebrow and said: 'He is not green, you idiot!'

'I know, but he is little, and you found him in the snow,' I said.

Satyar argued that since the kitten's fur was fuzzy and pinkish-orange in colour, we should call him Apricot instead, so that's what we did.

I put a soft towel in an empty shoebox and tucked him in. Shortly after, he started purring and fell asleep.

'Aunty Tangerine and Uncle have arrived!' Baba called out. 'Don't be rude—come and greet your elders!'

We went to the dining room; it was warm in there and a plume of smoke was hanging in the air from my uncle's cigarette, the smell mixing with Aunty Tangerine's perfume. My aunt was fluffing her hair in front of the mirror above the console when we entered.

'The city looks glorious in the snow,' she said. 'As I was getting ready to come here, Madame Avanesian and her family, my Armenian neighbours, were all dressed up and heading to church. I wished them a Merry Christmas and they thanked God for giving them snow for this beautiful night.' Two very old yet very different celebrations were unfolding that night: the Armenians were busy with their Christian rituals and customs while we celebrated the winter solstice.

We sat politely with the adults as they conversed about various things.

'Tea anyone?' Maman asked. As Madar was the elder, Maman was looking after the guests.

'If you have just brewed a fresh pot, I will have a really hot one, merci!' responded Aunty Tangerine.

Maman walked over to the tall samovar that was bubbling away on a side table in the corner. She placed teacups, saucers and teaspoons on a silver tray and started pouring the tea.

Baba and my uncle were speaking softly on the far side of the room, discussing current affairs. My uncle worked at the National Petroleum Company and was expressing concerns shared by his senior colleagues that Iraq had its eye on Khuzestan Province, one of the richest sources of Iran's oil.

'They are saying that Saddam Hussein thinks that the Arabic-speaking province of Khuzestan should become a part of Iraq,' my uncle said.

'He just wants our oil!' Maman said. 'Argh, those Arabs! There is no end to their greed. Since they invaded Persia fourteen centuries ago, they have been plotting to take more of our land. When will it end? Haven't they done enough damage? They forced our people to adopt a new religion, a new language, and tore apart our ancient culture.' She carried the antique silver tray to Madar and Aunty Tangerine and offered them cups of tea.

'Come and sit here, my dear,' said Madar as she took a sip from her tea, sucking on a sugar cube between her teeth. 'Let's not discuss politics tonight. Let us hope that the snow and the magic of this special night celebrating both Yalda and the birth of Christ will bring peace and harmony.'

'Amen—this is a holy night indeed,' Aunty Tangerine said.

'Christmas and Yalda Night are in fact one and the same!' Maman said. She never missed the opportunity to emphasise this point. She was a formidable woman. No one argued with her—she was very passionate in her views and held tight to the old beliefs.

That night, as on every Yalda Night, we stayed up late. Maman would not have it any other way. 'We must welcome the daybreak,' she said.

Baba kept yawning, and my uncle and Aunty Tangerine left after midnight. Maman turned the lights down, grabbed her *Divan-e Hafez* and started reading poems. Every year she would stay up until the first ray of light peered over the horizon.

I was exhausted and crawled into my bed in Madar's room. Apricot had found his way under my doona, and his tiny body made my bed warm and cosy.

Madar came to bed not long after. She came to kiss me goodnight and saw Apricot's little face next to mine. 'Oh! Who have we got here?' she said as she scratched Apricot's chin. He purred and rolled on to his back. 'You know you can't leave him here. I won't be able to look after him.'

'That's fine! I will take him,' I said.

'Hmm, I'm not sure how your Maman would feel about that!'

Madar then asked me to go and make her a hot-water bottle. 'My old bones are rattling tonight,' she said.

I put my coat on, pulled up my socks and left the bedroom.

Maman was still in the lounge room reading Hafez poems, taking notes as she often did. Baba had put a mattress on the floor and was fast asleep. Satyar had gone to Seyed Khanum's side of the house to watch TV.

I stepped outside. The ground was frozen and a sheet of ice covered the ground where more snow had fallen since the boys cleared the path. I went to the kitchen and filled the giant enamel kettle with water. It was very heavy, and I had to stand on a wooden step to place it on the stove.

It took ages for it to boil, as the water was ice-cold. When I had finally filled the hot-water bottle, I returned to the main building. As I was passing the spare room, I sensed someone watching me. I looked in, and Gretel was there by the window, her face shining white like the moon and the snow outside. I stood in the doorway and we looked at each other for what felt like an eternity until she moved away from the window.

By the time I got back to the bedroom, Madar was snoring. I slipped the hot-water bottle under her blanket and climbed back into bed, but I was wide awake now. I couldn't get Gretel's face out of my mind.

I got up and went to sit by the window. The sky was red, which meant more snow would fall. Maman used to say that a red sky meant the clouds were pregnant with bundles of snow. She was right—we always received a heavy snowfall when the sky was red.

Outside, all the roofs were covered in snow, thick white layers of it. Trees, bushes, pot plants, and the old ladder leaning against the outdoor toilet were all dressed in white, too. I loved watching the snow, listening to the silence it brought. The tunes you can hear in total silence are truly magical, that intense melody of nothingness. Looking at the clean sheets of snow, I spotted small pawprints, and wondered if Apricot's mum was looking for him.

I opened the window slightly to inhale the fresh crisp air, and Madar sat up and looked at me—she was a light sleeper. She pulled on her dressing-gown then came and sat next to me.

'Oh, it's cold, my love,' she complained.

'Yes, I know. But I want to listen to the snow, the soft hissing that it makes as it falls,' I said.

Madar wrapped her arm around my shoulder and kissed my forehead. A shivering silence enveloped us, broken every now and then by the sound of the melting snow dripping into the downpipe. Apricot came and curled up on my lap. My hands were cold, so I tucked them under his warm belly. I listened to him purring. There was a sadness in the air.

'I'm going back to bed,' Madar said. 'Don't stay up too long, and shut that window.'

Madar fell asleep as soon as her head hit the pillow. Her small face looked so peaceful. There was a story written in every line on her face, I knew, and I wished I could read them all.

I couldn't resist the urge to return to the spare room.

Gretel was by the window again, watching the snow.

'It's magical, isn't it?' I said.

'Jul *is* magical,' she said. 'That's when I met him.'

'Met who?' I asked. 'Jul?'

'No, met Valentin,' she elaborated. 'Jul is winter solstice, an old tradition. We had just returned to Visby, my birthplace, after fourteen years.'

My heart was beating fast. I didn't dare say anything in case the interruption caused her to stop speaking.

After a moment of silence, she pulled the rocking chair closer to the window and sat down.

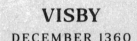

VISBY
DECEMBER 1360

W<small>E HAD RETURNED TO</small> Visby after sailing for many years with my father. It was the last days of December 1360, and Visby was covered in soft, feathery snow, the thickest white coat I had ever seen. The city wall looked tall and forbidding; I couldn't understand why it was there.

The wall around the centre of the town had been erected by the wealthy merchants to protect their assets from the country folk, like the farmers and fishermen. The merchants came from many countries, mainly Germany; my own father was one of them, I'm ashamed to say. He had arranged a grand residence for us in the heart of the town. I had my own room with clean sheets. A woman was also hired to help out with the housework.

Outside the wall, farmers were getting ready for the festival of Jul. Though Christianity had been practised in Gotland for quite some time, some of the Gotlanders were still following the old pagan traditions that had been upheld for many centuries. Some people had blended Jul and Christmas together—Christmas was the new Jul.

Inside the city walls, Visby was getting ready for Christmas celebrations. Large candles stood tall and proud outside St Karin's, a majestic church in Stora Torget, in the heart of Visby.

It was early in the evening and the night had drawn thick black curtains across the sky. Lanterns and fire pits were burning in every corner of Stora Torget as my mother and I walked around, enjoying the festive atmosphere. In the marketplace, people had gathered to watch a street performer swallowing flames. Another played tricks with a spear. Every now and then the oohs and the aahs of the crowd or the scream of an overexcited child would cut through the icy-cold air.

We heard someone calling my mother's name. 'Arngunna!' We pushed through the crowds looking for who had called, and saw a fishmonger with a bushy red beard. When we got closer to his stall, my mother recognised him. My mother had known Ulvar and his family before she married my father and moved into the city. Behind Ulvar, a young man was cleaning fish—he was sitting on a small wooden stool and seemed to be lost in his own world. Ulvar called him over and asked him to greet us. He was lean, with curly auburn hair. He said hello shyly, looking at the ground the whole time.

Ulvar grinned. 'My Sårk, Valentin, is a bit shy around nobility.'

My mother and Ulvar spoke for a while, and he invited her to go to his house, like the old days, when neighbours and close friends would gather to celebrate the end of the longest night of winter.

Since our return, my father had been dining with other merchants most nights till early hours in the morning. So, on the eve of Jul, my mother and I slipped out of the city and went to Ulvar's house. We had to do this secretly, as merchant families did not mingle with the farmers and fishermen.

Ulvar's family lived on top of a hill overlooking the Baltic Sea. Their humble cottage was made of wattle and daub and had a thatched roof. Rough wooden palings arranged diagonally and tied together with a rope formed a fencing around their land. Warmth and light emanated from the cottage. A large rosehip bush covered the house's front wall and ivy climbed the sides. A walnut tree stood a few metres away. Under its branches, an old timber bench faced the horizon.

When we arrived, Valentin was outside. He had a big bundle of firewood in his arms. He nodded and led us to the door, which was opened by Ulvar's wife Birgitta. She held up her lantern to see our faces, then embraced my mother and me and beckoned us inside.

There were a few other people already gathered around the large wooden table that stood in the middle of the small kitchen, near the fireplace. A large pot of soup was bubbling on the stove. Birgitta fussed over us, pouring drinks for everyone and offering sweets.

My mother and I sat with Ulvar's neighbours and their daughter, Stjärna. She was sixteen, I discovered, the same age as me. She had the sweetest smile and a gentle manner.

My mother had many tales to share from the years we had spent travelling around the region, bringing back spices and silks from the east, and she was soon the centre of attention. As the stories unfolded, a big Jul log kept on crackling in the fireplace.

As we got closer to midnight, everyone raised their cups to toast the occasion and my mother started wishing everyone a Merry Christmas. An uneasy silence fell over the room. 'It is Jul!' Valentin's grandmother Geirdís said, scowling. 'Since when do we celebrate Christmas here in Gotland? Our ancestors will be turning in their graves!' She turned away and spat in the fire.

'What are you saying, Arngunna?' Birgitta said. 'Have you forgotten your roots, sister?'

'No, I haven't,' my mother said softly. 'I'm sorry.'

'The winters had been long, dark and cruel to our ancestors,' Geirdís said. 'During the harsh winter months, the darkness and the light were in constant battle and the darkness managed to dominate the battleground. The sun became weak and defeated. This is why we have such long nights during winter and see only the palest sun during these months. During this whole time, though, the sun does not give up—she waits and perseveres, she restores her strength, and on the twenty-first of December the darkness relinquishes its power and its place to longer days and warmth. Tonight is a significant and glorious occasion as we welcome the rebirth of the sun and the return of the warmth. Our ancestors burned a Jul log throughout the night as a symbol of the returning light and warmth. The ashes from the log were then kept as a symbol of good luck and good health.' She gestured to the fire, to the burning log.

Glancing at Valentin, I saw he was immersed in the story. Every now and then he would look up and catch my eye, then lower his gaze. I was drawn to him and sensed he was drawn to me in turn. This shy and quiet young man was captivating.

A piece of the flaming log snapped and made a crackling noise before it fell. I caught and held Valentin's gaze. The spirit of Jul had lit a fire between us, I was sure of it.

Finally, the moment we had been waiting for was approaching. 'Come on now,' Birgitta said. 'We need to go outside—the sun will be rising in a few minutes and we can't miss it.'

We all stood and filed out of the cottage. Fires were still burning in pits around the fields and farmlands. A large group of locals had gathered on top of the hill, and others were approaching: young and old, all determined to keep this ancient tradition alive. The sky was still dark, ice and snow covered the ground, and the smell of wood smoke was thick in the air. People huddled in small groups facing the city wall, with lanterns in their hands. Within moments the first ray of sunlight peered over the wall and painted everything with a golden glow. People gasped and cheered at the sight. Valentin took a few small steps towards me. I looked over my shoulder and smiled at him. He was transfixed by the sunrise, his gaze soft and dreamy.

I felt a soft hand grasp mine—it was Stjärna, her eyes twinkling in the early morning light. We smiled at each other and watched the sunrise holding hands; I was excited to have found a friend.

Suddenly, my mother pulled at my kirtle. 'We must return, Gretel—your father will be home soon,' she said.

'Will you come to visit us again?' Stjärna asked me quietly.

'Yes,' I said. 'I will.'

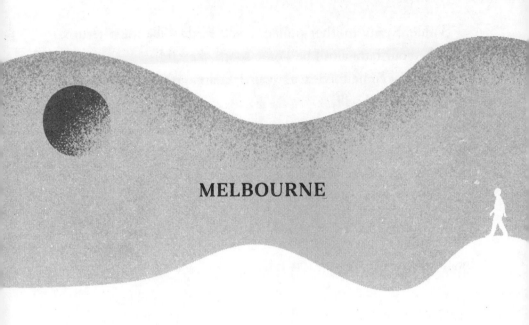

MELBOURNE

HABIBA AND HER NIECES attended their appointments for the DNA tests as requested. The report was sent to the embassy and I received a copy of it in an email. I was nervous about the results; my heart leaped out of my chest when I saw the email on my phone. On my way up to my office, I stop in the doorway of Habiba's store and tell her that the report has come back. 'Alhamdullilah!' she says.

'If you want to come upstairs with me now, we can read it together,' I say.

Habiba quickly instructs her assistant to mind the business and joins me in my office.

The report is ten pages long and contains lots of percentages and figures and estimates.

'What does all of this mean, Tishtar?' Habiba asks when I start reading them aloud.

I skip through all the scientific data and go to the last page.

'*Conclusion: based on all the variables and data collected, there is a ninety-seven per cent chance that Fowziah is related to Habiba, a ninety-eight per cent chance that Fatimah is related to Habiba, a ninety-six per cent chance that Fowziah and Fatimah are related with a ninety-five per cent chance that they are sisters.*' I scratch my stubble. 'It's good,' I say. 'Very good.'

'Good?!' Habiba retorts. 'A ninety-five per cent chance that they are sisters?! Ninety-five per cent? Are they joking?'

'It's my understanding that these tests are never a hundred per cent accurate,' I tell her. 'The clinicians who undertake these tests are reluctant to provide definitive reports. After all, science is always based on probabilities.'

'Why put people through these hoops then?' Habiba demands. 'What happens now?'

'Well, the report has been sent to the embassy. So now we just wait and see.'

Habiba gets up, rearranges her hijab and marches towards the door.

'Habiba?' I call.

She stops. 'These migration laws are written with the intent of stopping people from reuniting with their loved ones,' she says with her back to me. Her voice quavers.

'Habiba, please,' I say.

She raises her hand in farewell and walks out slowly.

I slump in my chair, staring at the report. I think back on all the cases I've handled over the years. They've all been family reunion or refugee cases. The circumstances of each are different, yet one consistent thread unites them: a sense of place, and the loss of that sense. I've searched for my own missing pages in others' stories. The more tales I've heard, the more I've come to realise how much us migrants all have in common. Always on the outside looking in—no longer part of the life we have left behind, not quite belonging to the new-found soil.

Why did I study law? I ask myself. More than two decades ago I came to Australia to continue my studies in visual arts—how had I gone from that to this?

☾

It was a warm day in early March when I met with the Dean of the Faculty of Arts at the University of Wollongong. My host greeted me on the steps and walked me to his office. Beautiful artwork was everywhere: a large Aboriginal painting on the wall; a sculpted figure on his desk which looked like a small version of him; a black-and-white photograph; and a playful Picasso-like oil painting. The afternoon sun was streaming through the window. That day, we talked at great length about my experience as a photographer of violations of human rights in Iran and my expectations from the course, what I hoped to achieve.

After I left his office, I walked to the pond near the library and lay on the grass in the shade. I was confused. I wasn't sure if what had just happened meant defeat or success. The Dean's reference to political oppression and human rights, in particular with respect to women and how they experienced Iran's totalitarian regime, dragged me back to a space I had left and didn't want to revisit again.

I got up and walked and walked in the heat until sunset, thinking about all the women who had suffered irreversible pain under the regime, from progressive politicians like Mrs Parsa to innocent young women like Sarve Bozorgy, from the thousands of women who had lost their sons, husbands, or brothers on battlefields or in prisons, to those like Maman, who were forced to give up their careers when they were in their prime.

I walked up to the lighthouse. It stood tall and strong. The ocean was wearing the orange glow of the sunset; its warmth resonated in me. I felt a small flame flickering inside my heart. What did it all mean? Where was I going?

When I returned to my flat, I shut myself away in the little darkroom I had set up. I processed the roll of black-and-white film I had shot that day.

Inhaling the dampness of the darkroom and the vinegary smell of photographic paper stabiliser, I handled the negatives as if they were fragile jewels. I placed them in the negative holder of the enlarger to print them on my favourite photographic paper. Before my curious eyes, the paper took a deep dive and swam in a pool of chemicals. The little timer on the wall ticked slowly, marking my anxiety as I waited. Soon, faces came to life, and all their stories and memories with them.

I had taken street shots, searching every face, every shadow, every corner for Gretel. She was nowhere to be seen.

I spent hours in the darkroom that night. All the photos I'd taken were either out of focus, underexposed, or overexposed. The faces in the photographs appeared to be mocking me. I became more and more agitated. I threw all the photos and negatives in the bin and poured all the chemicals down the drain.

The next morning I packed up all my photographic equipment. I made a sign, printed copies of it, and stuck it up around uni: I would sell all my equipment. I could no longer bear the pain of searching for her through my lens. I was done with photography.

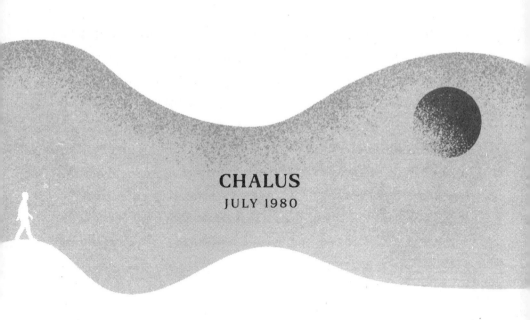

CHALUS

JULY 1980

EVERY YEAR, AS SOON as we finished our end-of-year exams in June, I started pestering my parents to leave dry, congested Tehran and travel north for our annual holiday. Often it would be August before we could get away, and I would spend the weeks in an agony of waiting.

After the exams in the summer of 1980, Maman and Baba started discussing what to pack, and Baba booked his car in for a service with Adolf, a local Armenian mechanic. Baba's 1963 Opel Rekord—a white two-door coupe with red vinyl upholstery—was his pride and joy, and he kept it in mint condition.

The night before we were due to leave, Baba packed the car. The boot was enormous, yet it filled quickly with everything Maman felt we had to take: pillows, sheets, towels, pots and pans, even though the seaside villa where we would stay along with Madar and Aunty Tangerine was fully furnished.

'For God's sake!' Baba complained. 'We are only going for two weeks, we are not moving up north permanently!'

Baba insisted that we would be leaving at 7 am sharp. 'I don't want to drive in the heat.'

Although he was good at concealing his excitement about the trip, I knew that my father was eager to return to his homeland, to be close to the sea, to eat the local food, to fill up his lungs with the sea air. As we drove, he regaled us with tales of his childhood growing up in the north.

The road from Tehran to the Caspian Sea first consisted of a couple of hundred kilometres of barren, dusty freeway. Then, a couple of hours into the journey, small towns started to pop up randomly like wild mushrooms. I saw old men sitting on benches outside the local tea houses, smoking hookah, discussing local affairs. Occasionally younger men running errands passed by and bowed to greet the elders. Local women doing the shopping hurried hither and thither, their small children in bright traditional attire clinging to the corners of their dresses like streamers in the wind: bright green, red, yellow, and blue.

Baba often varied the route we would take.

'Which way are we going this year, Baba?' I asked.

'Hezar Cham,' he responded.

'Oh, so we won't see the Zohreh and Taher fortress?' I said, disappointed.

'We can come home that way,' Baba promised.

'What fortress? Who is Zohreh?' asked Satyar.

'She is the subject of a tragic love story,' Maman said. 'Her family did not approve of her love for Taher. When she was told that he had been killed, she took her own life. But of course he was not dead. He found his way to the fortress, and when he discovered her dead body, Taher also took his own life.'

'Ah, it breaks my heart, that story,' said Aunty Tangerine.

Baba drove past the peak of Hezar Cham on a long winding road through the Alborz mountains that eventually took us to the Mazandaran Province on the shores of the Caspian Sea. Driving this road was not for the faint-hearted—its many twists and turns made it both terrifying and exhilarating.

As the road ascended, the scenery would gradually change. The rocky mountain ranges grew greener, there were more trees, and the air turned cooler and more humid. We usually stopped at the midway point for a break. Baba pulled into a little dirt road after a sharp turn. I was always amazed by his knowledge of the road—he knew exactly where to turn, though all the bends and curves looked the same to me.

Concealed behind some rocks was a little roadside kiosk. A samovar sat on a flat rock, like a monument, flanked by a tray full of small hourglass-shaped teacups, a bowl of unevenly cut sugar cubes, and a handful of teaspoons. Those who preferred cold drinks could choose from the bottles of yoghurt mixed with sparkling mineral water and dried mint, Pepsi, and Coca-Cola cooling in the mountain stream.

Refreshed after the stop, we piled back into the car. As we began our descent from the mountains I became impatient, craning my neck from the back seat to see if I could catch the first glimpse of the Caspian Sea.

'There it is! There it is!' I shouted at the first sighting.

Although there was still some way to go before we reached our destination, the smallest glimpse of the sea was enough to awaken my soul. The smell of salty sea air was tantalising, soft and tender as it seeped into my lungs.

The road continued along the coastline and we passed through several small towns on our way to our final destination, Chalus, a quaint seaside resort. *The coast of summer tales*, it was called in the ads. As we drove I could hear the local children calling out to the passing motorists, some selling the fish they or their parents had caught that day. Juicy watermelons and other locally grown summer fruits and herbs were on display at the roadside stalls. Other children called out, 'Room for rent,' as cars whizzed past.

Another hour or so of driving and the scenery resembled a picture postcard. On the left, mountains draped in velvety green blankets stood guard over the tea plantations on their slopes, the rice fields at their feet, and the farms in between. The slopes were also home to the local dairy herds: milky white cows with big black spots. To our right, waves gently caressed the pebbles, the seashells and the sand.

'White flags are up!' I cried. 'We can go for a swim!' Lifeguards raised white flags as a sign of safe waters; black flags were used when the sea was choppy and dangerous.

After hours of driving we finally arrived.

'Have you got the keys?' Baba asked Maman as she rummaged in her handbag. Baba's cousin had bought the villa a few years back. He would go there a few times a year to seek solitude. At other times of the year, he would let family members stay there. I snatched the keys out of Maman's hands and ran up the small steps to the verandah. The villa was a spacious two-storey building within three hundred metres of the sea. It had a small garden in which native flowers grew. During the day the sound of crickets competed with the roar of the waves in the background.

We opened the door to a musty smell. 'We have to air the place,' Maman said. I volunteered to run upstairs to open the bedroom windows, though really I just wanted an excuse to run out onto the terrace and take in the panoramic view of the sea.

After unpacking the car we had lunch and then walked down to the beach for a swim. We spent all afternoon in the water, until the sun at last vacated the sky for the moon. There was something deeply moving about watching the sunset while being wrapped in the warmth of the sea.

In the evening, we visited a local seaside cafe for dinner. Baba had particular places where he liked to take us. He believed that because the men knew him they would serve us the freshest food. It might have been true: he was from the region and knew his produce, and he also understood the local dialect better than the rest of us.

One little hut was the family favourite. Only a stone's throw away from the beach. It was simply furnished with a few metal chairs, an assortment of wooden tables covered with faded tablecloths, and fresh flowers in pickle jars-cum-vases. Two local fishermen ran the business. As soon as we entered, they'd rearrange their tables and chairs to accommodate the six of us. Bread would be served fresh from the oven, with local feta, and basil, mint, and tarragon from the garden. A couple of metres outside the hut there was a charcoal barbecue on which one of the brothers would grill skewers of marinated chicken, lamb, or fish. The adults always ordered mahi sefid (the local white fish) while Satyar had lamb and I had chicken marinated in lemon juice and saffron.

'How's fishing, my boy?' Baba asked the young proprietor.

'It's okay, uncle,' he replied in the northern dialect. 'Average, I'd say. The Russians take half, so we have to share!'

'We have to share nothing!' Maman piped up. 'The Caspian Sea is all ours! All of it, not half! We are the rightful owners of these waters! You must read the history books, my son—you will see that less than two centuries ago the government of the time gave substantial parts of our country to the Russians. I know this, I am a teacher!'

The man smiled politely, bowed, and took our order to his brother at the barbecue. Shortly afterwards, puffs of smoke filled the air and tomatoes blistered over the charcoal. The Caspian Sea was very quiet that night—you could just hear the waves touching the foreshore before retreating. Crickets sang a soft melody nearby; in the distance the mountains were fast asleep.

By the time we returned to the villa with bellies full of food, the full moon was high in the sky. We sat on the terrace, gazing at its glittering light on the sea, and sipped cups of tea. Baba recounted tales of family members who had lived in this region generations before us, and I tried to picture what life was like for our forebears, what they had seen in their day.

Madar was sitting silently in her recliner chair; I could tell from her strained expression that her arthritis was bothering her. 'What are you thinking about, Madar?' I asked.

'I was thinking how pleasant this is,' she said. 'It is a far cry from the harsh winters of my youth. We did not have the luxury of plumbing in our house—we had to buy water from a horse cart. Women then had to heat the water over the fire for cooking and bathing. We never washed clothes and sheets in warm water, though, as we had to be frugal with our firewood. When we didn't have enough money to buy water we used snow and ice from the yard. We were lucky that back then it snowed a lot more than it does nowadays. The arthritis in my hands now is a result of years spent washing dishes and clothes in icy-cold water outside in the yard.'

We knew from Maman that Madar was a strong woman. She had survived the First World War as a child then, as a young widow with three toddlers, she lived through the Second World War. Everyone in the family had the utmost respect for her; it was no small feat to have raised three children on her own with little money and no support.

'Madar, what was life like during the Second World War?' Satyar asked now.

'Oh, those times were truly tough on everyone,' Madar said as she gazed out at the sea. 'I had no tenants in the half of the house during that time because people had no money. In 1941, Hitler invaded the Soviet Union, and despite the fact that Iran was neutral, the Allied forces occupied Iran and used it as a base to push back Hitler's army and as a supply route. Tehran was full of foreign soldiers, some of whom got drunk at nights and roamed the streets. We were often woken during the night when they banged on our door looking for women. We didn't have the protection of a man, so your maman and her brothers hid under their blankets until the threat had passed. We never knew from one day to the next what lay ahead.'

'Madar, can you tell me more about the ones from across the water?' I asked.

'Enough now, both of you!' Maman intervened. 'Madar is tired, and you need to go to bed now, Tishtar, if you want to go for a swim again in the morning.' To Madar she said: 'He doesn't need to know about this stuff, any more than he does about Scandinavia—it is all history now.'

'But everyone needs to know the story of their people, their footprints in time,' Madar argued.

'Family history that old can't possibly be reliable; there were no birth records then for the common folk. We can't prove it and we don't need to.' Maman stood up abruptly and went back inside.

Satyar and I slept on fold-out beds in the main bedroom, leaving the two single beds for Maman and Baba. They came to bed late. I was still awake listening to the waves.

'Why don't you want me to know about things, Maman?' I asked.

'Hush,' she said. 'You are not a baby anymore—you need to grow out of this interest in nonsensical fairytales. Life is not some Zohreh and Taher fairytale. Look at what is happening to

Iran today! Our country, the land of heroes and riches is reduced to this.'

'But Maman, this is very real! I see and feel the things that you can't!' I said.

'Do you know what my worry is? That you will grow up with your head stuck in the clouds. You see life through an unrealistic lens! Stop dreaming—when will you listen? When your uncle was your age he wrote articles for the local newspaper to support our family!'

'He is only ten—leave him alone,' said Baba.

'I will have a word with my mother tomorrow—she has encouraged this fairytale nonsense!' said Maman.

I found it puzzling that Maman told the Zohreh and Tahir saga with an unmistakable passion but turned on her pragmatic voice when it came to my thoughts and feelings. I buried my head under the sheet. The sound of the waves drowned out Maman's warnings. *Maybe I will have nice adventures in my dreams tonight*, I said to myself as I dozed off.

☽

In the morning we visited the local shops. Lots of handmade baskets were hanging outside small shacks. The patterns and colours were so vibrant it was impossible to choose one. Some shops sold hand-carved wooden spoons and ladles, along with doormats, straw hats, and inflatable beach balls and tubes.

After buying things we didn't really need, we went back to the villa. It was a hot day, with humidity at ninety per cent; the sea was blue and calm. I was excited about going to the beach. While the adults had a siesta, Satyar and I went down to the shore. He hung out with the local boys his own age and ordered me to amuse myself on the sand. I occupied myself making sandcastles for a while, and when I was bored with that I lay on my towel and watched the activity around me. There were lots of boats and people in the water. Small children screamed with joy as they bobbed up and down in their inflatable tubes.

Turning to look along the beach, I saw a familiar figure in the distance: a young woman in a long white dress. The sea breeze was blowing her light-blonde hair across her face. It was Gretel. Rising to my feet, I started walking towards her. Her gaze was locked on the horizon, her eyes so blue it was as though she was carrying the sea within her. I took a few more steps but I couldn't seem to get any closer. It was as if there were an invisible barrier between us.

I heard Satyar calling me and turned to see him waving at me furiously, signalling that I should hurry back. When I looked back at Gretel, she was gone.

Walking back to join Satyar, I was excited and confused. I couldn't work out how Gretel had come to be there with us. I asked him if he had seen the pretty girl on the beach.

'Don't be stupid! You sat in the sun too long and your head is cooked! We'll both be in big trouble now; we've been gone for hours and Maman will not be happy.'

We hurried back to the villa. I took one last glance at the beach before we left; there was no sign of Gretel, though. I felt a tingling in my heart but couldn't understand what it meant.

As Satyar had predicted, we copped an earful from Maman when we returned—first because we had gone to the beach without letting anyone know where we were going, and then because we hadn't bothered with sunscreen.

In order to avoid another round of lectures, I crept away to Madar's room.

Madar was dozing when I entered, but she soon woke.

'Madar?' I said.

'Yes, my love?'

'I saw her earlier—she was on the shore looking at the waves.'

'Who?'

'Gretel! She must be the most beautiful person on earth, Madar—she is like a goddess!'

'Oh, listen to you! Goddess!' But she must have realised that I was serious, because she stopped her teasing. 'Okay, what do you mean?' she asked. 'What is this goddess business about?'

'Madar, I think she must have come from the heavens. Her eyes are so blue that you could drown in them.'

Madar studied me for a moment then pulled me into her arms. 'Hmm,' she said. 'Are you sure it was her? Maybe it was just someone who looks like Gretel. This is a holiday town, remember—a lot of people come here.'

I wrapped my arms around Madar's warm body and listened to her heartbeat, steady and strong and reassuring.

'I know it was her, Madar. I don't know why she is here, though.'

Madar ran her fingers through my curly hair.

'Will I ever be able to talk to her again, Madar?' I asked.

'Maybe one day. But you are very young still. When the time is right, when she is ready, and if it is meant to be, you will talk,' she said.

'She is very pretty, Madar.'

'Yes, she is, darling,' Madar agreed.

'Very pretty! Really pretty! But, Madar?'

'Yes, my love?'

'Please don't tell Maman about her. She wouldn't understand.'

☽

That night, the moon hung low in the sky, so bright, shining through the bushes, casting shadows on the wall next to my pillow. I listened to the crickets; their tune sounded like the saddest sonata. Something had changed, as though a warm river was flowing inside me. I fell asleep to the sound of the waves in the distance and wondered if Gretel would visit me in my dreams.

☽

For the rest of our stay in Chalus, I continued to go to the beach in the afternoon while Maman and Baba napped. I was hoping to see Gretel again, but she never appeared. At night, I sat on the terrace and looked at the glittering moonlight on the sea, wondering if she was strolling barefoot along the sand. In my heart of hearts, I was sure that I would see her again before we left for home.

On the last night of our holiday I sat on the terrace for hours, and she finally came.

'I've been waiting for you,' I said.

'I'm here now,' she replied. She walked to the edge of the terrace and leaned against the railing. 'The sea air brings back memories of long ago.'

'What kind?' I asked.

'Memories buried in the sand, laughter lost at sea.' Her eyes were distant.

'Tell me more, please.'

And as she stared out at the sea, with her back to me, she continued her story.

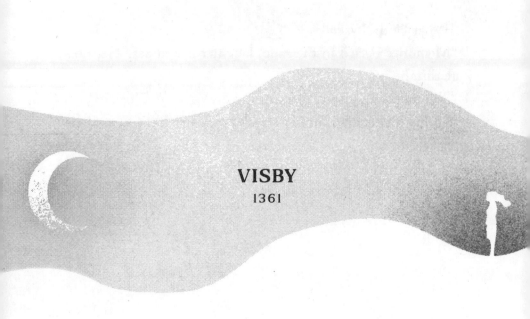

VISBY
1361

AFTER SPENDING THE NIGHT of Jul with Valentin and his family, I was keen to return to the countryside and learn more about how the people around the island lived. During our years away, Mother had told me about her life on Gotland and how much she yearned to return, but Father wouldn't allow it. He often spoke harshly to her; coming home late from his gatherings with other merchants he was often drunk, and he would use his fists on her. I was scared and didn't like how he treated her, but Mother told me that women must always obey their fathers and husbands.

One day, I left the house without telling anyone where I was going; I did not want to arouse the suspicion of my father's servants, who I knew would report my movements back to him. Accompanied only by my dog, Mishka, I slipped through the city gates and headed for the port, hoping to find Valentin.

I was captivated by all the activity around the quay, with the boats coming in, men yelling, carts moving around. I soon spied Valentin helping his father to clean the fish they had caught. Ulvar looked alarmed to see me wandering around on my own along the harbour, and in a low voice he told Valentin to escort me back to the gates. Valentin wiped his hands with his apron and without saying anything gestured for me to follow him.

A gentle breeze fanned the sea air towards the shore, and the waves washing against the pebbles made a soft soothing sound. Seagulls circled above.

'Where is your dog from?' Valentin asked eventually.

'Mishka?' I asked with excitement.

'Your dog has a name?' he mumbled, keeping his gaze down.

I explained that I'd found her when we were camping with other merchant families near Lake Ladoga. The area was always busy with trade, people from the east and west would meet and exchange goods. 'She used to wander around the campsite and I started feeding her. Soon she became a permanent part of our camp and when we started to pack to move again, we decided that she should come with us. We have had her for nearly three years now.'

Though he was still not saying much and I was talking the whole way, Valentin seemed interested in my stories of life travelling with my father. When we reached Lilla Strandporten, he stopped.

'This is as far as I can come. This is a quiet gate so I hope that no one will see you with me. Go now,' Valentin said.

I was fascinated by life in Visby; I had been gone for years and could barely remember anything about it. I asked him to tell me about the true Gotlanders, those who had lived on the island for centuries before the German merchants arrived and occupied the town.

☾

After this first excursion, I became more and more interested in life on the island. I would often sneak out to see Valentin at the harbour.

I had confided in our housekeeper, Valka, who lived in the country and would escort me out of Lilla Strandporten. She was surprised that I knew about this gate. When she told Mother that she was worried about my boldness, Mother told her that I had her warrior blood.

At first Valentin was guarded and would not say much, his answers were short and abrupt. The more questions I asked about life on the island, the more he started giving more detailed description of what life was like for his people. At the end of each visit, I would go home and tell Mother about all the things he had shared with me. Mother and Valka often exchanged glances seeing how elated I was after spending time with Valentin. Their looks and smiles always gave me a tingling sensation.

Mother and I often visited Birgitta and I would seek out Stjärna, as she and her mother worked on the farm and around the house. I watched her skilfully clean fish and stack them in the smoking hut. 'Come, don't just watch,' she said. 'Let me teach you how it's done.'

'Stjärna, do you get tired of working all day long?' I asked her as I clumsily copied her movements while preparing the fish.

'This is how it has always been,' she said simply. 'We women must work hard to produce what we need.'

I preferred their way of living to that of the merchants, I decided; I admired how they lived on what their land had to offer, and how skilled they were at sustaining themselves without needing to travel all over the world.

'Come, now I want to prepare the ingredients for a drink,' Stjärna said when all the fish were smoking. I followed her to a small hut that contained a few barrels. Stjärna reached for a goblet on a shelf and poured me a drink from one of the barrels.

I took a sip and recognised it as the drink I had tasted on the night of the Jul.

'We drink this in winter, to keep warm,' Stjärna said. 'We make it with cranberries we pick from the forest, plus wheat, malt, and honey from our own farm.'

I thought about all the years that Mother had been away from all of these old traditions and started understanding why she was longing to return to her soil, to be with her own people.

☾

One day I overheard Birgitta talking to my mother. 'It is only a matter of time before Karl Johann discovers what is going on!' she said. She was referring to my father. 'You are in denial, my sister! You don't want to admit that your husband does not approve of us country folk. But you know as well as I that there is no place for Valentin in Gretel's future—not as far as Karl Johann is concerned.'

'It will be fine,' my mother said.

'Arngunna! What about Stjärna?' Birgitta pleaded. 'We had plans and dreams for her and Valentin. We have all been waiting for them to grow up and start a family together. Stjärna's heart will be broken. This is not going to end well.'

Geirdís had been having nightmares, Birgitta confided. She would wake up screaming in the middle of the night. 'Oh, my child, these dreams are not good,' she would tell her daughter. 'Our ancestors are telling us something. It's not good, it's not good . . .'

Destiny will decide what should happen, my mother responded.

GILAN
JULY 1980

ON OUR WAY HOME from Chalus, Baba drove through Gilan
Province, where he had been born and raised. The route took a bit
longer, but the road was flatter and safer. Really, though, I think he
chose this road so that he could reconnect with his land and people;
even just driving through the region seemed to nourish his soul.

After driving through several small townships, we arrived at
Rudbar, a town with a history stretching back more than two
thousand years. Rudbar was famous for its olives, and every second
store had a large tray of olives, bottles of extra virgin oil, and bars
of olive soap on display, each shopkeeper claiming to offer the
best-quality products.

'You see that old fortress?' Maman said, pointing to the
remainders of an ancient fortress tucked away on a distant hill-
side. 'That's where Zohreh locked herself away.'

I was wedged between Madar and Satyar in the back seat and I had to crane my neck to see. Staring at the fortress I imagined the heartache and the pain the two lovers would have felt.

'Madar? What happened to Valentin in the end?' I asked. 'Did he suffer the same fate as Taher?'

Maman stirred in her seat and turned to face Madar. They exchanged a meaningful look but nothing was said aloud. Madar didn't respond to my question.

For most of the long drive home we were quiet. I was dreading going back to the dry, polluted city. The moment the Caspian Sea was out of sight I longed to return. 'When will be coming back again, Baba?' I asked.

Baba just shook his head. 'I don't know, son.'

I was frustrated; I had so many questions, but it seemed no one was prepared to provide me with answers.

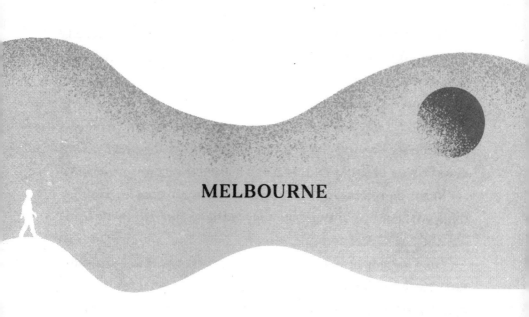

MELBOURNE

I WAIT ANXIOUSLY FOR the embassy in Nairobi to interrogate or dismiss the DNA results, but time passes with no response at all. It is May by the time I receive an email offering Fowziah and Fatimah a time and date for an interview.

Habiba has been keeping to herself, but I know from her strained expression when we nod to each other as I walk past her shop on the way to my office that the stress is starting to affect her.

As soon as I have read the email I run downstairs and burst into her shop, interrupt her conversation with her circle of women.

'Sorry! But we must talk!' I say, trying to catch my breath.

She sends the women away and ushers me to a chair. 'What is it, Tishtar?' she asks. 'Is it good news or bad?'

'They want to interview the girls,' I tell her.

She claps her hands together in excitement. 'See! I told you Allah would help! An interview is the final step. They would not interview them if they had any doubts!' Then, aware of my silence, she falters. 'Or would they?' she says.

'Habiba,' I say, 'nothing means anything until the whole process is complete. The interview is just another step. The case officer must be sure of the facts in order to make a thorough assessment.'

'What do you mean they must be sure?' she demands. 'Do they think we have been lying? Are they going to interrogate the girls like they have committed a crime?'

'No, I wouldn't call it interrogation, but they will want to make sure that what you have said in your statement is the truth. They might ask the girls questions about how they have been able to make contact with you, whether they are in touch with you—these types of questions.'

'They can ask me anything they like—I have only told the truth. Please send me the details of the meeting so I can inform my relative.' And Habiba shoos me out of her shop.

☾

Over the following two weeks I'm swamped with work, and I am surprised when Habiba barges into my office one morning with a box of sweets. 'Here, eat! We must celebrate!' she says.

I shake my head in confusion. 'What are we celebrating?' I ask.

'Mashallah! You forgot, didn't you? The girls had their interview yesterday! My relative said that it went really well, and that the case officer was very nice. Now put that laptop away and eat a sweet! One of the women from my shop will bring in

coffees in a minute and I want to tell you all about the interview.'
Then, without stopping to draw breath, she launches into her story.

'Allah be my witness, I was very nervous. I have performed
special prayers since you told me about the interview date. When
I told the girls about it, they were very worried. They thought
they were in trouble. Fatima said that their Swahili wasn't good
enough to do an interview with an official and Fowziah cried her
eyes out, thinking they were going to be kicked out of Kenya.
Over the past couple of weeks, Mum and I have spent so much
time with them on Skype, comforting them.

'The night of their interview, I set my alarm clock so that
I don't forget to wake them up. When I rang, my relative said
that they had been up since five in the morning. We stayed on
the phone with them until they arrived at the Australian High
Commission in Nairobi, where they had to turn off their mobile
phones. That's when my nerves really kicked in.

'I sat on the sofa and didn't know what to do with myself.
I imagined them sitting in the waiting room with no idea what
to expect. I kept checking the time. *Any minute now they will be
called to go in*, I said to Mum. *Be calm, my girl, Allah will be with
them*, she kept assuring me.

'She persuaded me to join her in the kitchen and we started
cooking. Every time my phone rang, I jumped out of my skin.
Finally my relative called. He put the girls on straight away and
they were buzzing with excitement.

'*The lady, Maryama, was very nice, she could speak Somali really
well!* said Fatimah. *She gave us a chocolate each and we showed her
your photos on our phone*, Fowziah added.

'When I heard the name, I thought praise Allah that a woman interviewed them. I am sure now that everything will be fine.'

'Habiba, that's wonderful but we must not get ahead of ourselves here.'

'Tishtar! Have faith! It will be okay, I know it in my heart.' She grins.

One of the women arrives with the coffee, and Habiba pushes the box of sweets in front of me. 'Eat, Tishtar. Eat!' she orders and proceeds with questions.

'Tishtar? Can I ask you something?'

'Yes?'

'How long have you been in Melbourne?'

'Hmm, a few years now, I think about six or seven, why do you ask?'

'What brought you here?'

'Work, I needed a change so when a job came up, I decided to move from NSW. Aren't you lucky!' I winked, she grinned.

'So, you have been here now all that time, you must have made a lot of friends?' she concludes.

'Nah not really, a couple of close ones but I like my peace and quiet.'

'You sound like an old man! People need people, one must be surrounded by lots of people! I'd die if our house was quiet!'

I check the time—it's nearly 4 pm; I will miss my train if I don't leave soon. I become uncomfortable. I don't want to be rude to Habiba, but I really need to get to the station.

'So, when are you going to get married, brother?' Habiba asks, leaning back in her seat.

'Habiba!' I say as I start packing my laptop. 'Not that conversation again!'

'Tishtar, you need to start a family!'

'I'm sorry, sister, but I must go,' I say. 'Thanks for the sweets, but I really have to go.'

☾

As on most days, I make it to the train just before the doors close. I'm sweaty and nervous. Will she get on? Will she see me? Will we talk?

The doors open at the next station and Gretel walks in. She walks past me as though I am a piece of furniture—insignificant and invisible.

My knees go weak and I sink into the nearest seat. It's the same every day.

TEHRAN

SEPTEMBER 1980

I WAS UPSTAIRS IN my bedroom doing my homework while Maman was in the kitchen baking saffron kaka. The aroma of cardamom and saffron coming from the kitchen was tantalising. Apricot was sitting under my feet playing with a cat toy—every now and then his claws would get stuck in my socks. Maman didn't know he was inside; I snuck him in when she wasn't looking.

Every now and then I stopped and spun the world globe that Madar had given me for my birthday. I located Iran and the Caspian Sea on the map; my mind sailed deep into the north as it often did.

My imaginary voyage took me to the northern parts of Europe. To Scandinavia, the mysterious wintry and cold landscape that so fascinated me. I was thinking about where Gretel and Valentin had lived when I heard Baba rush into the house. He told Maman that the airport had been shut down, and that Iran was under attack.

I went and sat on the stairs and watched my parents talking in the hallway. Maman's face was pale. 'But why?' she asked. 'What's happened?' Maman had so many questions, but Baba had few answers.

☾

Everything was happening so fast—Iraq had invaded a few towns along the western border and was attacking other cities in the vicinity. People were fleeing the border towns, heading towards the capital or to other big cities. Thousands were killed.

Satyar had turned eighteen that April, two months before he graduated from high school, and he was required to join the army before the end of the year; military service has always been compulsory in Iran. Earlier that year, at Maman's insistence, he had applied to study in Vienna and had got a student visa through the Austrian embassy in Tehran.

Baba had been reluctant at first. 'He is a bright student,' he'd said. 'The top of his class. Why can't he go to university here?'

'You seem to have forgotten that they have closed down the universities indefinitely,' Maman countered. 'He and all other bright students will be waiting a while for them to reopen.'

Eventually Baba gave in, as he always did. Now, it was imperative that Satyar leave for Austria before the borders closed.

I still remember the dark and windy afternoon when Baba packed Satyar's bags with much care and diligence, putting things in the suitcase and taking them out again, while Maman sat on a chair beside him overseeing the operations like a site supervisor. Baba even sewed a handful of US dollars into the lining of his winter jacket.

'Have you packed his action heroes notebook?' I asked.

'You take care of it for me until we see each other again,' said Satyar as he stuffed his favourite cassettes into the gaps between his clothes.

Finally, late in the afternoon of a cold October day, we took Satyar to the main bus terminal. From there, he and a group of twenty or so other young men like him would board a minibus and leave Iran for the safety of Europe. Some were bound for Germany while others, like Satyar, would travel to Austria. A strong autumn wind blew maple leaves around our feet. The boys got on the bus one by one. Baba pretended to be wiping dust from his eye, but I knew he was crying. The bus's automatic door hissed closed. We could see Satyar sitting by the window, waving to us. He was grinning.

The bus crawled out of the terminal, headed for the Turkish border. We stood there for a while with the other families that had come to bid their sons farewell. No one spoke a word. Gradually, the crowd dispersed and we all went home.

A few weeks after Satyar left, the government closed all the borders and no one was allowed to leave the country unless they had permanent residency in another country. The restrictions became tighter and harsher day by day.

My parents were not the only ones who had to say goodbye to their son so abruptly. Thousands of others had also arranged for their boys to be sent overseas. Many more lost their sons on the battlefield. Tehran's cemetery, along with cemeteries all over the country, expanded rapidly. They were frequented by grieving mothers, who came to talk to their fallen boys about the hopes and dreams for the future they had buried with them. Many of the soldiers who survived the war sustained physical and emotional scars that never healed.

Our country was already shrouded by the dark blanket of the Islamic Revolution, but war made everything worse. Relationships fell apart, as friends and family members either migrated or withdrew from society, too fearful to venture out. My mother's famous dinner parties ceased; only a handful of people still visited, my uncle and Aunty Tangerine among them, though even they came less frequently. Madar began to spend a lot more time at our house.

When we did gather, conversations no longer dwelled on fond memories of the past—they had been replaced by discussions about the political state of the country. Maman would talk endlessly about the mass killings of political activists or those perceived to be involved with some sort of insurgency, while Baba and my uncle analysed the progress of war according to reports from western media. The BBC and Voice of America broadcast views that were quite different from those in the local press.

'Iran will fall to Iraq in no time,' my uncle maintained. 'Saddam has the backing of the west.'

'Of course, as long as we have oil, we will always be a target,' Maman said. 'Iran is the jewel of the Middle East and everyone wants a piece of us.'

'We are doomed, basically,' Baba said gloomily. 'It does not matter who is at fault and who is backing whom. We are surrounded by the enemy, within and without. Simple as that!'

The furniture in our dining room was soon covered in sheets, as we no longer gathered there. Citizens of Tehran were ordered to black out their windows at night so the city wouldn't be a target for Iraqi fighter jets. Soon every window in the city was covered with thick curtains, blankets, sheets, or cardboard—whatever people could get their hands on. Most nights the power company would cut off the electricity to conceal the city in a blanket of darkness.

No one had heard from Satyar or the other young men on the bus since they'd left Tehran, and we were all starting to get anxious. The parents were constantly calling one another asking if anyone had any updates. There were no mobile phones or internet in those days, so it was harder to keep in touch.

One afternoon, a man came to our door saying he had news from Satyar and the other boys. Baba invited him in and Maman brought out a cup of tea straight away. The man put a sugar cube in his mouth and slurped a mouthful of hot tea. We tried to conceal our impatience as we waited for him to tell us what he knew. Finally he placed the cup back on the saucer with a clink. 'They have made it!' he said, a wide grin spreading beneath his bushy moustache. 'My son rang last night and said that your son and the other three boys who were destined for Vienna have all arrived safe and sound. But it wasn't smooth sailing. The driver drove them across the border to Turkey in the middle of the night, then stopped and demanded more money. When they refused to pay, he kicked them off the bus and drove off. Imagine! They waited there by the side of the road for hours in the freezing cold and total darkness, until a truck driver stopped and offered to take them to Istanbul. From there, they caught another bus and after three days they reached Vienna. They have found a place to stay for the moment.' He pulled out a piece of paper with the phone number of the house.

Maman could not wait for the man to leave so that we could call Vienna.

When we rang, a man with a deep voice answered the phone. Maman asked for Satyar. 'Ein moment, bitte, ein moment,' the man said.

After a few minutes Satyar came to the phone. He sounded excited as he told us that the temperature was minus twenty-five degrees. We gazed at each other in astonishment: that was a level of cold beyond our comprehension. Suddenly, our winters seemed insignificant.

☾

Before long, it was late November and our own winter had gained strength; a heavy snow had fallen. Our source of heating was a large kerosene wall heater. Because of the war, kerosene and gas were rationed and each household was entitled to only twenty litres of kerosene per fortnight which we had to use for cooking, heating, and washing. In order to make the little kerosene we had last as long as possible, we had to be frugal, only turning the heater on in the evenings. We were also very aware of the increased risk of fire from the kerosene if a bomb exploded nearby and the building shook violently. We sat in the small spare room where our TV was kept, although the TV was never turned on.

I would do my homework in one corner under a kerosene lamp as my parents spoke softly in the other corner. They listened to the radio to keep up-to-date with the latest news of our region. The broadcasts were frequently interrupted by announcements encouraging people to take shelter—anywhere secure they could find, for there were no purpose-built bomb shelters. The siren would suddenly blare, and a voice would boom ominously, '*Tavajoh! Tavajoh! The code you are hearing is code red! This means you must take shelter now!*' Baba had determined that it was best if we run outside to the yard. 'At least when the building falls down we won't be buried alive under tons of rubble,' he would say.

Running out to the yard at all hours of the night soon became the norm. If I was in the middle of my homework, I would just put my pen down and race outside. We would huddle on the steps leading to the garden and wait in the dark. I used to look up at the sky to see if I could spot the Iraqis' fighter jets. The anti-aircraft missiles lit up the sky like fireworks. Then the ground would shake as the bombs landed. The closer they fell, the more we felt it. The sensation was similar to being a passenger in an aeroplane as it is landing and you feel a thump as the wheels hit the tarmac. Once we heard the radio announcement that it was safe to come out of our 'shelters', we went back inside. I would pick up my pen and carry on with my homework.

Then the phone would ring. 'Allo? Are you okay?' Everyone routinely called around to check that close relatives were still alive.

My cousin lived on the twenty-second floor of a high rise in the centre of the city. She used to phone and report the location of the bomb blasts.

'What do you see, my dear?' Maman would ask nervously.

'Aunty, I think that they have bombed the south-west this time, around grand-uncle's house or thereabouts,' my cousin might report.

'Oh, dear God, we must ring them then . . .' Maman would respond. She would hang up and then, with shaky hands, dial my uncle's house. There was an anxious wait as the phone rang, then: 'Allo? Oh, thank God you are okay . . .'

Some nights I chose solitude over spending the final hours of the day in the TV room. Instead, I would quietly bring Apricot in from outside then light a candle and seek refuge in my bedroom. I had a small suitcase packed with the essentials in case we had to run for our lives. In my young mind, I had a plan. Should the situation escalate, we would walk and walk over the mountains and then voyage across the sea. I often consulted the globe. My mind would inevitably drift to the north. Since my encounter with Gretel, my compass had been directing my mind and soul in that direction.

When day broke, we dragged our sleep-deprived selves out of bed and resumed our normal routine. I would walk to school with my classmate from down the road; Maman no longer dropped me at school on her way to work. Because she refused to wear a hijab to school, she could no longer teach, and was forced to retire at the age of forty-five. She gradually fell into a dark depression and withdrew from the outside world, immersing herself in her writing and poetry. Baba, on the other hand, was more pragmatic and continued working. Really, he had no choice—how else were we going to survive financially? He not only had to support our family in Tehran; he was sending money to Satyar in Austria, too.

Each morning as I said goodbye to my parents, I would take a last look over my shoulder, never knowing whether we would see each other at the end of the day, whether the house would still be standing when I returned home from school. No one knew.

The sirens would go off frequently while we were at school. Teachers would pause their lessons, exams would come to a halt, and all sporting activities would stop as we ran to a safe corner in the school. When we were given the all clear, we resumed as though nothing had happened.

Coming home from school was scarier. There was always the risk of being bombed by Iraqi planes or snatched by the Revolutionary Guard for wearing Nike shoes, or being in possession of western music, or any other reason they could find to arrest someone. Often they didn't need a reason—they persecuted because they could.

The most common daily task for adults was sourcing food, as everything was rationed or otherwise available only at hefty prices on the black market. Each family was issued with a booklet of coupons according to the number of people in the household. With these we could purchase chicken, eggs, milk, rice, detergents, and sanitary products. Aunty Tangerine shared her coupons with us and her brother. Families who had only boys gave their sanitary products to those with girls in exchange for extra eggs. Everyone swapped coupons like they were collectable cards. Two chicken coupons in exchange for a bag of rice; one washing powder coupon in exchange for a dozen eggs. Those who had the financial means to buy extra in the black market did so at risk of being arrested and penalised. Others learned to live with what they had. I think people just got used to eating and washing less often.

When Baba wasn't at work, he would spend hours lining up to buy essentials with our allocated coupons. Sometimes, the shop-keeper would pull down the shutters announcing that supplies had run out before Baba reached the head of the line. It often just meant that the shopkeeper was selling his goods for three to four times more on the black market. Baba would come home empty-handed, sad and frustrated.

'Oh God, what are we reduced to?' Maman would cry. 'Not long ago, we had free education and food for every child! Now, not only can our children not attend school safely, they don't even have enough food to eat.'

She was referring to the Shah's White Revolution. At family gatherings, adults often talked about the groundbreaking reforms the Shah had implemented in the 1960s. The industrial expansion, voting rights for women, free education, breakfast for school-aged children, and plenty of jobs and housing opportunities for everyone. It was frightening and surreal to think that nearly two decades of reforms and prosperity had been wiped out so quickly. It was as though someone had pressed the rewind button on our country.

Our quiet evenings were full of trepidation. Every waking moment we expected to hear the sirens, or a phone call to tell us about someone who had died in a bomb blast or been arrested, imprisoned or executed.

☾

It was a dark winter day when Maman had a call from Mrs Bozorgy.

'Sarve hasn't come home from school,' Maman told us when she hung up, holding her head between her hands and rocking back and forth.

The phone rang again. Baba answered this time. 'I see, I see. Dear God,' he said as he put the phone down, his face white.

I put my pen down and stared at my parents.

'Who was it?' Maman asked.

'Apparently the Mujahedin held a demonstration near Sarve's school today,' Baba explained. 'People say that when kids left the school, they were faced with demonstrators distributing propaganda. Then the Revolutionary Guards swooped in and arrested all the demonstrators and everyone that was in the vicinity. Let's hope that Sarve has just gone to a friend's house and has forgotten to call her mother. You know what teenagers are like.'

After the successful installation of Khomeini as the Supreme Leader of Iran, it became apparent that the Mujahedin and the regime had different agendas for the country. The Mujahedin wanted to establish a democratic republic, whereas Khomeini was set on an Islamic republic. The two sides clashed, and the Mujahedin became increasingly agitated, ramping up their protests on the streets in retaliation. Many were arrested and killed without trial, while others fled to Iraq, where they found a safe base for their activities.

After hearing the news, Maman called Mrs Bozorgy again to make sure that they had called all of Sarve's friends to check on her whereabouts.

When she finished the call, Maman looked grave. 'It looks like Sarve has been arrested,' she reported. 'She was caught in the Mujahedin rally on her way home from school and was detained together with two other schoolfriends. The three girls' parents are worried sick.' Maman put a hand to her mouth. 'Oh, my dear God, save us from this brutal regime. They are only children, barely seventeen. What would they know about politics? What threat could they possibly pose to the regime?'

Later that night, the regime's grand prosecutor was on the TV news talking about the latest demonstrations. He appeared cold and heartless; he *was* cold and heartless. He announced that he had issued an order to all prisons commanding them to execute every single accused, without trial. Hundreds of them—thousands even. As far as the regime was concerned, they didn't deserve a trial: they were enemies of the state and had no right to defend the charges. My heart was pounding. I looked at Maman and Baba, hoping they would reassure me that he didn't really mean it. Baba was stone-faced and tears were streaming down Maman's cheek. My heart sank into my chest.

Mrs Bozorgy and her husband were never told what happened to Sarve. They never knew what crime she was accused of committing, when she was executed, or where she was buried. As far as the regime was concerned, she had never existed.

Still, Mrs Bozorgy held out hope. An exception might have been made, a pardon issued—perhaps Sarve was still alive in one of the city's many prisons. Mrs Bozorgy and her husband visited every prison in Tehran, and went from police station to police station, but they were always turned away.

Months after Sarve's disappearance, the Bozorgy family held an intimate gathering of very close friends in their house. When we arrived, the house was lit with candles. Red roses and tulips were in vases scattered around the room. 'Roses were Sarve's favourite,' her brother said.

When we had all sat down, Mrs Bozorgy began to speak:

'When we come home, I collapse on the bed. I draw the curtains and close my eyes. I remember her big green eyes when I first held her. I recall every birthday, when she first started school, then high school. What a bright student she was. Her father and I had so many hopes for her. I remember preparing lunch for her as she ate her breakfast that fateful morning. Then she walked out of the front gates, flicked her curls to one side, and waved goodbye. Everything after that is dark. I picture her being dragged away by her beautiful hair, frightened, huddling with her smart girlfriends in one of those dirty four-wheel drives. I walk in their shoes, blindfolded and thrown into a filthy prison cell, their inno-cent bodies being ravaged by dirty men in the name of religion.

'I live with them their final hour, waiting to be lined up before the firing squad. I live their last moments on this earth. Oh, what I would give to have been the one to receive those bullets in my chest. What I would give to have her body; to stroke her curls and say to her, *Fear no more, Mama is here*; to be able to give her to Mother Earth for eternal peace. I don't even know what day they shot her so that I can light a candle on her anniversary. All I know is that they always execute prisoners before dawn. Was it the very next day after their arrest? Two days later? More? Or maybe they didn't execute her? Maybe one of those sleazy bearded men spared her life and took her as a bride? She was too pretty to be killed, was she not? Surely even a mullah could see that. How can they just vanish like that? This a nightmare I cannot wake up from . . .'

Mrs Bozorgy couldn't go on. Her grief was terrible to witness.

Sarve and her two classmates had vanished forever, but they were just three among multitudes.

☾

The cost of living kept rising, and Baba took up private tutoring in the evenings to make ends meet. Retailers no longer sold goods at four times the price in secret—everything was put on the shelves and openly sold at the black market rate, including medicine and other essential health and hygiene products.

Madar's heart condition had worsened, and she relied on a particular medication which we could not find in the pharmacies. Baba would go to the southern districts of Tehran near the Grand Bazaar and negotiate a deal with street vendors in hidden laneways to get it.

While we struggled to stay alive, we were glad that Satyar was safe in Europe. International calls were very expensive in those days—phone cards and internet calls didn't exist—so we only managed to speak to him once a month. In between times, the occasional cards or letters he sent reminded us that he still actually existed. Maman and Baba ran to the door every day when they heard the postman's bike approaching, hoping that he would bring a letter from Vienna. When we did receive a letter, Maman would read it out loud. Then she and Baba would read it over and over again until the next one arrived.

I recall one of Satyar's early letters; I was listening from the top of the staircase as Maman read it.

'*It has now been four months since I left home. I am slowly getting better at German. It's a difficult language, but I am doing my best. I have no motivation, and the days are long. I search for a glimmer of hope and inspiration, but to no avail. When I see families together, I wonder if they know what it is like to be forced to leave behind all you love, not to have a choice. I am trying to figure out why I have come here. Have I come to study or have I fled the war and conflict? If the latter, then I am a coward, for thousands of other young men are fighting the enemy with their blood. I am in no mood to write more. Sorry. I love you. Your lonely son.*'

Maman was wiping tears from her cheeks as she put the letter away.

I received a postcard from Satyar one day in which he asked about Apricot; I was surprised that he still remembered him. He also wrote about the old cat that belonged to his landlady in Vienna. He described the cat as a big fat white cat like Kheppel, a cat we had years before Apricot. I was happy that he had befriended a cat who reminded him of home. That would bring him some joy, I thought.

☾

Aunty Tangerine dropped by once in a while. She was a shadow of her former self. She no longer wore red lipstick and colourful dresses or styled her hair. She still liked her tea scalding hot, though. She always looked worried, and carried her shopping basket with her at all times.

'I leave the apartment every afternoon to keep my mind occupied,' she said. 'I go up the road to the shops to fetch something. If I stay home, I'm just waiting for the next siren and wondering where the next bomb is going to land. The anxiety is unbearable. Will this nightmare ever end?'

Meantime, I was worried sick about Madar. Seyed Khanum and her family had moved to a small apartment in a more solid building, as Madar's house was no longer safe—the beams had caved in from the frequent shaking of the ground, and the ceiling in her kitchen had totally collapsed after a bomb exploded a few streets away. After much resistance, she reluctantly locked up her house and moved into a tiny apartment with a small balcony that belonged to an uncle of mine who had moved to the UK. It was a far cry from the enormous house and yard she was used to. Madar called it her prison cell.

'The neighbour blows her nose and it sounds like it's right next to my pillow!' she would complain.

The cooking smells from the tenant on the floor above bothered her too.

Maman changed the curtains, had all the furniture reupholstered, and new carpet laid, but none of it made any difference.

'Why don't you sit outside on sunny days?' Maman would ask her.

'This balcony isn't even large enough for me to stretch my arms without poking the neighbour in the eye!' Madar would respond.

'Why don't you take the calmatives prescribed by your doctor?' Maman asked.

Madar snorted. 'The donkey up the road knows more than that doctor!'

She hated everything about that apartment—she missed her own house. I stayed with her often, partly to escape my own house, and the sad atmosphere created by Maman's depression, and partly to spend time with my beloved grandmother.

I didn't mind the apartment, but I sometimes struggled to sleep, especially when I could hear Madar tossing and turning, cursing the universe.

When sleep was impossible, I would go out on the balcony and look at the sky. On clear nights I could spot the Big Bear, the Little Bear and the Saucepan. Madar had taught me about the constellations and I missed our nights under the stars. I hoped that she would overcome her grief and join me on the balcony so we could marvel at the night sky together. She used to tell me that the stars hold ancient stories deep in their hearts. Safe from invasions, protected from the chaos on earth. I wondered if the stars wept as they watched our country crumble.

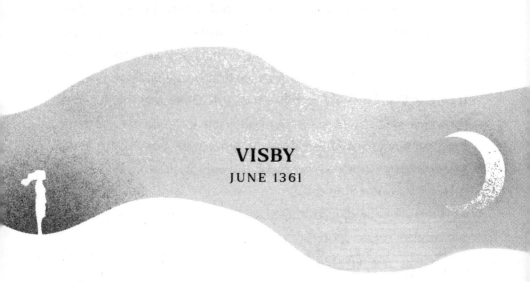

VISBY
JUNE 1361

A DARK CLOAK OF fear and dread was falling over Gotland. There were signs that the quiet life of the island's people was about to be disrupted. From the beginning of the summer of 1361, merchants who regularly travelled to Denmark had reported rumours that King Valdemar had set his sights on Visby.

One night, I was in the dining room with Mother waiting for Father to return home. A fire was crackling in the oven and every now and then I could hear the wood hissing in protest.

It was very late by the time Father returned. His mood was grim. He poured himself a drink and sat in his big armchair.

'What can you tell us?' Mother asked.

He shook his head. 'It's not looking good, Arngunna. Those close to the Danish court are saying that King Valdemar is coveting Visby's wealth. The merchants are quite concerned about the future of trade, and will fight tooth and nail to protect the city. It is thought the Danish will enter Gotland via Mästerby. We need to send an army to meet them there and stop them from progressing inland. According to local informants, there is a bog that the Danes would not be aware of. If we are able to steer them towards the bog, we can halt their advance. At the same time, we need to establish a line of defence outside the city walls to ensure they cannot be breached. I only hope we can find the necessary resources in time.'

The following day, Mother and I went to Ulvar's house so that my mother might share with them what she had learned.

Geirdís was rocking in her chair. Her big brown eyes were glowing in the candlelight, but a thick veil of sadness had enveloped her small face. The hunch on her back had grown bigger under the weight of her worries. She had long predicted that bad times were coming.

We all sat around the kitchen table. I was between Valentin and Stjärna; we held each other's hands tightly as my mother explained the threat to Visby.

'But we have the protection of King Magnus of Sweden!' Birgitta protested. 'We pay taxes!'

'It appears that as far as King Valdemar is concerned, the island and all its riches are ripe for the picking, and King Magnus doesn't intend to defend us. Some of the merchants have received letters from Sweden warning them of the danger looming. And the King's tax collectors have been warning us to get out while we can, predicting that the Danish army will eradicate us.'

Ulvar wasn't convinced. 'I don't trust those merchants! How do we know they're not just spreading these rumours to rattle us? Perhaps they think they can frighten us true Gotlanders into leaving our island so they can have it all to themselves!'

Although the days of civil war between the merchants and the islanders were long gone, the animosity remained strong.

'The men who have relayed these messages are as concerned about the future of Visby as you and me, Ulvar!' my mother said. 'Listen to me: these men have no reason to invent these stories. They are as much at risk as anyone.'

'I think there is some truth to what she is saying, Ulvar,' said Birgitta. 'There is no harm in being prepared.' She turned to my mother. 'Arngunna, what are the merchants proposing?' asked Birgitta.

'They want all the men, both young and old, to be ready to take up arms,' Mother said. 'Women and children will be sheltered in the churches and larger buildings within the city walls.'

Geirdís stirred in her chair. 'Guti shall Gotland claim . . .' I didn't understand what she meant. There was no time to ask questions.

I whispered to Valentin and Stjärna to meet me at Lilla Strandporten, the old city gate the following day.

☾

When I reached Lilla Strandporten, Valentin and Stjärna were already there, pacing.

'I'm sorry I'm late,' I said. 'I had to wait for Father to go out, so I could leave.'

It was a windy afternoon and we could see the small fishing boats bobbing up and down among the white caps on the sea.

'Now, we need to be prepared for what is ahead of us,' I said. 'You heard my mother yesterday: Visby is at imminent risk of Danish invasion.'

'What do you mean?' said Stjärna. 'How can we possibly prepare?'

I gestured to them to follow me.

I led them through narrow cobblestone streets until we arrived at St Karin's church in the heart of Stora Torget. I knew the narrow laneways leading to the church so well. Since we returned to Visby, I had been accompanying Valka during her trips to the market outside St. Karin's. The same spot that I had met Valentin for the first time. When Valka was busy bargaining with the stall holders, I would go inside the church and marvel at the blue stone walls and the high arches. I even had walked upstairs to the monks' bedroom once when they were praying.

We meandered through the quieter laneways and arrived at St. Karin's. 'This is it,' I said. 'We will be hiding in here while the men are on the front line ...'

The iron door of the church was half-open, and the afternoon sun shining through the stained-glass windows cast a rainbow on the walls and the floor. The sound of monks chanting echoed off the stone.

We walked quietly towards the east wing of the church. I had heard my father talking about concealing his gold coins inside the wall in that part of the church.

We spotted the door in the wall. Together we moved the benches and opened the heavy door. Valentin took a candle from the altar and we stepped inside the cold, dark room.

'So here we are—this is our shelter,' I said. 'If the Danes should approach the city, we will run inside the church and Father and his men will conceal this entrance. Then we will wait.'

We followed a narrow staircase up to the monks' room. It was a small room containing a few beds covered in woollen blankets. Through the window the whole town was visible.

'Everything will be fine,' I said, not very convincingly.

'We just have to pray that you are right, that we will be safe,' Stjärna said, her voice trembling.

We all knew our worst nightmare was unfolding before our eyes. We were scared; to find solace, the three of us sat on the cold floor and held each other's hands. No words were exchanged as we sat together in the flickering light of the candle. Our silent communion was interrupted when we were discovered by one of the monks. Although surprised by our presence, he did not admonish us. He gently escorted us out and closed the heavy door behind us. It was for our own protection he said as we parted.

☾

All day and into the night the town rang with the sound of blacksmiths banging and clanging iron to make weapons and chain mail. Hundreds of thousands of metal rings were linked together, as though they were connecting the threads of our history. Others worked day and night sharpening swords, spears and knives. It seemed that the division between the wealthy merchants and the country people had disappeared; people of the island had come together to defend our island home from invasion.

MELBOURNE

MONTHS PASS WITH NO communication from the Australian High Commission in Nairobi. Every week Habiba insists that I should email the case officer and find out how the case is progressing, but I am reluctant, as I know it will only annoy the case officer and do our application more harm than good.

'It has been nearly a year, Tishtar!' Habiba cries as December arrives with still no word; her hopes of seeing her nieces by Christmas have long been dashed.

'I know, Habiba. Let's wait until after the new year, then I will email the embassy.'

I send the email in the middle of January, and receive a response a few days later:

Dear Sir,

We have asked applicants to provide sufficient proof of their identity, and they have failed to comply. We now have to examine the case based on the information we have. You will be advised in due course of our decision.

Another two months passes before another email arrives from Nairobi. The subject line reads: 'Intention to Refuse Application'. When I see it I feel the walls of the building closing in on me.

As I open the attachment, I feel my ears burning with anxiety and fear. When I have finished reading the email I text Habiba and tell her we need to talk.

She replies that she is running errands in the city and won't be back till later this afternoon. I read the email over and over again, and each time I read it I grow more agitated and desperate.

It is four o'clock by the time Habiba enters my office; I will have to miss my train today.

'Now, Habiba, I need you to stay calm and focus, okay?' I say as she sits.

She nods, her eyes wide.

'They have given us twenty-one days to provide a response to this letter,' I explain. 'Remember the DNA test? They are saying there is a possibility the girls are only half-sisters, which means that one of them might have a father who is still alive and well, and therefore at least one of them is not an orphan.'

'How dare they!' Habiba erupts. 'My poor sister was a good woman. She did not sleep around! What do they want to do? Dig her up from the grave and question her faithfulness to her husband?! How else can I prove that Fatimah and Fowziah are sisters? Allah be my witness, we are not lying—their mother was a clean woman!' She burst into tears.

'Habiba, I know you are not lying,' I say. 'It is now my job to present a legal argument, and I promise you I will write the best submission I can.'

C

I spend hours at the computer, until I feel my head is going to explode. I look up case law and scour the policy advice manual the immigration department would have used to examine cases, but I can't find anything of any use. I ring a migration lawyer I have known for years for guidance.

'Shit, this doesn't look good,' she says when I have outlined the case.

'Yes, I know, but I need to do something. Do you have any ideas?'

'Not really. I never touch orphan relative cases—they are a nightmare and bound to fail. It sounds like in this instance the case officer is questioning the credibility of the applicants—that's where your focus should be.'

I sigh, defeated. 'Okay, thanks. I'll see what I can do.'

'Good luck!'

It is dark outside, and everyone in the building has gone. I pack my bag and leave the office. Nightlife in Sunshine is unfolding; the Vietnamese restaurants are full of diners. Outside the bottle shop a man with a stubby in his hand curses the shadows. 'Fucking morons!' he says as he staggers off.

I walk towards the station. A group of young Pasifika men are kicking a ball around, rap music blasting out of their Bluetooth speaker. Two personal safety officers approach and order them to move on. I don't understand why; they weren't bothering anyone.

The train is delayed, so I sit on the platform and wait. I wonder if Gretel had noticed that I wasn't on the usual train. Would she care?

A young Indian couple is standing a few metres away with their small baby in a pram. Next to them is an African family: a few children, two women in their forties, and an older lady, maybe an aunt or a grandmother.

Finally the train arrives and we all board. The African family sits near me; the little children play with their toys, the women with their phones. A man opposite keeps staring at them. After a few minutes he gets up and approaches the women, pointing to the Quiet Carriage sign on the wall. The family get up and move. The older lady seems confused.

After they leave, the man starts complaining aloud: 'Bloody refugees—they come here and don't bother to learn our way of life! They should make the English test compulsory before they let them in.'

'At least they didn't come by boat,' another person responds. 'The boat people are the worst.' He crushes his can of VB and throws it on the floor.

I am repulsed by their attitude, so I too get up to leave the carriage. They look me up and down as I walk past. I feel like pointing out that their ancestors too came by boat—and they showed very little respect for the way of life of Australia's first people.

The men's treatment of the African passengers reminds me of my early years in Australia. I lived in a block of flats in Wollongong; my flat was on the second floor. One day I was outside on my balcony hanging my washing on my small clothes rack when a busload of women arrived. They were nurses from Pakistan, sent by their government to Australia to undertake further training for a year. There were twenty-two of them, all accommodated in the apartment block, two to each flat.

The next morning I met a few of them in the stairwell as they were heading out. 'We are neighbours,' I said to them, for not only were we sharing the apartment block, our home countries shared a border.

They were a very warm and friendly bunch. On their second day they came to me to ask how to catch the bus to the university and to the town centre.

'How about tomorrow we catch the bus together and I will show you?' I said.

The next day was a Thursday and the shops stayed open till late, so in the early evening we caught the bus to Crown Street Mall. They were all dressed up in their finest traditional garments and were loud and chatty on the bus, climbing over one another to point out things along the way. Their very presence on the bus raised eyebrows, and some other passengers shook their heads.

We walked around the shopping mall for a few hours and I showed them where the cheapest supermarket was. It was getting late by the time we returned to the bus stop. While we were waiting, a dark Commodore slammed on the brakes in front of us. There were four men in the vehicle. The man in the front passenger seat wound down the window and yelled, 'Fuck off, curry munchers!' Then a back window came down and someone started throwing eggs at the women, who screamed and ran for cover. The men roared with laughter.

When they'd run out of eggs, the driver revved the engine and took off, tyres squealing, the sound of the men's laughter echoing in the bus shelter. When the bus arrived we got on, the women covered in egg. They were embarrassed; some were crying while others were helping each other to wipe the egg yolk from their faces. When we arrived at our building, everyone dispersed to their flats and hid behind closed doors.

Now I wonder what kind of future Fowziah and Fatimah will have if they are granted visas to come to Australia. Would they ever think that they were better off in the slums of Nairobi, where they were not abused because of the colour of their skin? Or would they be grateful for the new opportunities of life in the west?

My head is thumping when the train reaches South Geelong—I have a full-blown migraine. I am lucky to make it home in one piece; my vision is so blurred I can barely see the lines on the road.

Mr Cat is screaming for food. I feed him then take two Panadol Forte tablets and crawl into bed.

With Mr Cat sprawled next to me, I scroll through Facebook on my phone. I see a post from one of the Iranian groups based in Melbourne. Chaharshanbe Soori is to be held the following night and it looks like a large number of people are planning to attend. For thousands of years Persians have held the festival of fire on the eve of the last Wednesday of the Persian calendar year, just before Nowruz. Neighbours would gather to jump over bonfires. The Facebook post warns that the event might have to be cancelled due to high fire danger. We have been experiencing one of the hottest Marches on record, with the temperature sitting around thirty-five degrees for several days in a row. The comments beneath the post are entertaining. One user is protesting: *This is an ancient cultural celebration! They can't take it away from us!*

There is a risk of bushfire and we need to observe the weather forecast, the organiser has replied.

See? Those Iranians who migrated to Canada were smarter than us! No bushfire there in the middle of winter, another user has written, and many have reacted with the laughter emoji.

As I put my phone on the bedside table and prepare for sleep, I think it is somewhat strange to hold Chaharshanbe Soori in the middle of summer. It couldn't be more different from the celebrations of my childhood in Tehran.

Around the third week in March every year, those who lived in the country would gather twigs and dried bushes and sell them in bundles to the city folk. I remember seeing men with weather-beaten faces pushing large carts filled with such bundles along the city streets, while those who could not afford a cart would carry their bundles on their backs or spread them by the side of the road. The closer it got to sunset, the harder it was to find kindling for sale, and the prices went up accordingly.

Baba always sourced the best bundles. They were neither too big nor too small, were dry enough to catch fire easily but not so dry that they would burn to ash within minutes.

At about five in the afternoon, we would start getting ready for Chaharshanbe Soori. First, Baba would move his car out of the driveway and park it on the street. Then we would place five to six bundles of kindling about a metre apart on the driveway. I was always impatient and wanted to start the fire early, but Maman never allowed it. 'You have to wait until it is dark!' she would say firmly, then assign me tasks in the kitchen to pass the time. Usually Maman lit the fire, and we would then line up and jump over the flames, chanting, 'Your redness be mine and my paleness yours.' We addressed these words to the fire, wishing to exchange its warmth and glow for our ailments. When we got to the end of the line of fires, we would do it over again.

It gave me a special feeling to participate in this ritual; it felt almost pagan-like. I can still smell the wood smoke, and hear the crackling of thorny bushes going up in flames. Sometimes we would throw a big bundle of sticks and twigs on the fire and the flames would shoot up in the sky.

March 1980 was the last time we celebrated Chaharshanbe Soori. After this, it was forbidden due to the blackout orders. We were told that it had been banned to make sure that we didn't light the path for Iraqi planes, but in hindsight it was also likely the regime's way of eradicating an old Persian tradition.

With the camera I had received for my birthday the previous year, I took lots of photos that Chaharshanbe Soori night: flames dancing on Maman's face, Aunty Tangerine laughing, Satyar almost burning his curly hair. I still have one of the photos that I took of Madar. She is sitting on a camp chair, her chin resting on her palm, staring into the flames. Her head is tilted to the left; she looks very sad.

That night we sat by the fire and ate nuts, watching the flames until they died. Baba was always eager to clean it all up and bring his car in, but Maman never allowed him to put the fire out. 'The fire is sacred,' she'd remind him. 'We need to let it go out naturally. Otherwise the spirits will not find their way back.' Madar and Maman said prayers for those who had passed.

After nightfall, people roamed around the streets, banging spoons on metal bowls and knocking on doors, asking for sweets and mixed nuts. Maman always bought a big value pack and then made up tiny parcels of nuts for when people—mostly children—rang our doorbell.

When the fire had gone out, Satyar swept up the ashes with a dustpan and broom and scattered them in the garden.

'Do it gently and respectfully,' Maman told him.

Long after everyone had gone I remained sitting outside, enjoying the smell of wood smoke lingering in the air and listening to the sound of firecrackers being let off near and far. If someone had told me that as an adult I would have been celebrating Chaharshanbe on the other side of the world, I would never have believed them.

As I switched off the light and prepared myself for sleep, I wondered if Fatimah and Fowziah would have had any opportunity to learn about their Somali heritage, what traditions they would be leaving behind if they came to Australia, and how they would change and adapt them to their new country.

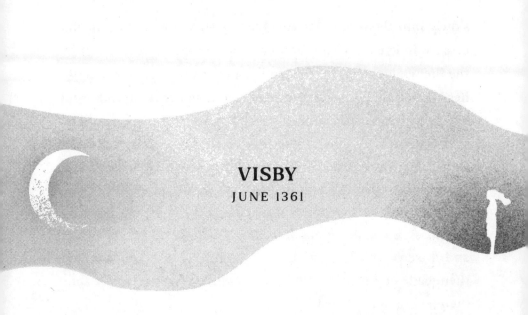

VISBY
JUNE 1361

WITH TENSIONS RISING IN Visby, Father and a few other merchants went to the mainland to ask for support from King Magnus. Every night in the lead up to his trip to Stockholm, Father had been talking about how insufficient the defence was on the island and that he and others wanted to ensure that the city was safe.

His absence meant that Mother and I had more freedom to venture out to the countryside. Mother enjoyed working with Birgitta on the farm during the day—reminded of her old life, which she missed—and in the evening we would join the family by the fire to eat and drink.

One night, we were sitting in the kitchen after dinner. Mother and Birgitta were knitting while Ulvar snored in the big rocking chair. Valentin was quiet as always, absent-mindedly carving a piece of wood, lost in thought. As I watched, Geirdís shuffled slowly into the room. She was like a restless owl at nights, and often wandered aimlessly through the cottage or came to sit by the fire while the rest of the family slept. Some nights they could hear her crying, pleading with Odin to give her peace. Her soul was in torment.

I watched her grasp Valentin's shoulders with her crooked fingers. She bent down and kissed his head. 'Min Sårk, min Guti, my one and only special Guti. You make good klappträ, Guti, very skilled with your hands, like your grandfather,' she said.

She then took a seat near him.

'Mårmår, why do you call me Guti?' Valentin asked.

His grandmother's eyes were fixed on the fireplace.

'Oh, nice fire crackling tonight. Tjelvar will be smiling; his fire is still alive,' Geirdís said.

Valentin frowned. 'Who?'

'Ah,' she said, 'you must know the tale of our ancestors! You must know how our island became what it is. You see, Tjelvar was the first person to come here. He soon discovered that the island was under a spell: it sank beneath the water during the day only to rise again at nights. But once Tjelvar brought fire to the island, Gotland never disappeared beneath the waves again.'

'What does that have to do with Guti?' Valentin asked.

'Ah,' said his grandmother, 'be patient and your Mårmår will tell you an old Saga.'

She continued, 'So, Tjelvar had a son named Háfdi who also came to live here with his wife Huistjärna. The first night they slept on the island she dreamed there were three snakes growing in her womb. She told Háfdi about her dream and he took it to mean that they would have three sons. He then said to his wife:

Everything in rings is bound.

Inhabited this land shall be;

We shall beget sons three . . .

One will be named Guti, and he will rule Gotland with his two brothers Graip and Gunnfjaun.

. . . Guti shall Gotland claim.

'When I was a young girl I dreamed that I would have a grandson one day, and that he would be named Guti. When you were born, I instantly knew you were the one from my dream. Your mother didn't listen to me when I told her she should name you Guti, but you have always been Guti to me. You have a big challenge ahead of you. But remember: Guti shall Gotland claim . . . You must hold your head high no matter what obstacles you encounter, and you will bring honour to your family.'

On the final day before Father's return I followed Stjärna around the farm. Together we groomed Valentin's horse—she was grey, like a piece of cloud.

'It looks as if the horse has taken a liking to you,' she said when I was brushing the horse's face.

'I love horses—I wish I could ride her,' I said.

'Why don't we?' And Stjärna helped me onto the horse's back, and together we rode him to the forest.

Since hearing Valentin's grandmother talking about the Guta Saga, I had not been able to stop thinking about the story. It had become obvious to me that Valentin's family wanted him and Stjärna to be together. I was drawn to Valentin, there was this deep longing for him that I couldn't resist.

After a while we stopped for the horse to have a bit of water and feed. The air was cool, so Stjärna gathered some kindling and lit a fire.

'There is nothing you can't do!' I said, and she smiled.

'What does the Guta Saga mean to you?' I asked her as we warmed ourselves by the flames.

'It's part of our being—it is our story,' she said. She tightened her shawl around her shoulders.

'And Guti?' I asked. My heart was thumping.

She poked the fire and remained silent. The golden glow of the fire made her more beautiful than ever—and she was blushing now. 'His heart is with you,' she said, 'and the rest remains a saga.' The smile had vanished from her face.

'Stjärna! What are you saying?' I gasped.

'He has been different since you came, he doesn't look at me anymore.'

I could not find anything to say to her.

Embers flew into the chill air. We watched the flames in silence until they died.

Stjärna covered the ashes with soil and extended her hand to me. I let her help me up. We mounted the horse and rode back to Ulvar's cottage. I put my arms around her waist and rested my head on her warm shoulder the whole way home.

MELBOURNE

MORE THAN TEN DAYS have passed since the case officer in Nairobi gave me three weeks in which to provide reasons as to why the girls' visa application should not be refused. But I am yet to find a compelling argument in the case law. Whenever I see Habiba she asks me how the submission is going and I say I am working on it. This is true; what I don't tell her is that I have failed to make any progress.

I study Habiba's statement, focusing on her recollection of the moment when she found out that the woman she thought was her mother was actually her aunt. I read over what Sumaya had said to her that day: *You see these sugar grains? Can you see where one family starts and ends? No, they are together. Nothing separates them, no demarcation. You have all of us, my child: we are your family.*

That image takes my mind to the village where Habiba grew up, the close-knit community she had described. I remember Madar, who had looked after her nephews as if they were her own children. I reflect on the role that aunties, uncles and elders play in First Nations communities. Western lawmakers would have little experience or understanding of how such communities operate, I realise.

A picture is taking shape in my head. I can see the village where Habiba's nieces were born. I imagine how young they would have been when they lost their beloved parents and how the villagers would have cared for them, even though they had scant resources to spare.

The case officer in Nairobi has applied a scientific calculation to conclude that the girls could possibly have a parent alive, somewhere. But what parent would willingly abandon their child amid all that bloodshed? It defies logic that Habiba's nieces could have a parent somewhere who knew the girls were alive and had not bothered to seek them out during all these years. Even if it were remotely possible that the girls had different fathers, given the number of people who had been killed during the conflict it was highly likely that that this additional parent would also be dead.

I spend the days left to me before the deadline writing a lengthy submission, one that appeals to the case officer's humanity, because the law provides no answers. I send it off with very little hope that it will succeed. And then the long wait begins.

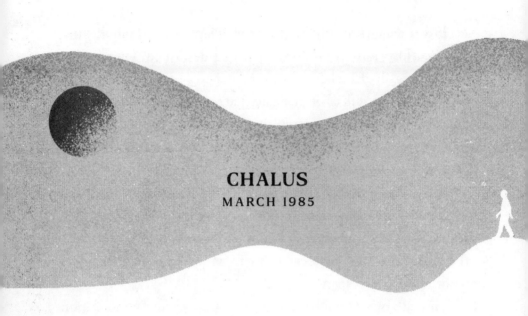

CHALUS
MARCH 1985

FIVE YEARS HAD PASSED since the war began. Contrary to the predictions of foreign analysts, who always seemed sure a ceasefire was imminent, the conflict had only intensified. Iran had remained defiant, despite pressure from the western governments that supported Iraq.

In the shadow of the conflict, I became a teenager and Satyar graduated from the University of Technology in Vienna with an engineering degree. He started working at Siemens.

'We didn't have children just for them to turn into photographs and a voice on the other side of the world,' Maman used to say as she wiped framed photographs of Satyar that were scattered around the house. Satyar on his sofa, or with his guitar, or at a party, or in a park, or outside the Vienna Opera House.

It was the last of the month of Esfand, days before Nowruz, and people were busy with spring cleaning. Carpets were scrubbed, curtains washed and hung back up, kitchen and bathroom cupboards emptied and wiped. Wardrobes and linen closets received a clean-out, too: unwanted clothes went to charity, while old towels and sheets were retired to be used as household rags.

It was hard to believe that we had been celebrating Nowruz for five years under a blanket of bombs and explosions. It was almost as though we had retreated underground and continued to live our normal lives while, above, people and places were being blown up.

'We have to keep the traditions alive until we take our last breath,' Maman said year after year, as she made Sabzeh. She would place a handful of wheat grains under a damp cloth days before Nowruz, and they would sprout into a small green patch: a symbol of life and peace. On the thirteenth day of the new year we would head out of town with our little bundle of green and release it in a river, wishing that our dreams would come true. That year, Nowruz would once again give people hope that the new year would bring an end to the pain and fear of war.

In the days before schools broke for Nowruz, the temperature had plummeted, and every living thing in the city was shivering. I had sat my last end-of-term exam and was walking home from school. The sky was dark red with a belly full of snow.

On the footpath, street vendors were selling goldfish and Sabzeh for Haft-seen, an arrangement of seven symbolic objects—including Sabzeh, goldfish, gold coins, sumac, samanoo, senjed and seeb—that were central to the Nowruz celebration. Each item symbolised an important aspect of one's journey: prosperity, peace, good health, life, wealth, and so on.

One vendor was selling steamed beetroot, while beside him an old man was selling clay pots and jugs.

I saw someone walking towards me through the crowd, and I found myself frozen to the spot as I realised it was Gretel. I couldn't believe it. She looked determined, as if she was on a mission. For a moment shorter than a heartbeat she stopped, searched my face as though I was a map or a street sign, and then continued walking.

I gasped for air, my lungs suddenly starved of oxygen.

'*This vessel would have been a lover like me one day / enchanted by a beauty. / This handle that you see wrapped around its neck / would have been an arm wrapped around the love of his life.*' The clay pot vendor recited Omar Khayyam's poem as he dusted his wares.

I looked at him—had he seen her, too? No, he couldn't have, I realised: he was blind.

'Ay ay ay, seek her in the shadows, follow the path and you will find her ...' the man said, gesturing in the direction that Gretel had gone.

I looked over my shoulder in the direction he was indicating— I could just make her out, walking quickly along the crowded footpath.

I ran after her, dodging women carrying shopping and schoolkids with their bags. I collided with a man and knocked his briefcase from his hand. It sprung open, documents scattering everywhere. He grabbed my arm and started yelling at me: 'You fucking idiot! Are you blind?! Why don't you watch where you're going?!' I tried to get away from him, my eyes following Gretel as she disappeared around a corner. By the time I was able to free myself from the man's hold, she was gone.

Despondent, I looked up at the sky—it could no longer bear the weight of the snow and had released the first flurry of snowflakes.

As I resumed walking home, the cold wind brushing against my face, I felt as if I were a different person now. I had altered, like leaves changing colour with the first hint of autumn. My brief encounter with Gretel had touched me deeply.

My dreams would soon become my reality, and my reality my dreams. I never learned the difference.

☾

The arrival of Nowruz didn't feel the same that year—the war had stolen the magic. The cities and towns along the border had been destroyed, and Tehran was flooded with people who had fled the fighting.

Baba's relatives in Gilan had been encouraging us to move north, as it was widely believed that Iraq wouldn't attack that region. Baba and Maman resisted their urging, but they did agree to spend the two weeks of the new year break in Chalus.

'A break from sirens and air raids will do us a world of good,' Maman said to Madar as they packed. 'Plus, we cannot allow the enemy to kill the spirit of Nowruz.'

Aunty Tangerine decided not to join us. 'I'd rather die in my own bed than on the road,' she said.

As we drove the winding road near Hezar Cham, the air felt different: cold and damp. Heavy fog had enveloped the Alborz mountains, and as we descended only the silhouette of cows was visible through the mist. The back seat of Baba's Opel felt too empty with only Madar and me for passengers.

When we arrived in Chalus the orange trees were covered in blossom, and Maman closed her eyes as she inhaled their tantalising scent.

'We should ask the locals if we can pick some, so we can make orange blossom marmalade while we are here,' Madar suggested.

'That's a great idea!' said Maman, and she asked Baba to pull over. A young local girl was selling zucchini and eggplants on the side of the road near a cottage. She had a round face covered in freckles framed by a scarf that had small flowers on it. She was wearing a green cardigan over a floral shirt, a brown skirt over dark trousers, and black gumboots covered in mud. Maman and Madar asked her if they could pick some blossoms from their tree. The little girl didn't say anything, but stood up and led them to the cottage. Her father opened the gate and let Maman and Madar inside. He had a kind face, tanned from working in the sun year-round. He grabbed a plastic bag and started plucking blossoms from his tree. Maman bought all the eggplants and zucchini from them, and gave them extra money for the blossoms.

'Stay for a cup of tea,' the man said in the usual hospitable countryside manner.

Maman and Madar declined, but thanked him, and Madar slipped a note into the little girl's pocket. The girl grinned and ducked her head shyly.

When we got to the villa, Maman and Madar boiled a large pot of water and added the blossoms to it, along with sugar. As the mixture simmered, the aroma of orange blossom seeped into every corner of the villa.

Baba and I rugged up and went to sit on the terrace and watch the sea. Baba fiddled with his small portable radio, trying to tune in to the BBC news. Reception was poor; people said that the regime interfered with radio frequencies to stop the flow of news from international sources.

I was thinking about Gretel and the evening that I saw her on the street. It felt like a lifetime ago. I was aching to see her again; I missed her terribly. I said to Baba that I was going to go for a walk.

'Okay, my boy, but don't go too far,' he said as he bent over his transmitter to hear the latest political analysis on the war.

When I reached the beach I took off my shoes and walked barefoot. I wanted to feel the sand between my toes. I walked to the water's edge and dipped my toes in the sea. The water was so cold and crisp that it pricked my skin like needles.

Turning to gaze along the deserted stretch of shore, I raised my hands in the air and called out: 'Where are you? When will I see you again? Can you hear me?'

There was no answer.

Sighing, I walked back to the villa.

I brushed the sand from my feet and went up to the terrace. Baba was wearing his beanie and had a lantern next to him. 'Well, well, you are back! Good boy!' He nodded.

We could hear a clinking of jars from the kitchen; Maman and Madar were pouring out the marmalade.

Not long after, they joined us on the terrace. Maman was carrying a tray with a small bowl of warm orange blossom marmalade, toast, butter and cups of Earl Grey tea, Madar's favourite. The marmalade's taste was out of this world.

Baba turned off the radio, and we ate in silence; even eating together wasn't the same anymore. None of us felt much joy this new year. Madar had a bellyache and went bed early. Maman cleaned the kitchen, then she too went to bed early with her small portable radio. Baba followed.

Too restless to sleep, I returned to the beach. The wind had picked up, and the sea was churning.

I walked along the shore, and there she was: Gretel. She was walking slowly up the beach ahead of me, with her arms wrapped around herself. I picked up my pace and before long we were side by side. We walked in silence, our shoulders almost touching. I waited for her to say something, but she was silent, and when I opened my own mouth to speak the words wouldn't come. My voice was trapped in my throat.

I stopped walking.

Where have you been all this time? I asked her silently.

She slowed and looked at me from the corner of her eye. I thought I saw a hint of a smile.

I reached out to take her hand in mine. Her palm was cold and damp from the sea spray.

There was a crack of thunder and lightning illuminated the sky, then the clouds opened to release a heavy downpour. Gretel allowed me to lead her to shelter beneath a tree, but as soon as the rain eased off she walked off without saying a word. I tried to call out to her but my words died in my throat. I clenched my hands into fists and screamed inside.

When I could no longer see her, I returned to the villa. I was soaking wet and cold as I crawled into bed in the room I was sharing with Madar.

☾

When I woke, Madar was sitting on her bed, reading. 'You went out last night,' she said, her eyes still fixed on her book. 'I gather that you were looking for her?'

I propped myself up on my elbow. 'How did you know?'

She just raised her eyebrows. 'You can't hide anything from this old woman!'

I couldn't see any point in continuing the conversation. I knew what she would say if I tried to ask her about Gretel: that I had to wait.

I rose, put my jumper on and went up to the terrace. Madar followed. We sat in silence for a while, staring out at the brooding sea.

'Madar?' I said finally.

'Yes, my darling?'

'Last night, Gretel and I were together for hours. We walked and walked. But then she slipped away without saying a word, and I found myself unable to speak. Will I ever be able to tell her that I am in love with her?'

Madar reached for my hand and squeezed it. She gazed at me with concern. 'In good time you will find the answers. You will know if she is the love of your life when the moment is right.'

She sat with me for a little while longer then said, 'It is too cold for me out here,' and she went back inside.

Despite the chill, I stayed outside, staring at the sea without really seeing it. Madar's voice was still ringing in my ears. *You will know if she is the love of your life when the moment is right.*

My thoughts were consumed by questions, and I was starting to wonder if I was doomed never to know the answers.

TEHRAN
MAY 1988

THE WAR HAD CLAIMED thousands of lives, destroyed hundreds of towns and cities along the Iran–Iraq border, and its ugly tentacles now stretched across the country. Nowhere was safe since the Iraqi army had started firing long-range missiles at cities deep inside Iran. It was hard to believe that, through it all, I had still managed to study and pass exams year after year, and at last was nearing the end of high school. The finish line was only steps away.

Maman was constantly reminding me of the importance of studying so I would earn a place at university. Iranian universities had reopened in 1983, and Maman was determined that I would follow an academic path. But to her despair I was still a dreamer. Once a high achiever at school, I had gradually lost interest in study. Year after year my grades declined, with the exception of history and geography—the only two subjects that engaged me.

One evening, while I was busy leafing through the world atlas when I should have been studying, I looked up to find my mother watching me, a frown on her face. 'Listen to me!' she said. 'Do you realise that these next couple of months are the most crucial time of your life? You need to concentrate! At this rate you will not only fail to get into university, you will fail high school altogether! Stop this daydreaming nonsense and focus on your future.'

But Maman didn't understand that my dreams were the only safe place I had left—the one place where missiles and bombs could not reach. So, despite her warnings, I continued to sail away to far-off places in my mind, searching for Gretel, and a home without conflict.

☾

A few nights later, a long-range missile landed in the street behind ours. In the pale light of morning, we discovered that there was nothing left but rubble: the whole block was demolished. The elderly sisters and their two cats, the family of five, the chickens, the vegetable garden: all were lost, reduced to dust. The only creature that had miraculously survived was the pet rooster. He was sitting on the high branch of a tree, his tiny eyes blinking nervously.

All of our windows had shattered. The blinds in my room had come off, thrown to the centre of the room. At Baba's insistence we had taken to sleeping under the staircase; if not for that, the shattered glass would've injured us.

While Baba and Maman cleared the debris, I looked for Apricot, but he was nowhere to be found. After a while I just stood frozen and stared at the flattened houses. A black cat emerged from the rubble and took off.

Madar came over later in the morning, and despite Maman's protest, she and I went for a walk around the block, hoping to find Apricot.

As we turned the corner into the street that had been bombed, I was hoping that the night before was nothing but a nightmare, that all the houses would still be standing, with their residents and all their animals.

But it wasn't to be. The street was full of rescue workers, still looking for bodies and survivors. The air smelled of death. I called Apricot. I called and called, but he didn't come.

Finally Madar pulled me away and we walked back home.

That night, and every night after that, we went to bed not knowing if we would still be alive in the morning.

One night in early May, we had assumed our usual positions under the stairs for the evening—Maman propped up on her pillow, listening to her small radio; Baba was staring at the ceiling in the dark, his right arm resting on his forehead; me with the blanket over my head, imagining myself far away—when we heard a loud bang, and the ground began to shake. We shot up.

'It's an earthquake, I think,' Baba said.

'Hush,' Maman whispered, as though being quiet would avert any risk.

We knew that missiles usually exploded a few seconds after they landed, so we waited.

The silence was deafening—all we could hear were our heartbeats.

'See? I told you it was an earthquake!' Baba said.

'Shhh!' Maman said.

Then the front door rattled.

Maman squeezed Baba's hand and pulled me close. I looked up and saw the panic and distress in her eyes.

The screen door stopped rattling, and we heard a faint meow.

'Apricot! Oh, thank God he's alive!' For a moment I was so happy that I forgot the peril we were in.

But as the sirens began to wail, Maman said, 'We must have a look and see what is going on.'

Cautiously, we stepped out onto the street.

A missile had landed two houses down from ours, but it had not exploded. Explosives experts had been summoned to disarm it.

'Attention! Attention, residents!' came an announcement over a megaphone. 'We're doing what we can to disarm the missile, but it could explode at any stage of the operation. Go back to your shelters until further notice.'

Some curious onlookers, heedless of the risk, stayed to watch the proceedings, but we went back to our beds.

Maman didn't argue when I insisted that Apricot stay inside with us.

We had just settled down again when the phone started ringing. 'Someone must want to check on us,' Maman said.

Baba answered. It was Bahman, his best friend. 'What is the matter, brother?' we heard Baba ask. Then, after a pause: 'Yes, yes, I'll come now.' He hung up.

'What's happened?' Maman asked anxiously. 'Are they okay?'

'It's Sara. She has been taken to the hospital,' Baba said. 'That's all I know.'

It was hours before he returned and was able to tell us what had happened.

Earlier that evening, Sara was getting ready to go to her friend's birthday party across the road. Through the window, she could see her classmates starting to arrive.

'Hurry up, Maman!' Sara pleaded with her mother, who was still fixing Sara's hair. 'Everyone else is there already! I am going to miss the birthday song!'

Then their building began to shake, and they could hear people screaming on the street. A missile had landed. It exploded as Sara looked on.

Sara did not move from the window. She stood there watching as rescue workers pulled the bodies of her friends and classmates from the rubble. Then she collapsed and was taken to the hospital.

Sara never talked or walked again. She died a few months later, still in her teens. Her young body just could not cope with the trauma. She never had the chance to go to university, to become a scientist as she had dreamed when we were younger.

I would often think about her in later years, and wonder how many shared Sara's experience. How many birthday candles were extinguished by bombs and missiles instead of children? How should we count the casualties of war? Do we only recognise those killed during the war, or do we keep counting long after it is officially over? Does war ever really end?

C

A few weeks before my final exams, I decided to go and stay with Madar. Maman's intensity had become unbearable, and the sound of her radio was driving me insane. For her part, Maman welcomed the suggestion—she thought I would be safer there; I'm not sure why she believed that apartment blocks were safer than houses.

It was very hard to get any sleep at night. The sound of the missile landing behind our house played in my head whenever I shut my eyes, and with the sounds came horrific images. But Madar helped me to establish a routine, and made me promise to study hard and not waste time. In return, she would cook me my favourite dishes, she promised. I worked hard to uphold my end of the bargain, but Madar couldn't say the same. She either burned the food or forgot to cook at all. Her memory was failing, but we all blamed the stress that everyone was experiencing. Some nights, all we had for dinner was bread with feta and a cup of tea, but I never complained. Just to be with Madar was a comfort.

I had brought my camera with me, and I took hundreds of pictures of Madar as we sat at the table together. She would talk and talk; the clicking of the shutter never annoyed her.

I also liked taking photos of her when she was talking on the phone. She would close her eyes and chat away with her relatives while I snapped away.

I took photos of her mending her woollen skirt, looking up and grinning at me. She was no shy flower in front of the camera.

Maman would ring me every night to make sure that I was studying. Baba would then ask me science questions over the phone, and then all at once it was over: my exams were finished.

I returned home to wait for my results, still uncertain about my future and with no motivation to think beyond graduation.

'It's nearly mid-July now,' Maman said, as though life were normal. 'Exam results should be released soon. While we wait, we should enrol you in language classes so you can improve your English. You never know when you might need it. We also need to think about what kind of degree you should enrol in.'

I rolled my eyes.

'They have bombed Azerbaijan with poison gas!' Baba called out from the TV room. 'Thousands of people are dead!'

Maman turned her ire in another direction. 'So much for peace talks!' she raged. 'Saddam has upped the ante. He isn't going to leave us alone. You watch—he will destroy the whole country.'

With the introduction of chemical weapons, the war took yet another nasty turn. We had thought the missiles that could flatten an entire block of homes in an instant were the worst that could befall us, but we hadn't reckoned on weapons that not only claimed the lives of thousands of innocent people, but also poisoned survivors, causing significant health issues for decades to come.

Not long after this, Iran accepted the ceasefire proposed by the UN. Maybe it was the poison gas that brought everything to a head, or maybe the governments of both countries had finally realised how pointless the whole conflict had been.

Some called the ceasefire defeat, others called it victory. Some merely called it a ceasefire. Did it really matter what it was called after eight years of bloodshed and destruction? After eight years of devastation and loss and a crippled economy?

I retreated to my room when we heard the news about the end of the war. As I lay on my bed, Gretel entered the room and lay beside me.

'What are you thinking?' she asked.

'I really don't know what the end of the war means for us,' I said. 'It's hard to imagine what a normal life looks like.'

'I understand,' she said.

VISBY
JULY 1361

THE MEN WHO WERE on standby on the outskirts of Visby sent a messenger on horseback announcing that the Danes were approaching. Masterby, not far from Visby, had fallen to the foreign soldiers and many farmers had been killed. With the fall of Masterby, it was time for us to go into hiding.

Father arranged for me and Mother to hide in St Karin's, but Mother refused, saying that first she must fetch our friends from the country and bring them to safety. I wanted to go with her, but she was adamant in her refusal: I must wait for them in the shelter.

Father took me to the church, and the monks led me up to their small room. It was cold and lonely. I sank to the floor and wrapped my arms around my knees, feeling helpless. Before long I heard footsteps and, not sure who it could be, I crawled behind the bunks so I wouldn't be seen.

Stjärna and her mother walked in with Geirdís. Stjärna was clinging to her mother, sobbing.

'What has happened to us, Mamma?' Stjärna cried. 'Since I was a little girl you have been telling me that I will have a good life on this island, that I will marry Valentin and we will raise a family together. You even drew a square on the soil and showed me where we would live. Look at us now. I have lost Valentin not only to another woman but to a war. And I will probably lose you and Fadar too. It was all a lie.'

'I know, I know, my love,' her mother said. 'But I didn't lie to you deliberately. You gave him your heart—and he gave it away to the wind. When we women give our hearts to someone, it is forever. But men, oh, they are different. A man's heart is like a boat, always sailing off in search of new horizons.'

She hugged her daughter, then said, 'Now I must leave you, my darling daughter. Birgitta and Arngunna have stayed behind to defend our farms while the men are defending the city, and I must join them.'

Stjärna stood by the window, and I knew she was watching her mother, hoping it would not be her last sight of her.

I emerged from my hiding place. 'Are you scared, Stjärna?' I whispered.

Stjärna gasped, startled by my sudden appearance, and then blushed as she realised I'd heard her conversation with her mother. 'Y-yes,' she stammered.

I put my arms around her and held her tight. 'I know. I am too. We all are. But everything will be fine.'

'Do you really think so?' Stjärna said, looking at me hopefully.

'Yes!' I assured her. 'My father and all his merchant friends are confident that this will blow over.'

When Geirdís and Stjärna fell asleep after midnight, I decided to go to Lilla Strandporten one more time, the gate where Valentin and I said goodbyes after my visits to the harbour. I was listening to the waves when I suddenly heard a rustling in the bushes next to the gate. Mishka yelped softly.

'What on earth are you doing here, Gretel?!' said Valentin as he grabbed me and held me tight. 'Why did you come out? What if they notice you are missing from the church?'

'Let's go to the forest, let's hide in the woods until all of this is over,' I said.

We jumped on his horse and headed for the forest. We stumbled over the deserted hunters' cabin.

It was raining, and by the time we arrived we were both cold and wet. It was freezing inside the cabin, and it smelled of damp timber.

I sat on a wooden stool and watched Valentin starting a fire in the oven with some kindling that had been left in a basket on the floor. Water was dripping from my hair. I was shivering from the cold. Soon the flames started dancing upwards. Mishka was sitting on my feet, licking her wet paws. 'This should warm you up,' said Valentin. 'I am going out to get some more firewood and secure the horse. Maybe take off the top layers, here, wrap yourself in this blanket.' He handed me a blanket and walked out.

When he returned, I was wrapped in the blanket and was undoing my plaits in front of the fire to dry my hair. Valentin stood in the doorway with a pile of logs in his arms. I turned around and said, 'I'm very cold—close the door, please. Come closer and hold me.'

He dropped the firewood on the floor, and approached me nervously, putting his cold work-roughened hands on my shoulders. He was breathing heavily.

I pressed my body against his and felt his hardness. He dropped his gaze, embarrassed. I wrapped my arms around his neck and whispered, 'I want this—I want to be close to you, Valentin. I know you want me too.'

He led me to the bed in the corner of the room and lay me down on a mattress stuffed with straw. I was trembling. 'I'm nervous, Valentin,' I whispered, and closed my eyes. He drew me close and I held tight to his neck as he entered me. I dug my nails in his back and felt the warmth of blood trickling down my thigh. I listened as his heavy breathing became more intense, until finally he groaned like a bear. He was still inside me when he fell asleep. The fire roared and hissed in the oven. It was dark and cold outside. I held him tight and drifted off to sleep in his arms.

☾

We returned to town well before sunrise. When we arrived at Lilla Strandporten, Valentin tied up the horse and we walked cautiously through the narrow laneways to Stora Torget. Most gates had already been shut and heavily guarded. He stopped a few metres from the door of the church. 'Before we part, I want you to have something,' he said. He took off his sun wheel necklace and placed it in my hand. 'Keep this with you. It is from my Mårmår. She gave it to me when I was born. I am meant to give it to the mother of my child. It is a family tradition. You must go inside now. Tell Stjärna that I love her too. When all of this is over, we will be together again.' He kissed me briefly then pushed me away gently.

The monks were praying in the chapel. I slipped through the door in the eastern wall and walked upstairs. When I entered the monks' room, Geirdís and Stjärna were still in bed. I climbed into a bunk and slipped under the blanket. Clutching the sun wheel pendant in my hand, I gave it a kiss then held it against my heart.

I was thinking of Valentin when I heard Stjärna whisper: 'I know you were gone all night. But I won't tell anyone, I promise. I know he has chosen you. All I want is for him to come back safe—I just want him to live. Promise to look after his heart, will you? I will be just a shadow from now on.'

'He loves you too, Stjärna,' I told her. 'He said as much. Nothing can break your bond.'

'Ay, ay, ay, young love . . .' Geirdís muttered.

Stjärna and I fell silent.

Before long, sleep claimed me. When I woke, Stjärna was gone.

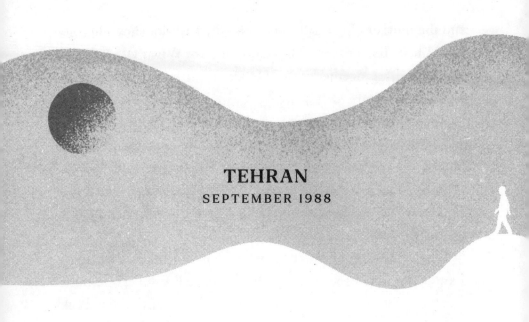

TEHRAN
SEPTEMBER 1988

AT THE START OF the summer of 1988, I enrolled in English classes. As much as I hated to admit it—and I would never give Maman the satisfaction of knowing—I found I enjoyed the lessons. I relished the challenge of expanding my vocabulary and improving my conversational skills. It felt as if doors were opening to me, though I couldn't say why.

That summer passed quickly, and by the end of it I knew what I wanted to study at university. I had fallen in love with photography and cinematography, and I was determined to do a degree in visual arts. Maman was not exactly overjoyed to hear this; she had wanted me to study medicine—or veterinary science, at least. She didn't bother to conceal her disappointment when I was accepted into the University of Arts and started a degree in photography. My cousins had been accepted into medicine and engineering. In Iran, where everyone hoped their children would become doctors or engineers, my uncle was the only one who congratulated me.

The University of Arts had a vigorous screening process; the board only ever accepted a small number of applications for each course, and applicants were required to go through two rounds of interviews. In 1988, a total of seven students were offered places: three women and four men. One guy was from Shiraz, another from Isfahan. Two of the young women were from Ahvaz and Kermanshah. Only Hooman was from Tehran, like me, and from day one I knew he and I would form a strong bond. Although we had come from all over, our group quickly became very close and supportive of one another.

The campus was located in the heart of Tehran's CBD. It comprised the central building, where most of the lectures took place, an auditorium for concerts and performances, as well as a small photographic lab located in the basement of the building. Two smaller buildings were devoted to graphic arts, including painting and drawing, and music. The first time I walked onto the grounds of the university I was taken aback by how small it was. I had always imagined a university to be ten times the size of a school, but this one wasn't.

Transitioning from high school to university was disorientating. I had gone from sharing classrooms and schoolyards with hundreds of pupils, all of the same gender, to sitting in lectures with only a handful of students of both genders, although women did sit on one side of the room and men on the other.

I was amazed by how quickly my lunch breaks had gone from fighting over an overused and worn-out basketball ring to having debates about painting and photography. From a reserved and shy adolescent, I was blossoming into a more confident and sophisticated adult. I was still very quiet, though.

Hooman and I developed a close friendship. He was very talented—he not only took stunning photographs, he also played piano beautifully. We bought our first cameras together from a little shopping arcade tucked away near the Grand Bazaar. Right from the start it was clear that we were going to pursue different photographic paths and styles. Even our choice of camera differed, and we spent many hours arguing in favour of a particular brand or model. Hooman favoured Nikon, while I insisted that Canon built better cameras. The women in our class preferred Minolta and Pentax.

Holding my first camera, a second-hand Canon AE-1, and taking black-and-white shots, was like having a superpower. I felt I could create and capture magic, what no one else could see, and claim it as my own. I was not alone in this: every day we raced to the basement lab and jostled for processing chemicals and equipment to develop our films. A couple of guys set themselves up with darkrooms at home, printing their photos whenever they wanted, but the rest of us had to endure long waits for our turn in the lab.

When we each had a batch of photos ready, we would gather around the long white bench, spread out our photos and analyse each other's work. It was amazing how encouraging we were of each other. There was never a sense of competition, never anyone denigrating the others.

It probably helped that we'd each developed our own unique style of photography. We were influenced by famous photographers. In this time before the internet, our only source of reference was the small library on campus, where a handful of books on famous international photographers and other artists were kept. Because the collection was so small, we were not permitted to borrow the books; instead we had to reserve a timeslot to view the books at the library.

Many books had been destroyed; in those that remained several pages of artwork might have been ripped out or covered in black ink, having been deemed morally corrupt by the Islamic council of the university. Everything related to the west had been destroyed in the early years of the Islamic Revolution. Women's body parts, including necks, bare shoulders or legs, were drawn over or cut out from the pages, rendering many articles and explanatory notes meaningless. We thought that this was just the norm, for we didn't know any better—we had never experienced what it was like to go to university before the revolution.

Despite our restricted access to their work, we managed to develop some sense of familiarity with the world's masters. I admired Avedon, because of my interest in portrait photography, while Hooman idolised Man Ray.

Occasionally someone's relative would go overseas and smuggle an art book back into the country for us. We would take turns to peruse the book while others watched out for the university guards. I too was lucky enough to receive a textbook from my uncle who lived in the UK. He had sent it to me with someone who was returning home to Iran. I was excited to share it with my classmates and took it to the campus. A couple of female students had just finished printing their photos and emerged from the darkroom. They had rolled up their sleeves to avoid staining them with chemicals, and the scarf of one of them had slipped back slightly so that a few strands of her hair were showing.

We'd become quite loud in our discussion, arguing about the techniques we were studying, when we noticed a bearded man we had never seen before start walking towards us. He was wearing beige trousers and a khaki shirt. I quickly stuffed the book in my backpack as the man came forward and ordered the women to cover their hair and then moved them on, jerking his head towards the stairs. He lingered for a while, going into the darkroom to see if anyone else was there, and coming to stand next to me as I fiddled with my camera. He smelled of stale sweat.

He didn't say a word, and I was relieved when he finally left.

I went outside and sat under a tree, recovering from the near-miss. Within minutes, I saw the man in beige trousers approaching. He announced that the head of the university wanted to see me, and he escorted me to his office.

When I entered, I saw the woman whose hair had been showing sitting in front of the university head, her head bowed, her hands folded in her lap. The man in beige trousers closed the door behind him and stood guard. The air was stifling. The smell of body odours and dirty feet hung low. The university head, a man with a big beard and big stomach, told me to take the seat next to the female student.

My palms were sweaty and my knees weak as I obeyed. I glanced at my classmate from the corner of my eye: she was as white as a sheet.

The university head finally broke the silence. 'What have you got to say in your defence?'

I swallowed. 'I'm not sure what I've done wrong,' I said.

'Let's stop playing games, shall we? You were seen entertaining female students with an immoral book.' His tone was calm and reasonable, but that seemed only to increase the threat.

'It was just a photography textbook,' I said.

'We don't provide you with adequate books? You feel you need to bring filth and nudity into the sacred grounds of this institution? Our brothers lost their lives for nothing? Show me the book,' he demanded.

I opened my pack and handed over the book.

'Besme Allah,' he said as opened the book. He flicked through the pages, ripping out a few as I looked on in horror. The female student started crying silently.

'Now, what is going on between you two?' he asked her.

'Nothing, brother, nothing—I swear to Allah,' she said.

'Hmm. I didn't expect this from you of all people. Your grandfather was a respected cleric, he would be turning in his grave to know you are flirting with men! I can't believe that your parents have allowed you to study photography. A woman's place is in the kitchen, not a photo lab. Haj Mustafa should know better!' He was sounding less calm now, his voice rising. 'But: if you apologise, and swear on the Qur'an to behave yourself, I will let you go.

But make no mistake, Brother Husseini here will let us know if such filthy acts are repeated! And I'll still have a word with your father tonight at the mosque.'

The bearded man in beige pants was Brother Husseini. I repeated his name in my head.

The female student was sobbing and apologising and begging for forgiveness.

The head of the university flicked his head and Brother Husseini escorted her out of the office.

He turned his attention back to me. 'I thought you were one of the good ones, but I was wrong—western immorality has corrupted you. We still have a long road ahead to fight the influence of the filth that comes from the west!' He threw my book in his top drawer and slammed it shut. 'Now, what are we going to do with you?'

I wasn't sure if he wanted me to stay silent or if he expected an answer. I chose silence.

'Do you know who I am?' he asked.

'The head of the university, brother,' I said.

'Smart! I also hold a position within the Revolutionary Guard as a senior prosecutor. I will grant you forgiveness this time, but only because you have not caused trouble before. However, if you should repeat your mistake, not only you will be expelled from this institution, you will end up in jail. As for the sister who was here earlier, you are not to approach her or speak with her ever again! Now go back to your class.'

I shot up from my seat; the back of my shirt was soaked with cold sweat.

'I hope your brother is planning to return from the west and serve Islam,' he murmured as I was leaving.

The hairs rose on the back of my neck; the bastard knew about Satyar. I shivered.

Brother Husseini was waiting for me outside the office. 'You will tell the others to behave modestly and not to engage in anti-Islam behaviour, won't you?' he said, with his face so close to mine our noses were almost touching.

I swallowed. 'Yes, brother.'

Within weeks the female student was married to the head of the university; she was his second wife. She left the campus, and we never saw her again.

☾

During the summer holidays our lecturer organised a photo-graphic expedition for a group of students from various faculties. He managed to sign up thirty students, and we all piled into a bus and headed for the Caspian Sea region in the middle of July.

I sat right at the back on a single seat. Hooman and Afshid, a girl who was studying graphic design, sat a few rows down from me. As we got closer to the coast the humidity intensified; the air on the bus was stifling, as it had no air-conditioning. We made frequent stops, which were a welcome relief. Hooman insisted that drinking hot tea would cool us down, and Afshid and I kept dismissing him. Afshid was loud and bubbly, joking and chatting with everyone.

We finally arrived at our accommodation—it was in the foothills of the mountains. The sound of cicadas filled the air; it was still very humid. I had a cold shower and put on fresh clothes.

Hooman gathered a group of us and we went for a hike up a mountain to take photos. I was scared of heights, and the distance between me and the group grew as I lagged behind. By the time we reached the summit, my knees were shaking, and I was dizzy. It was so hot and I felt like I couldn't breathe. I decided to turn back.

I sought shelter in a cool shaded area by a stream. I splashed my face and neck in the ice-cold water, then lay down on a wooden bench. I was listening to the cicadas when I heard Gretel's soft footsteps. Her face was flushed from the heat and strands of her golden-blonde hair were stuck to her forehead. She kneeled by the stream, scooped some water in her cupped hands and drank. Then, staring at the mountains, she said: 'It was a warm July day when the world closed in on us.'

VISBY
JULY 1361

27 July was the day our world fell apart. I watched from the window of the monks' quarters as people screamed and ran in all directions. The voices got louder: 'The Danes are coming! They'll be here within minutes!'

The Gotlandic army formed a strong line outside the city wall, holding all the weapons they had. They felt courageous, confident that together they could defeat the enemy. The Gotlanders fired arrows at the enemy soldiers on horseback, but they were unable to hide back the tide of Danes; within a short time, the Gotland army had suffered severe losses, with most of their men wounded or killed.

Inside our hidden chamber in St Karin's, Geirdís pleaded with Odin for protection:

'They've come for our island home

Their oars swish about violently
The summer breeze flees to an unknown horizon
The fish descend deep into the dark blue Baltic
They huddle tightly, not a word, not a whisper
A tiny fish flinches; "Hush!" reply the rest
The farmers clench their fists
Oh Odin, our island home. Oh, Odin.'

The Danish army roared in triumph as they slammed their fists on the city gates, behind which the merchants were cowering anxiously. Knowing they were routed, the merchants opened the gates and the Danish army entered the town in victory.

Inside St Karin's the silence was deafening. I ran to the door. 'Don't go, my girl, please don't go!' Geirdís called after me.

With Mishka at my heels, I ran outside the city gates to find Stjärna. When I reached the outskirts, all I could see were the bodies of the dead and injured. There was blood everywhere and smoke rising from the farms that the marauding Danes had set on fire. There was no sign of my mother and the other women.

I was frightened. I walked around, calling for my mother for Birgitta, for Stjärna helplessly. My heart was racing, my eyes burning from the heavy smoke. I heard Mishka barking outside Valentin's house I ran inside and spotted Stjärna: she was keening over the dead bodies of our mothers and Birgitta. I pulled Stjärna to her feet and held her in my arms. 'Stjärna, talk to me—please!' I pleaded. But Stjärna had lost her voice.

Father's loyal servant had informed him that I had left St Karin's. The servant had seen me heading towards the farm so

Father came to the burning scene and spotted us. He commanded his men to take us away from the scene. I wanted to say goodbye to my mother but he wouldn't allow me. His men took us back to our house in the city and locked all the doors and windows. Stjärna and I curled up together in my room and watched the flame on the candle grow tall with our breaths until finally, exhausted by our pain and anguish, we slept.

In the middle of the night, I woke to Father's voice and moved to stand by the door of the room to hear what was going on.

'Well?' Father was demanding impatiently of his servant.

The servant replied, 'It is all taken care of, master.'

'God help you if you are lying to me!'

'I would not dare, master! The peasant has been dealt with. He will never cause trouble again, master.'

My heart was pounding against my chest. I was praying that he wasn't talking about some innocent farmer. I could not believe how he was betraying the trust of the Gotlanders.

When Father returned to his bedroom, he spotted me in the doorway. 'I will send Valka to help you wash and put fresh clothes on,' he said. 'You look and smell like a filthy peasant!' His eyes raked over my torn and dirty clothes, pausing at my throat, where my collar was torn. He came closer, his eyes narrowed: he'd spotted the sun wheel pendant. He ripped the necklace from my neck. 'You are not allowed to wear this pagan rubbish!' he bellowed, his face suffused with rage. 'You are a Christian! You understand?!'

I retreated into the room and sat on the edge of the bed, next to Stjärna.

Her face was blackened from the smoke, her clothes ripped and stained with blood. Her eyes were wide open and she appeared to be frozen. I stroked her hair; she looked defeated and lost.

In a halting voice, she began to describe what had happened to her and our mothers.

A Danish soldier had grabbed Stjärna by her hair and dragged her inside Valentin's house. Her mother ran after them, intent on rescuing her daughter, and Birgitta and my mother rushed to her aid. The area was full of Danish soldiers. Suddenly four other soldiers joined in. Two of them held Birgitta back and another killed Stjärna's mother.

'You bastards!' my mother raged. 'Our men will cut your balls off! Just you wait!'

Stjärna struggled and kicked, trying to free herself from the soldier holding her. The soldier bashed her head against the wooden bench to subdue her, and she watched helplessly as the soldiers who had captured Birgitta raped her savagely on the kitchen table. When they were finished with her, one of the men hit her head with a skillet until her lifeless body fell to the floor.

'You may violate us, even kill us,' my mother screamed as the soldiers turned their attention to her, 'but you cannot touch our souls! You cannot claim the Gotlandic spirit! Our culture and our stories will live on!' She reached for a knife and stabbed one soldier in the leg. He screamed and kicked her in the head. She slumped to the floor.

Only Stjärna was alive now. The man who had seized her ripped off her clothes and pushed himself inside her. When he had finished, the others took it in turns to rape her, the last one attacking her so violently that she bled heavily.

Stjärna fell silent, haunted by the horrors she had seen and experienced. I faltered at the image she had given me of my mother's last moments, but then a powerful anger rose in me, and it gave me strength.

'Our mothers died heroes, Stjärna,' I said. 'They shed their blood to defend this island and its people. We should be proud to be their daughters; we must take it upon ourselves to follow in their footsteps, to honour their spirits and the land they loved.'

Stjärna blinked, then turned to look out the window.

A young swallow on the windowsill was calling out to another. Stjärna stretched her arm towards the small bird as it flew away.

'See, Stjärna?' I said. 'That little bird was a messenger from our mothers. She is letting us know that they are in a better place. They want us to be strong.'

A single tear rolled down Stjärna's cheek. I leaned over and put my head on her chest. There was something soothing and reassuring about the steady sound of her heartbeat.

☾

The next morning, Father summoned a physician to examine Stjärna, who still had not moved or spoken. The doctor reported that she had been severely wounded and had lost a considerable amount of blood.

I shuddered in the corner, and I felt my eyes widen with fear as the physician next approached me. 'Your father has asked that I examine you, too,' he told me.

The physician's assistant seized me and held me in a tight grip as his master inserted his fingers inside of me. He raised an eyebrow then nodded to his assistant, who released me.

Valka later told me that the physician had informed Father that I had lost my virginity, but not to rape. The violence Father had once turned on my mother was now directed at me.

Stjärna, meanwhile, was taken to an abbey in the country where the nuns looked after the wounded. I never saw her again.

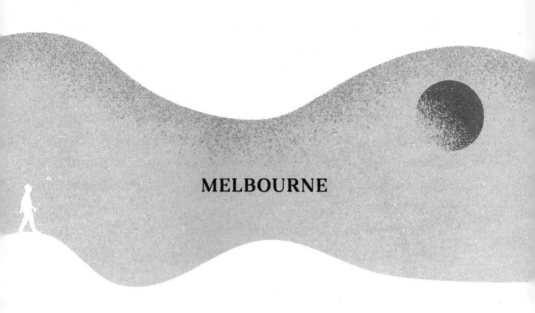

MELBOURNE

Months pass in which I receive no response to the submission I sent to the case officer handling Fowziah and Fatimah's visa application. Finally, as I am eating my lunch at my desk one day in October, I check my emails and find one from the Australian High Commission in Nairobi. The subject reads: *Visa Decision Notification—Orphan Relative Visa.*

I am too nervous to open it. None of the cases I have worked on to date has affected me as deeply as this one. Maybe it is because I know Habiba personally; it feels as if it involves close family members of my own. I get up and pace the small area between my desk and the window overlooking the train station. A drunk man is staggering along the footpath, swearing at imaginary people. Mrs Nga Chu is sweeping the pavement in front of her bakery, still screaming at Anh, who is inside. Sunshine is always bustling, morning or afternoon: I can easily find myself distracted for hours watching the goings-on outside.

But as much as I crave distraction, I know I must face whatever news the email contains. I return to my desk. My hands are shaking so that I struggle to open the letter attached to the email.

When I read the first paragraph, I can't believe it. I know Habiba has gone away for a few days, so I can't go downstairs to give her the news in person. I call her instead. She answers after a couple of rings.

'Tishtar?' she says. 'Is everything alright?'

I take a deep breath. 'I have some news for you, Habiba. I've just received an email from Nairobi.'

'Oh,' says Habiba. I hear her swallow nervously. 'And?'

'The girls have been granted a visa! They can come to you as soon as you purchase two airline tickets for them!' Tears are streaming down my face as I share the joyous news.

'Oh Alhamdullilah, Alhamdullilah, Alhamdullilah, a hundred times over!' she shouts. 'I am lost for words, Tishtar! Thank you! Thank you! God bless you and your family!'

TEHRAN

NOVEMBER 1992

In my final year of university I was regularly invited to gatherings at my fellow students' homes, to parties where forbidden western music was played, where alcohol was consumed secretly, where girls and boys danced together in low light. We all knew that at any moment we could be raided by the Revolutionary Guard and that we would all be arrested, beaten and imprisoned for crimes of immorality. Many gatherings had been raided, and while in detention young people had been lashed by power cables. The number of lashes a person received correlated to the seriousness of the crime they were accused of; it might be anywhere from eighty to two hundred lashes. Women received a slightly lower number of lashes—probably the only time that women were shown any consideration. Many victims suffered long-term injuries to their spines and lower backs.

Students who were arrested and accused of the crime of immorality were expelled from university for life and would never be able to get a job anywhere in the country. But despite the risks, we were young and fearless; we had survived eight years of war, as well as relentless harassment by Brother Husseini and other bearded men on and off the campus. We felt tough enough to defy them. Besides, if you are conditioned to believe that on any given day your life could end, you live life to the fullest. Why wouldn't you, when you have nothing left to lose?

It was at Afshid's birthday party that I was introduced to Sousan. When I arrived at the house I could hear the beat of the music vibrating the windows. Uncle Behrooz, Afshid's father, opened the door and gave me a firm handshake. He was a tall man with dark brown eyes and a dense beard. We called him Uncle because we were very fond of him and he treated us almost like his own kids.

'Come in, come in, son!' he said as he wrapped his arm around my shoulders. 'What would you like to drink? Vodka or whisky?'

'Just a soda, merci,' I said.

'What nonsense is that?' Afshid's mum said as she joined us. She had a cigarette in her right hand and a glass of sherry in the left. 'Why not something stronger, Tishtar joon?'

'I'd better not. The guards are everywhere at night,' I said.

'I'll drive you home, son,' Uncle Behrooz said. 'Let me fetch you a whisky; I recently received a new shipment from London.' He winked at me.

He returned with two glasses and handed one to me. 'Salute!' he said as he raised his glass.

I took a sip and it warmed me up inside. 'How did you manage to get it through customs?' I asked.

'Money talks, son,' he said.

'But the Revolutionary Guards?'

'Even they can't resist a few crisp notes!' He grinned.

I went and sat on a stool in a corner, watching everyone dance. There was a plume of cigarette smoke hanging over the lounge room, and the air smelled sweetly of perfume and food. There was a large dining table with a huge spread of food. Afshid's mum must have spent hours in the kitchen.

Hooman came and sat next to me. 'What do you think about the girls?' he asked.

'Yeah, they seem nice,' I said.

'What about that one?' He tilted his head in the direction of a girl who was dancing with Afshid.

'She's good-looking,' I said. She was very attractive; her hair was light brown, and she had hazel eyes.

'Afshid says she has noticed you,' he said.

'Me?'

'She noticed that you are sitting all by yourself, and it has intrigued her. Afshid wants to introduce her to you.'

I grinned and took a sip of my whisky.

'It's a yes, then?' Hooman said.

'Nah, nah, I'm okay.'

'Oh, come on! Just say hello—she won't bite.' Hooman laughed as he walked away.

Afshid's dad suddenly switched off the music and dimmed the lights. 'Hush, everyone,' he said, as he grabbed his coat and went outside.

A few people gathered around the window. 'What's going on?' someone called out.

'It's pitch-dark, I can't see a thing,' another said.

Everyone started murmuring softly.

Suddenly Uncle Behrooz reappeared, accompanied by two bearded men. Both were dressed in military uniforms and were carrying guns. Their faces were hard; one was frowning and the other scanned the room, seeming disgusted by what he saw.

Uncle Behrooz guided the men to his study and nodded to his wife. She grabbed a few containers from the kitchen and frantically made food parcels. The rest of us remained still and silent, too frightened to talk.

My palms were sweaty and I felt hot. I knew I would be taken away to prison. I rehearsed in my mind what I would say, how I would explain why I was drinking alcohol and why I was in the company of girls who had no hijab. I wondered how many lashes I would receive and how Maman and Baba would take the news.

Minutes went past. It felt like an eternity before the men came out of the study. Their faces had softened; the one who had scanned the room kept his eyes on the carpet while the other walked ahead of him. Afshid's mum gave them food and Uncle Behrooz walked them out. He patted them on the shoulder and slid envelopes into their jacket pockets.

When he returned he asked us to keep the music down, and soon everyone started dancing again. I was so unsettled that I reached for my glass and drank the rest of my whisky in one go.

Before I knew it the party was in full swing once more.

Hooman and Afshid brought the young woman over to meet me.

'Shit, that was close,' I said.

'My dad looked after them,' Afshid said.

'Fuck the mullahs!' Hooman roared like a lion as he raised his glass.

The woman smiled and flicked her hair back.

'Tishtar, this is my dear friend Sousan,' Afshid said.

'Hello, Sousan,' I said.

Hooman and Afshid drifted off, leaving us alone; Hooman winked at me as they left, and Afshid pinched Sousan's arm.

'So, I hear you are a photographer?' Sousan said.

'Yes, and you?' I said.

'I'm studying graphic design at a different university from yours. Do you take portraits?'

'Yes, mainly in the studio, though. I would love to take some outdoors, but it's risky.'

'Maybe one day you can take some of me?' she suggested, her eyes gleaming.

I was stunned by her directness.

'I don't know how we would get you into the studio on our campus without anyone noticing.'

'Oh, I'm sure we'll think of something,' she said with a smile.

We spoke for a long time that night, and Sousan didn't try to hide her interest in me. She wrote her phone number on a napkin before she left and handed it to me.

☾

'So?' Hooman asked the next day when he saw me.

'What?' I said.

He shook his head in mock disappointment. 'A gorgeous girl gives you her phone number and you do nothing? I'm going to see Afshid this weekend—you will come too. Sousan will be there.'

'I really don't like these types of arrangements,' I said.

'You don't like any arrangements! Be there!'

☾

When I arrived at Afshid's house that weekend, she screamed with joy. 'I'm so glad you came!' she said, kissing me on the left cheek then the right.

It was a hot afternoon; Afshid's house was west-facing and the afternoon sun was strong. There was a power outage so we couldn't use the evaporative cooler. I kept going to the bathroom to splash my face with cold water.

We played cards for hours but Sousan never turned up. I was very uncomfortable; something was bothering me but I couldn't put my finger on it.

'I'm gonna go,' I said as evening fell.

'Stay, we are going to get pizza,' Afshid called out from the kitchen.

'Nah, merci, I'm not really hungry,' I said.

'Sorry, brother! I don't know why she didn't come,' Hooman said.

'I have an assignment due anyway; I need to get it done,' I said.

When I got home I had a cold shower and went to my room. It was stifling—the cooling system had failed and my room was boiling hot. I grabbed my notes and sat next to the fan, but I couldn't concentrate. I went to the lounge room, where Maman was writing. 'Want ice cream?' I asked.

'You know I never say no to ice cream!' she said with a big smile. I filled two bowls with bastani and we started eating.

'I thought you were going to stay at Afshid's for dinner,' Maman said.

'Nah, I have to finish this assignment,' I replied.

'What's the task?'

'We each have selected a piece of literature,' I said. 'I need to write an essay examining the characters and analyse why the author has portrayed them the way he has, in the context of the time the story is set.'

'Oh, that's interesting! And what have you chosen?'

'*Romeo and Juliet.*'

'Argh, Shakespeare! Walk your own soil before you venture elsewhere.'

'Meaning?' I said, scooping up the last mouthful of bastani.

'You should have looked to Persian literature. You should embrace your own heritage.'

'But I was interested in the theme.'

'The theme? Did you know that Nizami wrote *Khosrow and Shirin* in the twelfth century, long before Shakespeare was even born?' She got up and walked to her bookshelf, ran her fingers along the spines, and pulled out Nizami's book. When she returned to her chair she opened it and started reading aloud. She had a habit of doing this. She would begin reading from an article, an essay or a book without asking if you were interested. I seldom objected, though. With her melodic voice and dramatic flair, her recitals were always compelling.

'*Khosrow's grandfather visited him in his dreams one night,*' she read. '*He promised him a beautiful wife and the kingdom of Persia. After this, his close friend returns from Armenia and tells him about Mahin Banoo, the Queen of Armenia, and her beautiful niece Shirin. Hearing the description of Shirin, Khosrow falls in love with her. In his subsequent assignment to Armenia, his friend shows Shirin a portrait of Khosrow and she falls in love with him. She flees Armenia to go to Persia to be with Khosrow. At the same time, Khosrow runs away from Persia to escape punishment and heads towards Armenia. The lovers keep heading in opposite directions and miss each other each time.*'

Maman put the book down and went to the bathroom. In her absence, I grabbed the book and started reading where she had left off.

'Oh, you don't want me to read?' she asked when she came back. I handed her back the book and she continued.

'*So, Khosrow and Shirin finally meet in Armenia after Khosrow flees Persia when it is overthrown by Bahram Choobin. But Shirin tells Khosrow that he should reclaim his kingdom from Bahram, so he sets off. While he is trying to find allies to reclaim Persia, he promises Caesar he will marry his daughter Miriam.*'

'Very confusing, too many characters,' I complained.

'Ah! But wait till you hear the end. I won't read all of it.' Maman went on: '*By now so many years had passed. By the time Khosrow gets to Shirin's palace, his son from Miriam is all grown up and falls in love with Shirin. Out of jealousy he murders his father so that he can marry Shirin. She in turn kills herself so that she doesn't have to marry him. The old lovers are buried in the same grave so that they can be together.*' Maman put the book down.

'Quite a complex story,' I said.

'Yes. So what do you think Nizami is trying to do here?' Maman asked.

'Well, it's not the tragic love story it appears to be on the surface,' I observed. 'It's subtly illustrating the politics of the time, and the war and conflict and the power play between the empires.'

'And, most importantly, it's crucial to pay attention to the role of women in the narrative and how they are portrayed,' Maman said. 'They are not the weak subordinate type that is often described in stories. Persian women were monarchs and generals during this period of history. They were outspoken and independent, heroines and forces to be reckoned with, until the Arab invasion, when these powerful women were deliberately suppressed.'

It was long past midnight when we finished discussing the role of women in Ancient Persia and in classic literature. My head was spinning, and I said that I was going to bed.

'Goodnight, darling. We can talk some more about your assignment tomorrow,' Maman said as she kissed my forehead.

I went to bed but found myself unable to sleep; the temperature in my room felt like it was a thousand degrees.

Light from the lounge room was still seeping through the gap under my bedroom door when I got up again and went to the kitchen for a cold drink; Maman was still awake too.

'I can't sleep!' I complained. 'It's so damn hot in this house!'

'Well, when I told Baba to buy a house in the northern suburbs, there was a reason for it!' Maman was scribbling in her notebook.

'Maman?' I said.

'Yes?'

'Why don't you go back to teaching?'

'There is no place for me in an education system monitored and controlled by the fanatical regime.'

'But not every teacher is a supporter of this regime,' I said.

'No, but by wearing a scarf and agreeing to teach their curriculum, I would be bowing to them. I won't do it!' she said defiantly.

I sprawled on the couch in front of the fan and drifted off to the sound of her pen scratching the paper.

☾

In the following weeks, Hooman organised several times for Sousan and I to meet at Afshid's. I came up with excuses time after time to avoid going but Hooman wouldn't have a bar of it. I gave in and each time I turned up, Sousan didn't. She had all sorts of excuses for failing to appear: she was held up in class, or she was expected at home, or she'd simply forgotten.

Afshid didn't give up, though—she continued to invite me over, and one day Sousan actually came. She arrived very late, took off her hijab and helped herself to a drink from the fridge. She seemed very comfortable in Afshid's house.

We were already eating when Sousan arrived—Afshid's mum always put on a big spread for us. Sousan leaned over and pinched a piece of food from my plate, and she and Afshid started giggling.

After dinner, Uncle Behrooz put on a video for us to watch—a western movie that he had smuggled into the country together with the other contraband.

After that night, Sousan and I continued seeing each other at Afshid's house. Sousan always teased me: when we played cards she would snatch the cards out of my hands and make me wrestle them off her; she'd hide my wallet in obscure places in Afshid's room and tickle me while I was searching for it. When we played cards or watched movies, she would sit very close to me, her thighs pressing against mine.

Once when I was in the studio practising taking photos with a large-format Sinar camera, Hooman and Afshid burst in, laughing. Behind them was a woman wearing a long black chador. When she removed it, I realised that it was Sousan. Afshid had smuggled her past security without them noticing that Sousan wasn't a student at our university.

'God! You are out of your mind! Brother Husseini was here a minute ago!' I said.

'Nah, he just left,' Hooman said. 'Only the old guard is at the gate, and we gave him some cigarettes and a big container of soup—he was grateful.'

I took portraits of all of them that afternoon. I shot Hooman smoking a cigarette, Humphrey Bogart-style. Afshid had borrowed her mum's fur coat, while Sousan wore a pair of long silk gloves, dark-red lipstick and a low-cut top that barely concealed her breasts.

Sousan and I began to meet outside Afshid's house, though trying to arrange a time to meet was a battle and a half, as I had to ring her family's home. If her mother or father answered the phone, I had to hang up. Her sister was our go-between; if she answered the call, she would put Sousan on the line. We spent hours talking on the phone when her parents weren't home. If they were nearby when I rang, her sister would say that I had the wrong number, and I would hang up.

For months we met up secretly in less crowded parks, as it was illegal for men and women to have a relationship out of wedlock. If arrested, penalties could range anything from two hundred lashes to imprisonment or even death—by stoning for women and by hanging for men.

Sometimes, Sousan would come over to my house when Maman and Baba weren't home. One evening, when Maman and Baba arrived home with Madar, Maman sniffed the air suspiciously. 'I can smell perfume,' she said.

'It's my deodorant—I just had a shower,' I said.

'Since when you do wear female deodorant? I wasn't born yesterday. You will bring disgrace to our family. The neighbours are talking.'

I walked away and went to my room.

Shortly after, Madar came in and sat on the floor.

'What is going on?' she asked softly.

I told her the truth; I always did.

232

'This is not an attempt to replace Gretel, is it?' She narrowed her eyes.

'No, Madar! I really like Sousan,' I said.

'Well, it's about time I met this young lady. Bring her over for a cup of tea.'

I took Sousan to Madar's house the following day, and frequently after that. This caused a lot of arguments between Maman and Madar. 'It is better if it is under our eyes than God knows where,' Madar would say.

Meeting at Madar's place gave us the time and space in which to explore each other intimately. One afternoon when Madar had taken a strong painkiller and gone to bed to rest, we went to the spare room. At first we just lay on the bed, listening to music. But Sousan's musky perfume was tantalising, and we started kissing. It was the first time we had been able to touch each other. It was illegal to show any physical affection in public—even married couples would get into trouble simply for holding hands.

Sousan climbed on top of me, her lips warm on mine, her long hair enveloping me. She unbuttoned her shirt. Her skin was soft and smooth. I unhooked her bra and she rolled onto her back. My hands wandered all over her body. I slid a hand inside her pants, and found her warm and wet. I started to unzip my jeans.

She pushed me away. 'No, not that. You can't, not that,' she said. 'Here, let me . . .' she whispered in my ear.

Afterwards, she went to the bathroom to clean up.

Madar had woken up by now, and she came looking for us in the spare room.

'Why have you drawn the curtains?' she asked, her eyes taking in the rumpled sheets with obvious disapproval.

Sousan returned from the bathroom and, seeing Madar, she blushed.

'Let's have some tea,' I suggested hastily.

We drank our tea in an awkward silence. Madar seemed very upset.

As soon as we'd finished, Sousan and I left the flat.

We walked in silence. 'What's wrong?' Sousan asked.

'Nothing, just a bit of a headache,' I lied. I was thinking about how I'd let Madar down. I escorted Sousan to the taxi rank, then walked all the way home, which took me over an hour. I was torn. I wanted to be with Sousan, but something wasn't right; a strong energy was pulling me away from her.

When I arrived home, Maman was in a foul mood. I said hello but she ignored me; I knew something was seriously bothering her.

'We need to talk,' she said. 'I just got off the phone with Sousan's sister, and she said that you have tried to get her sister into bed!' Maman's voice was getting louder and louder.

Baba was watching the news on TV, but I could tell by his pale face and the way he kept clearing his throat nervously that he was listening.

'This is disgraceful! I don't know what we have done to deserve this! You should be ashamed of yourself!' Maman kept on screaming and cursing, until finally I left the room.

I tossed and turned all night. At first light, I rose, had a shower and left the house. It was very early still; I walked and walked, until I reached Sousan's university campus. When she saw me, her face was ashen. She told me to meet her in the park later in the afternoon.

'Why did your sister betray us?' I asked when we met.

'My lips were swollen, and she saw the stain on my clothes, and she figured out what had happened,' Sousan explained.

☾

We continued to see each other, but were more secretive than ever, meeting only on the street, and far from where either of us lived. I didn't take her to Madar's again. We were always on the lookout for the Revolutionary Guards. If we spotted one of their vehicles, we would quickly separate until they were out of sight.

A few months went past. Maman and Baba had gone up to Baba's hometown of Rasht for a funeral, and were staying overnight, so Sousan came to our house after her classes.

When she arrived, she took me to my room and took off her top. 'I want you to come all over me,' she said. She unbuckled my belt and kneeled on the floor. But I couldn't do it—all I could see was Gretel's face before me. Her eyes were penetrating my soul.

'What's the matter?' Sousan asked.

'I don't know,' I replied.

She took my hands and placed them over her breasts. Her nipples were hard.

I lay down on the bed and closed my eyes. She started kissing my neck and ears. Her lips were burning. I wanted to be with her, but all I could think of was Gretel. I rolled onto my side and squeezed my pillow.

'Don't you want this?' Sousan asked.

I didn't answer.

'What's wrong?'

'I can't do it,' I said, my voice muffled in the pillow.

I got up and went to stand by the window. The sun had gone down, though a streak of orange was still left in the sky. The traffic was getting heavier and louder outside.

'There is no air here,' I complained and opened the window. Cars were tooting their horns continuously, and police were trying to manage the gridlock.

'Are you going to tell me what's going on?' Sousan said.

I didn't respond.

'Are you already bored with me?'

I was silent.

She started to pull her clothes on. As she did, she glanced at me and gave me a venomous look.

'It's someone else isn't it? That's what it is all about, isn't it?' she said. 'Ever since we got together, this has been between us, this lingering shadow that never goes away!'

'Come here,' I said, and tried to embrace her.

'Fuck off, you bastard—you just wanted to get between my legs! I practically threw myself at your feet, and your mind has been elsewhere this whole time!' She ran from the room. A few seconds later, I heard the front door slam.

☾

I tried to call her house dozens of times to clear the air and apologise, but her mother kept answering the phone. I went to her university campus, but she was always surrounded by friends and ignored my attempts to talk to her. Maman guessed that we had broken up, and she expressed her relief, saying that it was for the best. 'In time you will forget her and you will be thankful for this,' she said.

After a month, Afshid asked me to leave Sousan alone. 'Sorry, Tishtar, but there is no point pursuing her. She has made up her mind. Hooman and I have tried to talk to her about you, but she won't have a bar of it.'

I was upset, yet relieved. I felt confused, but had clarity at the same time. I wanted her back, but was happy that she had ended it.

One by one my peers were getting married and engaged, either to women they had chosen themselves or women their families had selected for them. I kept myself aloof; after my experience with Sousan, I wasn't keen on entering into a relationship with anyone else.

'There's plenty of fish in the sea!' Hooman said. He was constantly trying to fix me up with other girls, but I resisted. 'You are not still lusting after the Nordic girl, are you?' he said.

I didn't reply. I had told him a bit about Gretel when I sketched her in our drawing class at uni.

'Brother, you are strange. This is going nowhere.'

I knew already that I was strange. And it was true what Sousan had said on the day she broke up with me: Gretel had been a shadow between us. I could not imagine wanting anyone as I wanted her. Everywhere I went, I searched for her. The dreamer in me always imagined her as the subject of my photos. Each time I developed pictures in the darkroom I hoped her image would magically emerge from the processing tray. But it never did.

C

Our university days were drawing to a close.

At the end of the final semester, we were required to present a portfolio and a written thesis to a panel of judges. I presented a series of portraits, all in black and white, accompanied by a research paper on the history of black-and-white portrait photography in both America and Iran. I had examined the use of light and shadow, the choice of people in the photos, their facial expressions, and emulated the series in my own collection.

We were called in to the auditorium one by one to hang our collection. The judges then considered our work and asked questions about it. I received good feedback from them, though one said that my photography was somewhat cautious. 'Don't let anything get in the way of freedom of expression,' he advised. 'Take your portrait photography to the next level—don't hold back.' He had been a political activist in his youth and was fearless; he spoke his mind and was not fazed by Brother Husseini's lingering presence on campus.

After we graduated, our little circle fell apart. Afshid was hired by a graphic design company in Toronto and migrated to Canada. Hooman went to Austria to undertake postgraduate study at the Vienna Konservatorium, one of the elite music academies in the world. He became an accomplished conductor and works with the Vienna Philharmonic Orchestra; his talent in music far surpassed his considerable photographic talent.

When Hooman and Afshid left Iran, the grim reality of life as a photographer dawned on me. Unless I took photos at people's weddings, there were not many opportunities for aspiring photographers. I did a few industrial photo shoots with one of my former lecturers, but going to factories and taking photos of steel and wood was hardly inspiring. Becoming an academic didn't interest me either, though this was the path a few of my peers had taken.

One day I went for a walk and started taking some street shots. As I was taking photos I noticed a four-wheel drive pull up. The Revolutionary Guards patrolled the streets in white Nissan four-wheel drives. Whenever you saw a white Nissan with four bearded men or four women in black chadors, your heart would stop. The brothers were licensed to interrogate men and women, whereas the sisters only had authority to address women on matters of immorality.

Two bearded brothers in khaki uniforms stepped out of the vehicle and approached me. One asked me why I was taking photos. I said I was a photographer and was just taking pictures of the cityscape. 'Well, you can't take photos here. There is an all-female high school nearby and it is against Sharia to take photos of the opposite sex.'

There were no schools in sight, plus it was early in the evening, so the school would have been shut in any case. But I knew that it was pointless to argue, so I apologised and started walking away.

One of the brothers called after me. 'Not so fast! You need to hand over your camera.'

His offsider snatched my camera from my hands.

'No, please, that is the only camera I have! I'll give you the film, if that's the issue.'

They looked at each other, and one tried to open the film compartment, but didn't know how to. Reluctantly they gave my camera back. I wound on the film, opened the compartment and removed it. I watched in despair as one of them stamped it beneath his heel. I had spent days taking street shots.

'Consider yourself lucky,' he said. 'Now keep walking and don't ever try this nonsense again.'

As they drove away, I felt hollow. I had had enough. I could no longer bear to be censored, monitored, and denied basic freedoms. I had to leave, I decided.

Walking home that night, I saw a sign on an office building: MIGRATION SERVICES, AUSTRALIA & CANADA. It seemed like fate.

I went upstairs and entered a small and stuffy office. A woman was behind a desk, typing away. She had a mountain of files in front of her. She looked up and greeted me.

'Do you have an appointment?' she asked.

'No, I just saw the sign. How do I find more information?'

'Well, you need to speak with Mr Najafi. He happens to have had a cancellation, so you can see him in fifteen minutes if you'd like.'

I took a seat in the waiting area. There were brochures of universities and touristy sites in Canada and Australia. Glossy magazines with beautifully attired people in modern offices overlooking Sydney Harbour. There were people running in green parks, surfing, skiing, snowboarding, eating at cafes and restaurants. In every picture they were smiling, as if they had not a worry in the world—no brothers or sisters on patrol, no interrogations, no threat of imprisonment and beatings for minor offences. I felt a knot in my stomach.

'You can go in now,' the woman said, gesturing to the office behind her.

I entered the room. Mr Najafi was a man in his late fifties. He had a bald head and a round belly. He was smoking a pipe and drinking coffee. Like the receptionist, he had a mountain of folders on his desk.

'Please, sit,' he said as he released a puff of smoke. 'How can I help you?'

I cleared my throat and told him that I was interested in leaving Iran.

He pulled out a notepad and started asking questions, writing down my replies.

'Well, it sounds like you will qualify,' he said. 'Your score is high enough.'

'What do you mean?' I asked.

'Based on the information you've provided, you would qualify to migrate as a skilled worker. But we need to have your qualifications assessed. You'll also need to undertake an English language test and provide supporting documents to prove your identity.'

'How long will all of this take?'

'If there are no hold-ups, it should take six to twelve months,' he said.

'That long?'

'The migration process is time-consuming, young man.'

'Which country should I choose?'

'Your score and situation match Australia's criteria.'

He made it sound simple. I couldn't believe that it was really possible to gain entry to a country like Canada or Australia.

'I assume that you have done your military service?' he said.

'No, I have been studying.'

'Ah, that changes things,' he said. 'You won't be permitted to leave the country unless you pay a huge penalty and buy your discharge from service.'

'I will have to see what I can do,' I said, and left his office.

☾

When I told my parents that I had decided to move to Australia, they didn't hesitate to express their disapproval.

'But you have military service obligations!' Baba said.

'It's too far! Why not the US or England?' Maman asked. 'We know no one in Australia!'

'We have everything here!' Baba protested.

'Do we, Baba?' I asked. 'Do we really?'

The news spread fast among our close family members. My uncle came over most afternoons to try to convince me to stay. Aunty Tangerine joined the chorus, pleading with me not to leave.

It was impossible for them to imagine me so far away when Satyar had already left home long ago and was never coming back. I think my parents had secretly hoped that I would stay and be with them as they grew old. They had somehow adjusted to the horror of life in the Islamic Republic of Iran and thought I would cope too.

Madar's eyes grew cloudy when I told her that I was going to Australia. 'Does this have anything to do with Gretel?' she asked.

'I can't live in this hellhole anymore, Madar,' I replied.

'That doesn't answer my question.'

'Madar! Gretel stopped visiting me a long time ago. Too long to even remember when the last time was! I have been waiting! My heart is telling me that she is not coming back, that I must find her,' I said.

She held my hand and asked me to think about it a bit more. 'You don't know if she will be in Australia though, do you?' she said.

'Madar, I just know I have to leave. Can I borrow money from you to pay the penalty of not undertaking military service?'

Madar held me tight, kissed my forehead, and said she would see what she could do.

When I told my close friends of my intentions, I got mixed reactions. 'Oh, come on! You are not serious!' some said.

Hooman urged me to migrate to Europe, where culture and art were appreciated. *Go and talk to Uncle Behrooz—he will give you proper advice, not like this fat Mr Najafi you described,* he wrote in one of his letters.

I saw the sense in this, and rang Uncle Behrooz to ask if I could meet with him. He invited me to drop by and see him that same day.

I hadn't seen Afshid's parents since her farewell party. It was a strange feeling to walk into their house without hearing my friend's loud laughter and the sound of music pumping.

Afshid's mum made some tea, and then the three of us sat in the living room and I told them why I had come.

'I want to seek your advice,' I said. 'I have decided to leave Iran. I want to further my studies in visual arts, to read uncensored textbooks and learn about the work of great artists. Above all, I want to be able to live and breathe like a normal human being.

To listen to any music I want, to talk to girls without the fear of being arrested and punished.'

'Ah, your mother will be heartbroken,' Afshid's mother said.

'Where are you planning to go?' her husband asked.

'I have been thinking of Australia or Canada.'

Uncle Behrooz thought Europe was a better option. 'But it will cost you a fair bit,' he warned. 'A visa to go to the UK or Germany will be more expensive than these other countries.'

'And that's in addition to my military service penalty,' I said.

'Oh, that's a minor cost. I can take care of that. I have a few contacts.' He patted me on the back.

After the revolution, there were two sets of prices for everything: the official rate and the black market rate. I presumed Uncle Behrooz was referring to the latter, but I had no idea how much it might be.

When I returned home, Baba had already had a call from Uncle Behrooz about my military service penalty. 'I will sell our old rugs and gather the money,' he said, holding back his tears.

I hung my head low; I was embarrassed that my parents had to resort to selling their household possessions to finance my exit, but I knew there was no way I could afford to pay for it myself, and I would never feel free and happy in Iran. I went to my room and put some music on.

Madar followed and came to sit next to me on the bed.

'Baba and Maman love you so very much. You are all they have left,' she said. 'It is never easy to say goodbye to your flesh and blood, especially when they are moving so far away.'

I put my arms around Madar and we cried together in silence. It got dark outside. I could hear the pots and pans in the kitchen: Maman was preparing dinner.

The next day I went and visited Mr Najafi again and told him of my decision: I was going to apply for an Australian visa.

☾

Over the next few weeks I was kept busy gathering all my academic and school transcripts while Baba went with Uncle Behrooz to see a man Afshid's father knew in the Department of Defence. It was always about who you knew.

Their visits were frequent and often fruitless—the man they needed to see would be at midday prayers, or not in the office that day, or he would be in a meeting, and they would come home disappointed.

Finally, after several trips to the Department of Defence, Baba and Uncle Behrooz were successful, and I was excused from military service. But there was still no news from Australia.

I went to Afshid's house to thank Uncle Behrooz for everything he had done for me. He embraced me warmly and scolded me for bringing him a present.

'This is the only thing I can do to thank you,' I said.

'The best way to thank me is to go to Australia and make us proud. These mullahs have destroyed Iranians' image in the world. Help to restore the standing we once had,' he told me.

As I was leaving, Afshid's mum handed me an envelope. 'It is a letter from Sousan. She sent it here. I guess she wasn't sure if you would receive it otherwise,' she said.

I shoved the letter in my pocket.

Alone in my room that evening, I pulled it out. I recalled every-thing that had happened between us. What could she want to say to me now? It was all too late; there was no point in looking back. I tore up the letter without reading it.

C

While waiting for my visa, I accepted a photography assignment from a former fellow student. He rang our house one day and said he needed help taking a series of shots at an industrial site for a glossy publication they were putting together. It was a mammoth task: we had to go to the factory early in the morning before the workers arrived to photograph the site and the machinery. Then, throughout the day, we would take shots of workers in various settings. We worked long hours; I would come home late at night and go straight to bed, rising again before dawn. The project occupied my mind for a few months.

Meanwhile, Madar had taken a bad turn. Her memory was rapidly failing and it was becoming dangerous for her to live in her flat by herself. We insisted that she stay at our place, but she would leave and catch a taxi back to her apartment. No sooner did she arrive than she would be calling us, crying her eyes out, and we would go and fetch her back.

I came home one evening after a long day of taking photos and went to the kitchen to warm up my dinner. Maman and Baba were sitting in the lounge room drinking tea; they'd already eaten. Maman looked sadder than usual, but I didn't probe for a reason—I assumed she was just sad about me leaving.

When I finished my dinner, Maman told me that she was going to stay at Madar's flat for a while. The doctors had advised that it was best for Madar to be in her own place, that she would be comfortable there. It was clear Madar was deteriorating rapidly.

After that, Baba and I ate our meals at Madar's place most days.

One evening, we had just arrived home from Madar's when Maman rang and asked us to go back there. When we entered the flat, Madar was on the floor in the bathroom. She had fallen asleep there and Maman wasn't able to rouse her.

An ambulance was called but the paramedics told us not to worry, that Madar just needed some rest. We decided it was no longer feasible for Maman to look after Madar on her own, so we brought Madar back to our place once more.

While her physical health improved slightly, she was becoming increasingly confused and disorientated. As I was washing the dishes after dinner, I heard Madar say to Maman, 'Excuse me, madam, who is that man in your kitchen?'

I stood frozen with a plate in my hand. I turned to see Madar in the kitchen doorway, looking at me as though I were a stranger.

Maman didn't respond, but tears started streaming down her face.

'Is he a home help?' Madar asked.

'No, Madar, he isn't,' Baba replied. He didn't say anything else.

Maman brought the empty teacups to the kitchen and stood next to me. I wrapped my arm around her and she put her head on my shoulder.

That night we found Madar sleeping on the floor of the bathroom again. She had taken her pillow with her this time, and arranged it so her head was next to the toilet bowl. We could no longer bear to see her like this, and we didn't have the skills to care for her in the way she needed. The time had come for her to go to a nursing home.

☾

My uncle found a place in the northern suburbs, where the air quality was better; the facility was clean and reputable.

We took Madar to her flat to pack her things. She was very calm and quiet—it was quite eerie. As we left the building, she turned around and glanced at her flat. 'Goodbye, home,' she said, and then she slowly shuffled to the car. There was no point telling her that she might return, as we all knew that it would have been a lie.

Madar and I sat in the back of my uncle's car, and Maman in the front. I held back my tears all the way to the nursing home. When we arrived at the facility, a woman in her fifties came out and greeted my uncle.

'Hello, Doctor,' my uncle said.

The woman embraced Madar and took her hand. She led us to a large room where an empty bed was awaiting Madar's arrival. Maman and my uncle went to the office to do the paperwork and two nurses helped Madar into the bed. They asked me to wait outside so that they could put comfortable clothes on her.

I sat in the corridor; a man was being wheeled out of the men's section. He had an oxygen tank attached to him, tubes hanging out his nose. His eyes were lifeless, his face ghostly.

By the time Maman and my uncle returned, the nurses had finished dressing Madar. She was sitting on her bed in a dressing-gown, and she looked so lonely. A wave of shame and anger washed over me; I hated that we weren't able to look after her ourselves. Instead we were surrendering her to bunch of strangers. What did they know about her? Who would she tell her tales to?

I could no longer bear to see her there. Leaving my mother and uncle behind, I returned to the city. Instead of going home, I went straight to Madar's flat and sat in the empty lounge room, remembering all the time I had spent there.

Signs of my grandmother were everywhere. An unfinished cup of tea was still sitting on the coffee table with an opened packet of biscuits, her favourites. She had a sweet tooth, like me.

I cleared the coffee table and washed the cup in the sink.

Next I went into the spare room; the air smelled like sleep and mothballs. I remembered the time I had lain on the bed with Sousan in that room.

I went to Madar's room. It smelled of her Coty perfume. Her Bakelite radio was sitting on her small chest of drawers; I turned it on and pulled her photo album out of the bookcase.

I lay on her bed and looked at the photographs: Madar as a young woman with her two sisters with 1930s hairdos; Madar with Baba Bozorg, a date in 1935 written on the back; a picture of Maman and my two uncles aged between two and five; several photos taken at the weddings of her nieces and nephews; Madar on a fishing boat on the Caspian Sea, laughing and holding on to her the seat. There were some more recent photos, too, taken during her trip to London to visit my uncle, her youngest. These would have been taken before the revolution, as Uncle had impressive sideburns and flared jeans.

I fell asleep on Madar's bed, holding her pillow. Her handkerchief was under it, and it smelled of her valerian. This made me laugh as I drifted off—I recalled the first time I'd encountered its potent smell and how she was annoyed with me for pulling faces.

I was woken up by the phone ringing. I sat on the bed and didn't know what to do. It rang and rang and eventually stopped.

It was dark outside; I turned on the bedside lamp and put the photo album back in the bookcase. The wardrobe was open, and on the bottom shelf there was a small green metal safe where Madar had always kept her money. I lifted the lid and saw the old yellow tin containing the necklace with the sun wheel pedant. My heart started beating hard. I took the tin out, and opened it. The small velvet pouch was still inside. I took the sun wheel out and held it in my hand. I felt as though it was burning my palm—the same burning sensation I'd felt when I held it at the age of eight.

I closed my palm and squeezed it. *It's just you and me now*, I thought as I kissed the pendant and put it back in its pouch. I tucked the pouch back in its tin, drew the curtains and left Madar's flat.

☾

Two months after Madar was taken to the nursing home, my visa was granted, and so I went to see her for the last time. She was wearing a white gown and was propped up in her bed. She rubbed her hands, examining them closely—she was in her own world. There were six other women in the large room, which overlooked a beautiful garden. Madar's bed was closest to the window—my uncle had seen to that. We all knew how much she hated to be cooped up.

I kissed her head. Her hair was soft and smelled of olive soap. She had lost a lot of weight—she was all bones.

'What time is it?' she asked.

'Nearly five,' I said.

'Oh, time for a cup of tea then,' she said.

I went to fetch a cup of tea for her. One of the workers chucked a teabag in a melamine cup and held it under the hot tap.

'Don't you have a teapot?' I asked. 'Madar likes her Earl Grey tea-leaves brewed in a teapot.'

'This is not a hotel,' the woman snapped.

My heart ached. Madar had never had her tea in anything other than her beautiful fine bone china, the set that her father had brought back from Baku. I took the disgusting tea to Madar. She wrapped her crooked fingers around the cup and took a sip.

'Madar, I'm leaving,' I said, the lump in my throat getting bigger.

'Oh, be careful,' she said. 'Make sure you don't get lost.'

'I promise,' I said. 'I promise.' I couldn't bear to say anything else.

When she'd finished her tea she dozed off. I sat there and watched her small face, so peaceful. Her bony chest rose and fell gently, like the sea on a calm day.

The day was drawing to a close. The pale orange glow from the sunset lit up Madar's face. I kissed her for the last time and left the nursing home.

☾

I was determined to bid farewell to all my most beloved places before my departure to Australia, so I decided to visit the villa by the Caspian Sea where we had spent so many happy holidays. Since the escalation of the war no one had been there, and Baba's cousin had abandoned it.

I borrowed the key from him and made the journey on my own. Maman didn't think it was a good idea—she was worried something bad might happen to me: a lunatic truck driver might run into the coach taking me to Chalus; I might get caught in a rip while swimming; I might be hit by a motorcyclist while walking the streets. 'I'll be fine, Maman,' I assured her.

I arrived at the villa to find the gates rusty and covered in sea salt—they creaked as I opened them. The local family who had kept an eye on all the villas in the area and guarded the gates had been dismissed; now rubbish was strewn everywhere and some villas were covered in graffiti, while many had broken windows and damaged doors. I walked up to our villa: overgrown grass concealed the driveway, and it had an air of neglect, but it seemed otherwise unscathed.

I opened the door and entered, and immediately breathed in the familiar smell of sea salt, damp, and old furniture.

I went straight upstairs, like I always had as a kid, heading for the terrace. The door was jammed, but I forced it open and went outside. A gentle sea breeze embraced me; the sea was very calm. The water level had risen so that the beach was much closer, only a couple of hundred metres away from the villa. We used to have to walk at least four hundred metres to reach the water. We had heard about the rising water level for over a decade, but I hadn't imagined the extent of it. Maman blamed the Russians: 'It's all their dredging and God knows what else.' The villa vanished under water a few years after I left; it couldn't have been the fault of the Russians, but Maman knew nothing about climate change.

I went to the bedroom and opened the windows, and looked around the room. I could almost see Maman's colourful clothes, sheets and towels lying around.

I stripped the bed. The sheets were filthy. I blamed the previous visitors for not cleaning up after themselves, unlike Maman who always left the place sparkling clean.

It was late in the afternoon and I was hungry, so I ate a hardboiled egg Maman had packed for me and went back to the terrace. The recliner chairs were still there, and I unfolded a pair. I sank into one of them and closed my eyes. I could hear Madar's soft footsteps approaching. I opened my eyes and the empty recliner chair next to me greeted me in silence.

I leaned back and drifted away, recalling all the summer holidays we'd spent here. I could hear Aunty Tangerine's cheery laughter, see Baba's big grin as he tucked in to the local food. I remembered browsing the Saturday markets for the best watermelons; Satyar hanging out with the local boys at the beach and getting into trouble with Maman for smoking or for staying out in the sun all day. Memories of Maman cutting up watermelon and putting it in the fridge first thing in the morning so that it was nice and cold.

I smiled thinking of how it took her forever to get ready to go for a swim: first she had to put on sunscreen, lots of it, then she would wrap a towel around her waist and pull on a shirt over her bathers, as she thought it would be immodest to show flesh, especially in the regional areas. Then we would walk together to the beach. I would run straight into the sea, but Maman would enter the water very slowly, still covered in her towel and shirt. She would only take them off once she was waist deep in the water. Satyar would take her towel and shirt back to the beach, and fetch them for her when she was ready to return to the sand.

We often stayed in the water till sunset; I never wanted to come out. We would return to the villa exhausted. We had to wash all the sand off in the outdoor shower (except for Maman, who would have a 'proper' wash in the bathroom inside), then we would gather in the living room and eat watermelon. I can still taste the sweetness of its juice mixed with the sea salt on my lips. How I wished that I had taken more photos back then and preserved all those moments.

Listening to the waves, I fell asleep on the recliner chair, and when I woke up the sun was going down. I decided to go for a walk along the foreshore.

As I walked along the sand, I noticed a long canvas partition had been erected, splitting the beach in half and running out into the water. When I drew closer I spotted a sign. *Brothers* was written above an arrow pointing to the left side of the partition, and *Sisters* above the arrow pointing to the right. The regime had divided the beach so that women and men didn't mix. There were further warnings on the Sisters side:

All sisters must observe the Islamic rules and adhere to utmost modesty. They must be fully clothed, covered from head to toe. No hair or skin may be on display, for evil.

The sign stopped short of saying that should anyone fail to obey the rules they would be severely punished under Sharia law, but it was implied.

I walked past the partition; there was no one in the water on either side.

A few hundred metres further along the beach, I saw the ruins of the old lighthouse, which had been swamped by the rising sea.

The lighthouse had been the marker for our walks. It was about three kilometres from the villa. If we were tired, we knew not to go as far as the lighthouse. When we were full of energy, we would go way past it, almost as far as the next township.

I went up close to the lighthouse; only its skeleton remained. 'Do you remember me?' I whispered.

The images of the past will never rust away, it seemed to say, as it buried its head deeper in the sand like an ancient sea creature.

I bid goodnight to the lighthouse and decided to head to the small restaurant where we used to go to for meals. When I approached the hut, a young man greeted me and showed me to a table. I looked around for the two brothers who ran the place, but I couldn't see them anywhere.

The young man brought a plate of hot lavash bread, feta and herbs, and a bottle of water.

'Where are the owners?' I asked him.

'My baba has gone to town to get a few things,' he said politely. As soon as he referred to his father, I recognised him: he was a young child when we used to go there; he was in his late teens now.

'And your uncle?' I asked.

'He passed away,' he said as gave the table another wipe.

'My condolences. We always came here when I was young: my baba would not go anywhere else.'

'*Tashakor*,' he said, thanking me, and then left me to eat. I was starving by then; the smell of hot bread with fresh herbs was tantalising.

I had just scooped up the last bit of feta when the young man's father arrived. He ordered his son to unpack the car and glanced in my direction. I rose to my feet to greet him. He squinted at me then placed his hand on his chest. 'Welcome, welcome! I can't believe it! You are all grown up!' he said. 'Where is your family?'

'I've come on my own. They are back in Tehran.'

I pulled up a chair for him and he sat on the edge as a sign of respect. His hair had gone grey on the sides, and his eyes didn't have the same spark anymore.

'Your son told me about your dear brother—so young to be taken away,' I said. 'Was it an illness?'

'Ahhh,' he sighed, and dropped his head.

'What happened?'

'My beloved brother was executed. The Revolutionary Guards came for him in the middle of the night. He had been following the pro-monarchists and a local bastard gave him away. He was hanged in the town centre, just up the road, where everyone could see. No trial, no nothing. Every time I drive past the town centre, I see his body dangling from the crane. Nothing will ever erase that image.'

I felt I was going to throw up. I put my hand on his shoulder, but no words came out. No words could possibly be adequate.

256

'It's been six years now, but it's like it happened yesterday,' he said hoarsely.

His son brought tea for us and we drank and talked for a long time. He told me how he had continued running the business to make his brother proud. I told him that I would soon be leaving Iran.

We both were so immersed in our chat that we lost track of time. It was nearly ten o'clock when he suddenly realised that I hadn't ordered a meal yet. Despite the late hour, he insisted on cooking for me himself. Going over to the barbecue, he rolled up his sleeves and fanned the coals. He summoned his son to bring some skewers and he arranged them on the grill. I watched his face soften behind the smoke rising from the blistering tomatoes; the smell of onions and chicken marinated in lemon and saffron filled the air.

I pulled my camera out of my pack and began to take photos. His hairy arms turning the skewers over burning coals; the lines on his forehead; his dark eyes under bushy eyebrows; his large, scarred hands fanning the sizzling chicken; tomatoes bursting out of their skin, dripping red tears into the fire; the young man watching from the kitchen window in the background.

When he was nearly done, he called out to his son and said something in the local dialect. The young man brought over a large enamel tray and placed it on the table. There was a bowl of labneh mixed with dried shallots, more bread and feta and herbs, a plate of smoked rice, and a jug of doogh. He put a single plate on the table and one set of cutlery.

'I'm not going to eat alone—please share this meal with me,' I said to the older man. I almost had to beg until he finally agreed and sat down.

We said very little as we ate. When we were finished, his son served us more tea and cleared the table. The man lit a cigarette and offered me one. The moon was slowly rising, lighting up the sea. The waves slapped the sand every now and then, making a loud splashing sound.

'The water is much closer than I recall,' I said.

'Yes, not long before this hut will go under.' He blew smoke into the air.

'They say it's the Russians causing it.'

'I wouldn't put it past them—they have been interfering with these waters for over a century now.'

'What will you do if the water rises further?'

'Ah, it may be for the best. The memories will be buried in the sand forever.' He sighed.

We sat side by side in silence and smoked.

It was past midnight when I left the hut. The man embraced me and refused to accept any money for the meal.

When I was back at the villa I realised that there was no power. I searched for matches, but they were all damp. I rummaged in the cupboards but couldn't find so much as a cigarette lighter to light the small lantern. The moon had risen—it was a bright white ball lighting the villa. I grabbed a can of Pepsi and went up to the terrace.

I had just lowered myself into the recliner when I heard familiar footsteps. I turned to see Gretel standing behind me, gazing out to sea. Her expression was unreadable.

'Here we are again,' she said.

'You have been gone for years,' I said.

'Maybe it was for the best.'

'How can you be so cold?! I have been waiting, searching! You have captivated me ever since I was a little boy. I have thought of little else but you for years. But each time I try to hold on to you, you vanish into thin air. Why?'

'There is only so much I can tell you. The rest is up to you to solve.'

'But how?!'

'I'll tell you all I know. After tonight, you need to set things right.'

'What things?'

'Remember how your grandmother always said that you need to be patient, and the answers would come?'

She pulled over the other recliner and sat. She looked breathtakingly beautiful. I leaned over and touched her face; she looked down.

I moved closer, until my lips were almost touching hers. My heart was pumping. She pulled away.

It was a warm afternoon in the middle of October; I was packing my suitcase for my flight to Sydney the next day. I was sitting on the red floral handmade carpet in my bedroom with all my stuff scattered around the room. I was overwhelmed with the task and I kept unpacking things that I thought I wouldn't need to take. Then as soon as I took them out, I felt that I had to put them back in again.

I started putting all my books, clothes, cassettes and photo albums in the suitcase. Soon the suitcase started overflowing and there was hardly any room left for all the spices and herbs Maman wanted me to take.

'Maman! I am not going to a stranded island! They will have shops!' I said to her as she kept piling things in the bedroom. 'You would not find these over there! I know!' she'd respond.

Leaving is not as simple as moving out of a house you grew up in, it's not packing your bags and boxes to go and live a few suburbs away or another town. It's not taking a gap year to go and travel the world and coming back all grown up and worldly.

It's pulling out all your roots from the soil that has nurtured you for as long as you have lived, and hacking away at it till nothing holds you down. You are so consumed with the mission of severing your ties that you don't even take notice of what you are leaving behind, the shattered pieces of the past, the unwrapped hopes for the future

It's migrating to an unknown destination so so far away, dreaming, thinking, hoping that your wounded roots will heal and grow once more on foreign soil.

It's about knowing that there is no coming back, not in a year, not in a few years, not ever in fact.

So then, what do you pack? What do you leave behind? How much is too much? Is everything going to be enough at all?

I looked at the mess around me and lay on the floor, staring at the ceiling.

I spotted the outline of the glow stars on the ceiling of my bedroom.

Madar had bought them for me. Whenever she slept in my room, we would talk about them at nights until the glow faded or till I fell asleep. When I was old enough not to look at the glow stars on my ceiling, we painted over them. This is how we conceal the past, with memories trapped underneath.

I was half-asleep when Maman came to the room and put a light blanket over me.

'It's warm Maman!' I protested.

'Don't be fooled by the warm autumn days, it's always cool at nightfall. You don't wanna get sick just before your flight.'

'Yeah right,' I moaned as I rolled to my side.

'I can't believe you are leaving the nest,' she said.

'Maman! Please! Don't make it more difficult!'

She started rearranging my suitcase and noticed Madar's yellow tin with the sun wheel necklace in it. Silence grew between us.

'Oh Maman! I am sorry I took this from Madar's house, I should have told you,' I said eventually.

'It's okay, my love. Madar would have wanted you to have it. The sun wheel will keep you safe. But promise me that you will take time to find yourself,' she said.

I looked at her puzzled.

'I know you have been searching for Gretel, I really hope that you will not spend the rest of your years chasing this impossible dream.'

'I know you have been searching for Gretel, I really hope that you will not spend the rest of your years chasing this impossible dream.'

'Gretel? Maman? But how do you know?' I could hear my heart thrumming inside my ears.

'Oh, my love, mothers know everything. I carried your heart for nine months, you don't need to tell me anything, your heart beats within mine, you are a piece of me.'

She then took a note out of her pocket and started reading a short poem that she had written that night.

My sweet dove
Full of life, elated and ambitious
As you fly away from this nest
On the wild wings of love and hope
Will you hear these silent tears, the untold stories?
Will you remember this lonely nest one day?

When she finished, she folded the piece of paper and placed it in the palm of my hand.

'I wrote this for you,' she said softly.

A big droplet of tear fell on my hand, I didn't know if it was hers or mine. We held each other and cried in silence.

VISBY

DECEMBER 1361

A FEW MONTHS HAD passed since the Danes occupied Visby. It happened so fast, within hours they had claimed and looted the city. Within days they had taken control as though nothing had happened. Many lives were lost and Visby came under the rule of King Valdemar of Denmark.

I had not seen or heard of Valentin since the invasion and every day I pleaded with Father to find out what had happened to him, but he would refuse to discuss Valentin with me.

One afternoon I was in the kitchen with Valka when I heard my father's servant report to him in the dining room. He was giving updates about Valentin. As soon as I heard Valentin's name I leaped towards the dining room.

'Please don't, dear Gretel,' Valka said. 'You will only make things worse for both of you.'

I knew she was right, so instead of confronting my father I stood near the doorway to listen.

The servant was saying that the jailers had gone to the cabin where Valentin was kept imprisoned for months, and they kicked him in the back to wake him up. When he opened his eyes, he started asking where he was and why they had brought him there, until one of the men silenced him with a blow. They chained his wrists and ankles, dragged him out of the hut, and threw him into the back of a cart in order to transport him to the city's main jail. When he asked what crime he had committed, they told him he had been accused of abducting and raping a noble girl. Me.

I felt as if a sword had been plunged into my stomach. It was all my fault—I was the one who'd asked him to go to the cabin that night. I had wanted to give myself to him.

I started crying. I wanted to run into the dining room and scream the truth at my father, but Valka held me tight and didn't let go. I rested my face on her shoulder and sobbed. I knew what punishment awaited my beloved Valentin: he would be hanged in Stora Torget.

Another month went by and my father had frequent visits from various stallholders and merchants who all gladly received bribes from him to invent stories about Valentin and his father. They were accused of being dishonest in the market and of stealing goods, allegations which Father then used to make things worse for Valentin.

I was still locked up in the house. My father had ordered his men to watch all the doors and windows, and I was confined to the kitchen or my own room. Valka made me promise not to do anything silly.

Father was drinking a lot more and wasn't planning on resuming trade. As a merchant, he was in a good position to negotiate with the Danes, but instead he gambled and brought prostitutes home. I had to block my ears against the sound of women giggling and my father groaning in the same bed my beloved mother had shared with him.

As time passed, his fortune began to decline, and soon debtors started knocking on our door. Another frequent visitor was Valentin's uncle, who was also a merchant. He was turned away each time, but he persisted, until finally my father agreed to see him.

Valentin's uncle offered my father a deal: he would free him from debt in exchange for Valentin's release. Father's cooperation was needed for the court to pardon him.

I heard my father roar like a wild bear, but after several minutes his bellowing ceased.

A short while later, Valka came to tell me that my father had accepted the offer. I could barely contain my joy, and Valka and I held each other and wept with relief. I pleaded with Valka to help me escape so that I could see Valentin, but she refused, saying that it wasn't safe. Instead, she promised me to bring news from the outside.

Days later, Valka returned to my room. She had encountered a servant from Valentin's uncle's house at the market. On his release from prison, Valentin's uncle had taken his nephew to his house— but the young man was in a terrible condition, the servant said, unable to walk and suffering a severe stomach wound.

Tears streamed down my face as I heard this. What I would have given to tend his wounds myself!

I asked Valka if Valentin had asked about me, and she said that the servant told her he had: my name was the first word to cross his lips when he was carried from the cell. His uncle reassured him that I was safe and alive. The servant had also said Valentin's uncle had arranged for Stjärna to be moved to his house.

I was glad that Stjärna was there with him—she would comfort him and he would do the same for her.

When Valka left my room that day, I had no idea that I would never see her again. But barely any time passed before my father summoned me to outline his plans. 'We will be leaving this hellhole tonight,' he declared.

'But, Father,' I began.

'Not a word or I'll cut your throat!' he screamed. 'We are going to Germany, and that is final! You will do as you are told. Your future husband is awaiting your arrival. You will be delivered to him as soon as we disembark and from that day forth I never want to lay eyes on you again. You have brought disgrace and shame to my name, and I am lucky that someone of his status has agreed to take you as his wife, knowing that you are not a virgin!'

I kneeled at his feet and begged him to change his mind, but he ordered me from the room.

At nightfall he ordered his men to bring the carriage around. As he forced me into it, I wished I had taken a knife from the kitchen and ended my life, but it was too late.

As the carriage bounced and swayed over the cobblestones, I felt nauseous. I closed my eyes and listened to the clatter of the horses' hooves. As they slowed near Lilla Strandporten, our beloved old gate, I heard a voice. I was certain that it was Valentin's—he was calling me! I pressed my face to the window and caught a fleeting glimpse of him. Then the driver whipped the horses hard and they sped up, heading for the harbour. We left Visby that night.

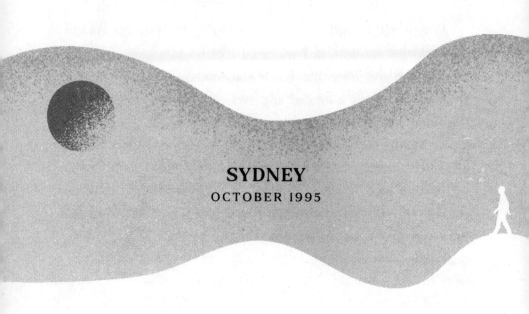

SYDNEY

OCTOBER 1995

When I entered the arrival hall at Sydney Airport, the humidity hit me in the face—it reminded me of arriving at the Caspian Sea.

Uncle Behrooz had found a connection, and so a friend of a friend of his was waiting to collect me. At the back of the crowd of people waiting for their loved ones, I saw a tall man holding up a piece of card with my name on it. I waved to him and hurried over. We shook hands and he led me to his car, a station wagon.

He was not very talkative, which suited me, as I was so jet-lagged I could barely keep my eyes open. About an hour into the trip he pulled over to have a cigarette and invited me to get out too. We were at a lookout which I later learned was called Stanwell Tops. The view was breathtaking: the wide blue ocean stretched across the horizon.

The driver stepped away from me and made a phone call. I heard him say 'lots of luggage' to the person he was talking to. I figured he was talking about me, but I didn't think two suitcases and a portfolio bag was too much for someone who was immigrating from more than twelve thousand kilometres away.

When the man finished his cigarette, we got back in the car and drove down the escarpment to Wollongong. Uncle Behrooz's connection had arranged for me to stay for a short time with an Australian family in Unanderra, a suburb of Wollongong, until I got my bearings.

We pulled up at a house on a hill; Unanderra had many hills and this was one of the steepest. A blonde woman in her mid-fifties greeted me; her name was Jenny, and she was very warm and friendly. She showed me to a room in the lower part of the house, separate from where she and her family lived.

She said that she had come home during her lunch break to greet me, and that she had to go back to work. 'Make yourself a cuppa,' she said, 'and I'll be home this arvo, around four-ish.'

I took a shower and went to the kitchen to look for the 'cuppa'. I searched in the pantry and every cupboard but to no avail. *Maybe she has run out and hasn't realised*, I thought, and went back to my room.

Between three and four in the afternoon I could hear people arriving upstairs. Before long there were many voices; it sounded like a huge gathering, I could hear footsteps and the clatter of dishes in the kitchen.

After a while, Jenny came down to see me. 'How are you settling in?' she asked.

'Well, thank you,' I said.

'You haven't had anything?'

'No, I couldn't find the cuppa you mentioned.'

She laughed. 'Oh, that! I just meant you should help yourself to a cup of tea or coffee.'

So a 'cuppa' was a 'cup of'. I realised the English I had learned in Tehran was not going to help me to decode the local lingo in Australia.

☾

Despite my exhaustion, that night I couldn't sleep. I had a shower and went to bed then stared for hours at the shadows outside my bedroom window. At just after six in the morning, I heard the family getting ready for work: the sound of water running, voices in the kitchen, footsteps, followed by car engines—one, two, three, four, five of them, until finally the house was silent.

When I was sure I was alone, I emerged from my room and went to make myself some coffee and toast. Everything felt strange, though I couldn't put my finger on one thing in particular. Forty-eight hours ago I was in my own home, having breakfast with Maman and Baba. Now I was in someone else's house, a stranger in a foreign country. I looked out the window. A bird was sitting in a tree, laughing. Was it enjoying itself or was it mocking me?

☾

A few days after my arrival, Jenny took me to the University of Wollongong—she worked there, and I'd been accepted as a student to study Visual Arts. The campus was enormous, so big that there was a shuttle bus to take students from the southern entrance of the campus to the northern part.

Seeing students walking around freely, or lazing on the lush green grass, I recalled my days at the University of Arts in Tehran: the watchful gazes of the morality guards, the censored textbooks, the segregation of male and female students, and the controlling of thoughts and minds by the oppressive regime. Suddenly, that world—my world—seemed so far away and almost surreal, as though it had never existed.

☾

When I wasn't at uni I would walk around town, exploring my surrounds. My favourite spot was the Crown Street Mall—I would load up my camera with a new film and take street shots, or sit on a bench and just watch people walking past. In the centre of the mall was a spot where a lot of young people congregated, just outside the Sanity music store. It was bizarre to hear music blasting out and see people buying any music they liked. After years of buying illegal copies of western music in dark side streets and listening to it behind closed doors, it felt almost overwhelming to walk into Sanity and browse all the CDs.

I would often go to Wollongong City Beach to watch the sunset. The sand was soft and white, much paler than the sand on the shore of the Caspian Sea. I would walk all the way up to the lighthouse perched on top of a green hill overlooking the ocean. The lighthouse became my confidant and best friend. My only friend. I used to sit at its foot and share my stories and thoughts with it. Later on, I'd go there at night, especially when there was a full moon, and spend hours watching the light glittering on the ocean, and listening to the waves roaring.

Eventually I moved into a studio apartment at the base of Mount Keira. My small window looked out onto the majestic mountain. I would wake up to the sound of kookaburras—the laughing bird I had seen on my first morning—and watch the mist rise from the mountain throughout the day. At dusk I would listen to the lonely, sad tune of currawongs as the sun sank behind the peak.

Maman and Baba called me every Sunday evening around 6 pm. It was a gloomy, overcast Sunday evening when they rang to give me the news of Madar's passing. First Baba spoke to me, and then he gave the phone to Maman.

'Maman? What happened?!' I asked.

'We visited Madar at the nursing home yesterday,' she said. 'She was sitting on her chair near the window, looking at the garden. When she saw us, she asked why you hadn't come to visit her lately. Her Alzheimer's had advanced, was getting worse and worse, and she forgot almost everyone, but she always remembered you. As we were leaving, she grabbed my hand and said: *Tishtar is a very special boy, never forget that.* She loved you more than any of her other grandchildren.' Maman sighed. 'Shortly after we left the nursing home, she passed away. But her spirit will always watch over you.'

The grief of losing Madar was like being run over by a truck. I didn't know what to say or to do. I felt so lonely. Madar was my rock, and now she was gone. Who would I tell now if I found Gretel? Who would I share my stories with, if not Madar?

After we hung up, I sat by the window, and listened to the currawongs. I watched the darkening sky until there was no light left. I didn't turn on the lamps, didn't want to face the reality of what had happened. I don't know how long I sat there, or at what point I went to bed, but I woke the next morning with a thumping headache.

That night I visited the lighthouse. It stood tall and assured, as ever; I needed its strength. It was a windy night and I sought shelter close to the bushes at its base. I was missing Madar; her passing had brought raw emotions to the surface. My soul was churned up like the ocean. Overcome with grief, I started sobbing.

Below, the ocean roared. My gaze followed the path the lighthouse lit as it cast its glow over the water. I heard Madar's voice in my head. *Follow your heart and the answers will be revealed.* I called to her, but the sound of the ocean drowned out my voice.

'Let her go,' said Gretel softly, her breath warm on my neck. 'Let her rest in peace.' She wrapped her arms around my waist, and I drew her close. We spoke, in silence, about a life long gone, and a life yet to come.

She squeezed my hand and stood, and I followed her back to my flat. I listened to our footsteps as we walked: slow, steady, in sync. When we entered my flat, I sat on the edge of my bed and watched Gretel light a candle.

'I have never stopped wanting you,' I said.

'Hush now, you are tired.' Her golden hair, tied back in a single plait that rested on her shoulder, shimmered in the candlelight.

'I have looked for you in every corner,' I said, my voice trembling. 'Searched every face. Every shadow I saw I thought was yours. Every head of golden hair I saw I was sure was yours. With every photo I took, I hoped to find you. If only I could tell Madar that you are here.'

'She knows,' Gretel said, as she traced my lips with her fingers.

Her hand was warm, her breathing heavy. I could hear her heartbeat. I drew her close and she clung to me like ivy. My whole being seeped through her, and I poured my heart and soul into her until I became invisible.

'Your touch hasn't changed,' Gretel whispered in my ear, as she drifted away like an autumn leaf on a windy day.

☾

Two years after arriving in Australia, I had my conversation with the Dean of the arts faculty and changed my course of study. The Faculty of Law was situated in the northern section of the campus, at the foot of Mount Keira. It wasn't until I started my law degree that I learned about the Aboriginal significance of the site. An elder welcomed us to country on our first day and gave us each a gum leaf. She told us the story of Mount Keira—which she referred to as Geera—and the five islands that scattered in the ocean nearby. She told us that the five islands, together with Geera, were daughters of Oola Boola Woo, the west wind. Aunty explained that the west wind and his family lived on top of the

Illawarra escarpment, and she described how the five sisters of Geera were turned into stones and thrown into the sea, forming the five islands, while Geera looked on for years and years until she turned into stone and formed the mountain that can be seen today.

I was immersed in the tale, and Aunty's calm and reassuring voice reminded me of Madar. I had to blink back my tears as she spoke. I wished she could stay all day, sharing the stories of the land—her land. I wish I could remember her name; I wish I had written it down.

☾

I started working different jobs during the day to cover my expenses. I did all sorts of things, from door to door sales to pizza delivery, and took night classes. Sometimes after the lectures I would go and sit beneath the lighthouse, listening to the waves. Hearing Aunty talk about the waters surrounding Wollongong had changed how the ocean sounded to me. I could now hear the waves speak millions of words. It was as though she had unlocked a door between me and the water. Aunty had told us that the water carries memories, and I could feel that in the way the waves danced and swirled all the way to the horizon. Night after night, I heard the waves sharing stories with each other and with the sand. Sometimes I would even hear the wind catching a story and taking it to the top of Mount Keira—messages from her sisters, those five islands that sat gracefully in the ocean.

Sitting there, I would talk to Madar, especially about Gretel and my longing for her. It had been nearly two years since her last visit; I searched for her in my dreams, and would light a candle and look for her in the shadows dancing on the wall, but to no avail. I was alone. Sometimes I would hear the lighthouse emit a deep sigh, flashing its light over the water. I wondered if this was its way of telling me to journey across the ocean to find answers.

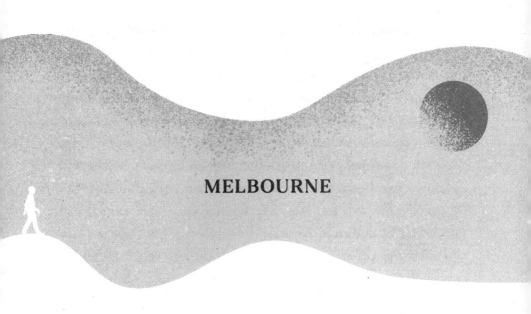

MELBOURNE

THE MORNING FLEW BY, and I've spent most of the afternoon staring out the window, watching the storm clouds wrestling in the sky.

'You still here?' Habiba says from the doorway, making me jump.

'Yes. I can't seem to concentrate,' I say.

'Go home,' she says, and she walks over to the desk and shuts the lid of my laptop. 'There is no point sitting here when your mind is elsewhere.'

'Tell me, Habiba: where is home?'

'You are being too philosophical now! Ya Allah, Ya Allah, Tishtar! Here, take your jacket! You are tired and don't know what you are talking about.' She orders me out of the office.

As I follow her down the stairs, she says: 'Not long before Fowziah and Fatimah come! You must meet them!'

'I can't wait,' I say, and then walk to the train station.

☾

The rain splashes into the train carriage every time the doors open, creating a puddle of water on the floor. The smell of wet garments mixed with body odours fills the air. Raindrops roll down the train windows. Sometimes the drops join one another and run down in a hurry, like children having fun on a slide; you can almost hear the little droplets' cheerful laughter. Other drops travel solo, either by choice or because the wind changes their route.

I'm drifting off when the train stops at the next station. A crowd of people enter, some hurrying to secure a seat while others shuffle around near the door. Water drips from their umbrellas and jackets, making the puddle near the door bigger.

Today there is no sign of Gretel on the train. Maman's voice echoes in my head: *Stop dreaming—life doesn't work like that.*

Months have melted away like snow in early spring. Almost every day Gretel and I catch the same train, though she never appears to notice me, rendering me invisible.

I take my phone out of my pocket and flick through my playlist, picking a song to match my mood as I gaze at the dark and unforgiving sky outside. As we pull into the next station, there is an announcement: '*Attention, passengers: this train will terminate here due to a boom gate malfunction ahead. Please check in with staff for updates.*'

People exchange looks of disbelief. Some immediately get on their phones to make alternative travel arrangements; others huff in frustration. I file off the train with the others, and lean against a lamppost as gradually the crowd disperses. Soon the platform is deserted. My mind is blank; I am incapable of forming a plan to get home.

Out of the corner of my eye I see someone approaching. I look up: it is her. She is walking straight towards me, and she is smiling. Her lips are moving, but I can't hear a thing.

'So, we meet again,' she says calmly as she draws near. She sits on a bench nearby.

I walk over and join her.

'Gretel, you've been riding on this train for months now,' I say. 'I've tried and tried to catch your attention, but you keep slipping away.'

She smiles, and shrugs.

'Why now?' I say. 'Why here? It's been years since that night we spent together.'

'And you still haven't fulfilled your task,' she says.

I frown. 'What do you mean?'

'I've got no more to say to you.' She smirks.

'Is this all a joke to you? Am I just a game you have been playing for decades? You come and go as you please, playing with my heart as though it means nothing!'

'Things are not that simple. This isn't just about you and me. One day you will understand.'

The whole world starts to spin; I can't breathe. A train is approaching the platform. When it comes to a halt, Gretel starts walking towards it.

I sit, watching her leave, helpless to stop her.

Before she boards the train, she turns to look at me.

'Please stay!' I beg. I search her face for a hint of explanation or emotion, but I can't read her expression.

She turns and steps into the carriage.

My heart slows down; I can barely feel it beating.

I hear heavy footsteps approaching. I look to my left and see a young man running towards the departing train. He is calling out, but his voice is drowned by the sound of the engine. I sense his despair. I look for the conductor; perhaps the young man needs assistance. Then the whistle sounds and the train pulls away. Soon there is nothing left of it but a light flickering far away. Then it is swallowed by the darkness.

I look at the young man. *Who are you?* I wonder. *Why are you running after the train? Do you know her?*

I examine him closely: he is a teenager, I realise, about sixteen or seventeen, of medium height, with quite a solid build; his auburn hair is thick and curly, and he is wearing a woollen tunic and dark britches. He is soaking wet and he holds his cap in his hands, pressing it to his chest.

He stares after the train, unsure. Finally he turns and walks away. As the darkness envelops him I feel a tightness in my chest. I get to my feet and walk up and down the platform looking for him. He is not there.

'What just happened?' I ask myself aloud. I no longer know if I am asleep or awake. I can't feel my legs; my jaw is trembling. I reach for my phone in my pocket, thinking I will call my parents, to make sure I wasn't dreaming, but when I dial their number there is no answer. I dial again, but the call rings out. I feel I have lost contact with reality—if I even know what reality is.

I return to the bench where Gretel and I had sat earlier. I look at the spot where she'd been while we talked. Had we really talked? Was she really here? Nothing makes sense.

I dial my parents' number for a third time. It rings and rings, and then I hear Maman's voice. I collect myself: I want to tell her everything, and to find out whether I am awake or asleep. Instead I hear her say: '*Please leave a message.*'

I am on my own.

As I board the next train to Geelong, I take one more look at the bench where we were sitting; it looks vacant and lonely. I scan the platform again for the young man; he is not there.

☾

Hours after I left the office, I finally arrive home. I light a few candles and collapse on the sofa. My head is full—I can't get the events of the day out of my mind. It was all very strange: familiar and foreign at the same time.

I am staring at my bookshelf; my gaze drifts over the spines of the books and then I stop as I see the yellow tin containing the sun wheel necklace. I go to the shelf and pick it up, remembering the first time I saw it in Madar's spare room. I open the lid, take the sun wheel out of its black velvet pouch and hold it tight in my palm. My heart is racing.

I ring my parents again, and Maman answers this time.

'Maman? Gretel talked to me tonight!' I say without preamble.

'What do you mean?' she asks. 'Gretel?! How can this be? What is this?'

I know I am not making any sense, but I keep going. 'Maman, we talked tonight, at the train station!'

'Well, she chose you all those years ago for a reason, and shared with you all she knew,' Maman says. 'You need to embrace it, to walk the path until you find the answers.'

'What is it that I am supposed to do?'

'That's for you to discover,' Maman says. 'Remember what Madar used to say? Follow your heart and the answers will be revealed.'

☾

It has been weeks since my last conversation with Gretel. I have boarded the train each day thinking about her and left the train with a heavy soul. I have been curious, anxious, sad, and elated all at once. Every day I have rushed to the train station hoping to see her, but she never comes.

I lie awake at night, thinking, my thoughts getting louder and louder. *You must go there. You must go to Visby*, I tell myself. *Follow your heart and the answers will be revealed*, Madar's voice says.

And so I make my decision. I will leave the office early and go to the travel agent at Sunshine Plaza. I am packing up my computer when I hear footsteps coming up the stairs. I hear whispers and then Habiba's voice saying, 'Yallah, yallah.' Her friendly face appears in my doorway, beaming with happiness. She is wearing a red scarf with bright colours.

'Tishtar!' she says. 'You have visitors!'

She steps aside, and two tall slender young women appear, smiling shyly.

I look at Habiba in disbelief. 'They are here!'

'Yes!' Habiba sings as she pushes them forward. 'Alhamdulillah!'

I am lost for words. I sit down again, and the girls each take a seat.

I stare at them in astonishment. It is hard to believe that they are actually here right in front of me in my office, no longer just names on forms and emails. Even though I cannot help but think how many more like them are still struggling to survive back in Somalia, or in refugee camps in Kenya, I am happy for them.

I ask them about their journey, but they are too shy to speak. Fowziah looks at Habiba and whispers something.

'She is saying she is excited to meet the good lawyer! Like in the movies they saw on TV in Kenya!' Habiba explains.

'You know, I think we are very lucky that the case officer opened her heart and heard your story. It was the plight of your circumstances that won the case, not my legal skills. The law school did not prepare me for cases like this,' I respond.

Habiba tells the girls to go downstairs, then drops into a seat by my desk. 'So, what's new with you, Tishtar?'

'I have decided to go to Sweden,' I say.

'What?! You can't leave! I have more clients for you!'

'I'm not leaving forever, sister. Just going for a visit.'

'But it will be in the middle of winter there!'

'I know, I know, but I have to go. It is very important that I go at this time. Oh, sister, this is a long story. Maybe one day I will tell you. Maybe I will even write about it!'

'I knew that you had been burdened by something. You are always lost in your thoughts. But promise you won't get any ideas about staying in Sweden!' She gives me a shrewd look. 'Is there a lady there waiting for you?'

'Oh, Habiba, I don't know. Like I said, it's a long story.'

'Ah, you men! Can't make decisions. My brother is the same. Don't waste time!' She gets to her feet and leaves my office, and I hurry to the travel agent and book a flight to Stockholm. I am on a quest to find the missing pieces of the puzzle.

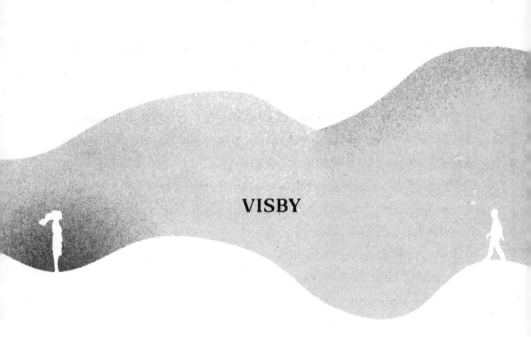

VISBY

I HAVE A FOUR-HOUR wait at Stockholm Airport, and it feels
like I am there for four thousand hours. Eventually I board a
small aircraft that carries my restless soul through the dark winter
sky to Visby.

I disembark and walk into the small airport. The arrival
hall is the smallest I have ever seen, only slightly bigger than
a lounge room. I feel like Gulliver on Lilliput Island. The hall
has worn-out timber panelling with lines of old writing faintly
visible in parts. I sense the ancient pieces of timber elbowing one
another, wondering who I am and what I am doing there. Under
their watchful gaze I collect my suitcase and step outside.

It is nearly eleven in the evening and the temperature is one
degree. I breathe in the air—it is so cold it burns my nostrils and

cuts through my lungs like a sharp knife. It smells familiar. I feel the mist on my face, and look up at the sky. All I can see is black velvet. A starless night.

Then I hear a 'Hej!' followed by a string of unfamiliar words. It is a taxi driver, standing with her hands on her hips, awaiting my response. She is tall and athletic-looking, with long blonde hair tied back, a strong face and piercing eyes. She is wearing a green woollen jumper, black jeans and black leather boots.

She must realise from the dazed expression on my face that I don't understand the local language, because she switches to English. 'Going to your hotel?' she asks with a smile.

'Yes! Thank you.'

'Okay!' she says. She heaves my suitcase into the boot as if it weighs nothing, while I slide into the front passenger seat.

She takes off like a gangster.

'Is the hotel far?' I ask.

'Nothing is ever far in Visby!' she says with a chuckle. 'Where have you come from?'

She nearly runs the car off the road when I say Australia.

'You are joking,' she says.

When I have managed to convince her that I am not playing any games, she says that I am mad to come to Visby in the middle of winter. 'Let me guess: you wanted a white Christmas!' she says. 'Strange man! Why would you leave the beach to come here? Then again, I must admit I don't like your snakes and spiders. I would much rather freeze here all year round than encounter those.'

She is driving so fast I can barely catch my breath, and when she suddenly slams on the brakes outside my hotel I jerk forward, my head nearly hitting the dashboard. She laughs. 'You have come a long way; you must be very tired. You will sleep well tonight!'

As I pay her, she hands me her card. 'Here. Call me if you want me to drive you around the island.' She gets in her car and drives off, tyres squealing.

I open the front door of the hotel with the security code provided for late arrivals. A warm welcome note inside the medieval entrance greets me, and gives me the instructions for breakfast and room service. Enclosed is the key for room 101, on the first floor.

I carry my suitcase up one flight of stairs, and open the door to a warm, cosy room almost entirely taken up by a queen-size bed. I cross the room and pull back the curtains to see that I have a view of Visby Harbour below. I open the window; the cold freezing air seeps into my lungs. *What am I doing just sitting here?* I ask myself.

Despite the late hour, I put on a puffer jacket and leave the hotel. I start walking; I can hear waves. I follow the sound down the hill towards the harbour.

Boats of varying sizes are bobbing in the small swell, their lights flickering in the dark and their reflections shivering in the freezing water. I am so exhausted after my flights that I can barely lift my legs, but I keep on walking, following the path to the Visby wall. As I get closer I grow more and more anxious. My heartbeats grow faster and louder. It is past midnight and there is not a soul around. I pass rows of small houses, some half-timbered, preserved from the medieval period, others built later but keeping the same style. All the windows are lit with candle-shaped lights.

Every now and then I spot a small lantern or a candle burning on the front steps of a tiny house.

I walk and walk, taking deep breaths. The cobblestone streets, the narrow laneways, the smell of wood smoke, the cold fresh air in my lungs: it all feels achingly familiar.

My path takes me to Lilla Strandporten. Two stone sheep greet me in silence. I touch the arch, and feel its pain. I hear what it had heard, I see what it had seen.

There is a rustle in the bush next to the stone sheep. My eyes search the area but I see nothing. I continue walking.

It is nearly 3 am when I finally return to my hotel. I collapse onto the bed and stare at the ceiling until I fall asleep.

I wake countless times in the night. Each time I sit up, feeling that this is all nothing but a dream. I get out of bed, look out the window: yes, the harbour is still glowing in the dark. A giant Gotland ferry is snoozing by the pier. *I really am in Visby*, I say to myself.

On the stroke of 7 am, I head downstairs for breakfast and a strong coffee. I am the only one in the dining area, but I hear the clatter of pots and pans in the kitchen. When I get up to make a fresh cup of coffee, I look through the little kitchen window and see the back of the hostess's head. She is wearing her thick blonde hair in a single plait.

A few minutes later she enters the dining room carrying a basket of rye bread hot from the oven. I smile at her and her serious face lights up.

'God morgon,' she says.

'Hello!' I say in English. 'I'm Tishtar, visiting from Australia.'

'Oh! Hello, I'm Veronica. All the way from Australia!' She too is intrigued by my visit to Visby in the coldest month of the year. 'Well, welcome. We have a few guests, so you will bump into them shortly. Enjoy your breakfast.'

She goes back to the kitchen, and I sip my coffee.

After a while she comes out of the kitchen again and looks at me curiously. 'Why Visby?' she asks. 'Why now?'

'I'm trying to piece together an old story,' I say. 'I have six days to find out as much as I can about this town.'

Veronica frowns. 'What do you want to know?'

'I am interested in life in Visby around the time of the Battle of Visby.'

She purses her lips and wipes her hands on her apron. I'm not sure if she thinks I am having her on. 'You have come all the way here for that? Surely, you could have found what you wanted online!' She pauses. 'Hmm. Wait one moment!' She rushes to a narrow bookshelf in the corner of the dining area, peers at the spines and grabs a book. She returns and pulls up a chair near mine.

She places the book in front of me.

'But it's in Swedish!' I say.

'Okay, then I will tell you what I know,' she says. 'Where we are meeting today, inside the medieval wall is where all the noble families lived. My ancestors, the local fishermen and farmers, lived outside the wall, they had very little or no access to the city centre unless they had a stall at the local market. They were always very careful not to get into trouble with the law for there would be harsh punishment.'

'Tell me more about crime and punishment in those days.'

'The wall that you see all around the inner town was built by the merchants to protect their assets and warehouses,' Veronica says. 'Stealing and adultery were considered serious crimes. If one was accused of stealing something or for taking a woman without her family's approval, he would go under the guillotine or he would have to pay a hefty fine. Most people didn't have a lot of money to pay big fines so would end up losing their heads. This wall is a tourist attraction today, but it has a painful history. When you walk along it you will see that some parts have crumbled: even the stones could no longer bear the pain, and collapsed over the centuries.

'The new settlers trampled all over our land. Their wealth and power gave them the license to do whatever they liked, at the expense of the rightful owners of the land. They received no share of the island's growing prosperity.

'But despite the increase in trade and the regular movement of large commercial ships in and out of the port, the farmers focused on their harvest and the fishermen continued to ply their trade; they knew the temper of the sea, its good days and bad, its currents and its waves, just like their ancestors did.' Veronica suddenly stops. She checks the time and says that she has to go back to her tasks in the kitchen. 'Go! Go now, you must see as much of the town as you can before it gets dark!'

'Dark? It's not even eight o'clock!'

'Ah, it's winter. The sun sets at about three in the afternoon!' she says. 'Now, there is a monument outside the southern part of the wall in honour of those who lost their lives in the battle of

Visby. They say the blood spilled streamed down the hill to that spot. You must see it. Go!'

Then she hurries back to the kitchen.

I go back to my room and put on so many layers of warm clothes that I am almost unable to move.

Stepping out of the front door I almost take a tumble. The front steps are slippery with ice and I don't have proper snow shoes on. To my right is a narrow street that leads to the town centre, but I head towards the harbour again, following the route I had taken the previous night. I walk along the water. The seagulls have woken up and are flying in small groups over the Baltic Sea. Occasionally I can hear the clanking of a bicycle chain as someone glides past. A cat peers at me from atop a wall. Otherwise, the town is quiet. I follow the wall, reading various explanatory signs that have been erected for tourists.

I cannot get Veronica's voice out of my head. If one was accused of taking a woman without her family's approval, he would go under the guillotine . . . I think of the horror Valentin would have experienced having been accused of taking advantage of Gretel, how helpless she would have felt witnessing her father's refusal to grant him pardon.

Suddenly I hear footsteps behind me. It sounds like someone is out for an early morning jog, and so I move aside to make room. But no one passes me. I look around but the sound of footsteps has stopped. Blaming my fatigue and jet lag, I keep going. A few seconds later I hear the footsteps again. I halt. The footsteps stop too. *I am not going mad*, I tell myself. I resume walking. The footsteps are still following me.

I keep walking until I reach the northern part of the wall. Now the trees and the grass are bathed in sunshine. At the top of a hill I pause. From here I can see the dark blue waters of the Baltic Sea shimmering in the sun. I head towards the promenade. I feel a heaviness in my chest, a terrible pain, as though an eagle has seized my heart with its talons.

I finally reach the foreshore, and walk along the water. There is a gentle breeze bringing small waves to the shore. I stand and listen to the pebbles rolling with the tide. The seagulls are circling, and a pair of white swans float gracefully on the water.

I can hear nothing and everything at the same time. I see a small fishing boat anchored a bit further up. I am sure that I see a lone figure behind an old tree; his shadow stretching along the wall like a needle. Something draws me to him; I start walking and the shadow retreats from me. I stop, wondering if he would prefer to be left alone. But then he slows and turns his head slightly as if to check that I am following. We keep walking in silence until we arrive at the outskirts of town. The figure enters a small farmhouse on top of a hill overlooking the Baltic Sea. He closes the door behind him.

A humble cottage built of wattle and daub, with a thatched roof, rests on a parcel of farmland. It is exactly as Gretel had described Valentin's family home, with a rosehip bush out the front and ivy climbing the sides.

There is a walnut tree a few metres away, and I go and sit on the old timber bench beneath it. I am gazing out to sea when I hear the creak of the cottage door as it opens and then shuts. I stay still and silent.

Then, a voice speaks: 'I spent a lifetime nursing the tree of my dreams, watched it spread its limbs, looked on as it grew tall and proud, dressed in colourful tales. Then the autumn chill arrived, unannounced. It unleashed its angry wind and ravaged my tree. The tree trembled in fear; it shivered as it was stripped naked. Some leaves flew far away, out of reach, out of touch, out of sight. Others stayed close, crept close to one another, lost their colour and soul, dried up and broken. Whatever happened to my tree of dreams?'

The voice falls silent, and its owner takes a seat next to me. He smells of wood smoke. From the corner of my eye I catch a glimpse of his auburn curls. I turn to face him nervously. He is wearing a black tunic. It is the young man I saw on the train platform the last time I spoke with Gretel. He stares blankly at a spot between dreams and clouds. I can't quite follow his gaze; it is not of this world. My chest tightens as I realise it is Valentin. Tears start streaming down my face, and strong emotions wash through me. I wipe my tears with my sleeve, and then notice that my companion is gone.

I glance back at the cottage. Its door is wide open and it is dark inside.

I start walking again until I arrive at Lilla Strandporten. The old gate looks just as beautiful as it did the night before. I touch the wall and feel it is weeping inside. A modern hotel has been erected immediately behind it. The guests inside would be admiring the beauty of the gate and enjoying its proximity to the promenade, no doubt. I can almost hear cameras clicking, capturing happy snaps to upload to various social media platforms. Do the cameras also capture the pain and the hurt that has been washed away with time? The loss of innocent lives? The bloodshed? The betrayals, the acts of cruelty, the broken hearts? Could technology ever advance to a point where it can capture the invisible?

I walk up the narrow laneways towards Stora Torget. St Karin's is still standing tall. I have arranged to meet a local guide, Jon, who has agreed to show me the interior of the church.

'This church was stunning back in the day!' says a man who I take to be Jon as he climbs out of his car.

'It is breathtaking still—the savagery of time has not diminished its beauty and charm,' I respond passionately.

Jon smiles as he unlocks the front gate. He seems very know-ledgeable as he recounts the history of this monastery, as he refers to it. He unlocks a heavy wooden door and asks me to follow. I walk through it after him. The sun is shining through the broken roof, casting shadows on the floor. Jon starts to describe the religious services that once took place in what are now ruins. He points at the stone basin that would have been used for baptism.

'Where is the upstairs room?' I ask.

'Oh, we will go there in a second. I must turn the lights on first.'

We climb up a small set of stairs and enter the room where the monks would have slept. I picture Geirdís sitting near the small window calling to Odin.

Jon suddenly stops. 'Wait—how did you know there was an upstairs room? Have you been here before?'

I don't know how to respond. 'I must have read it somewhere,' I say. I hope he won't ask any more questions, am relieved when his phone rings. He excuses himself to take the call and leaves me alone. I stand in the small room where Stjärna and Gretel whispered to each other in fear. I can almost hear the monks downstairs, chanting. I sense Geirdís's big brown eyes darting about in the dark as she rocks back and forth, whispering, '*Inhabited this land shall be . . . Guti shall Gotland claim . . .*'

I look through the small window and I am sure that Valentin is standing in the middle of the square outside. He seems puzzled.

☾

Every day I search for Gretel in vain. The silence is deafening. I walk by the water, I walk along the wall, I walk through the trees, but I hear nothing. She has vanished into the past. Have I upset her spirit? Have I gone too far?

On my last day in Visby, I decide to hire a car and drive out to Tofta Beach. I pass a densely forested nature reserve and picture Valentin and Gretel in the abandoned cabin a few kilometres outside the town. I park the car near a kiosk and start walking towards the beach.

Snow has covered the sand, a soft powdery coat set against the steel-blue backdrop of the sea. The sun is a faint yellow circle high in the sky, too shy or too cold to emerge.

I walk until I reach a fishing hut. Its door is open, and I walk in. There is a stool near the window overlooking the Baltic Sea. I hear a sigh.

'So, you finally came,' the voice says.

My heart leaps out of my chest.

She is wearing a black dress, looking at the horizon. I can only see her silhouette in the darkness of the cabin.

She looks at me, her expression unreadable.

'Gretel!' I say, my voice quavering. 'I've turned over every stone for answers. I have talked to the stars, the waves, the clouds, the sunsets, the moon. I searched every corner, every day. I waited and waited to see you again, and here we are. I have found you and you are still out of reach.'

She doesn't say a word. She gets up and walks out of the cabin. I run after her. 'Please come back,' I beg.

'There is nothing left to say,' she whispers as she walks away.

When I step outside it is snowing and I can't see anything; Gretel has been swallowed by the thick fog and the snow. The temperature is plummeting fast.

The snowfall is growing heavier, and I can barely stand under the weight of it. I sink to my knees on the frozen beach.

☾

When I return from Tofta Beach, I go to a small grocery store near the hotel and buy myself a bottle of mineral water. It is a cold evening and the air in Visby is so still that the whole town appears frozen. I turn in early, pulling the big fluffy doona over my ears and watching the snowflakes melt against the window. My bones slowly warm up.

I lie awake for a long time; as fatigued as I am, sleep eludes me.

In the end I decide to go for a walk and catch a last glimpse of Visby at night. I rug up and leave the hotel. Icy snowflakes brush against my face as they dance in the cold night air. Some melt there; others fall to my shoulders.

I reach the top of the hill, where I had sat a few days earlier and Valentin spoke to me for the first and last time.

Candles are burning inside the cottage. A small stream of smoke drifts from the chimney. Through the window, I see the light of a lantern. I walk towards it.

As I draw near, the front door opens and a face looks out: it is an elderly woman. I gasp when she addresses me.

'Oh, Valentin,' she says. 'Good, you are home. I was getting worried.'

Beckoning me inside, she turns and shuffles back to her chair near the fire. A dog lies at her feet, licking its paws. I take a deep breath and enter the cottage.

'Make the boy a hot drink, Stjärna,' the old woman says.

I glance to see who she is addressing. Stjärna tilts her head and smiles at me. Her blue eyes twinkle in the low light. I feel I am disintegrating into the air: she is as beautiful as Gretel had described her; even more so.

'I will do it right now, Geirdís,' she says.

I swallow. I can hear my heartbeat inside my head.

Geirdís gets up and goes to the window again. I try to move aside but my feet are pinned to the floor. She stands next to me, examining the darkened sky with anxious eyes. 'Oh Valentin, look at those menacing clouds out there ... I hope your father is safe out in that stormy sea. But I must not fear, for he is an experienced seaman. He should return soon; he would have caught many fish today. Your grandfather used to say that stormy days in mid-winter are the best time to fish. Very dangerous, but fruitful.'

I glance at Stjärna and she smiles.

'Is your mother still out on the farm?' Geirdís asks. 'She'd better be coming in or she will get snowed under. Those angry clouds are not going to wait for her to finish her chores. Maybe you and Stjärna can go and give her a hand. What do you say, Guti?'

I can't utter a word; I stand frozen.

Stjärna comes and wraps her arms around Geirdís and leads her back to the chair, 'Now, my dear Geirdís,' she says, 'I will make us a hot drink and we will sit here and watch the snow together.' She spreads a green blanket on the old woman's lap then pulls out a stool for me and places it next to the fireplace. 'Here, sit and warm yourself. You have been out in that cold all night,' she says, smiling at me. I hold her gaze; her eyes so blue and her smile so warm, like none I have never seen before.

Stjärna returns to the kitchen, still talking. 'Oh, look, I'm going to make us rosehip and cherry blossom tea. Rosehip from our own bush right outside and cherry blossoms from the tiny tree out there too. Our land is very generous to us, isn't it? We get everything from it.'

Stjärna comes back with three cups and sits on the floor between Geirdís and me. She hands me a cup. My fingers touch hers; her hand is warm and soft.

'*Everything in ring is bound.*
Inhabited this land shall be;
Guti shall Gotland claim . . .'

Geirdís recites the lines quietly while gazing at the steam rising from her cup. She takes one sip of her tea and closes her eyes. I watch her chest rise and fall, the fire hissing and sighing next to her.

Stjärna puts another blanket on Geirdís's lap and says, 'Your poor Mårmår doesn't remember anything. She has forgotten the ordeal that we have gone through. But I think it's good that she doesn't recall. She must be at peace, if she doesn't remember that everyone has been killed.'

She kneels next to me, puts her head on my knee and takes my hand. 'Oh, Valentin, what happened to us?' she asks. 'That dark day in July when the enemy ripped us apart, they took all our dreams away, they drowned our souls. I feel as if I died over and over again during that horrific time.

'But you know, Valentin, ever since I was a little girl I knew we were meant for each other. Mama told me that the night you were born the white star shone in the sky. It was a sign from our ancestors, their way of showing us the path. When I was born a year later the white star hung low in the sky, so they named me Stjärna. Geirdís made sure that our parents followed the path shown by the spirits. That's how it was decided that we were meant for each other. And as you grew into a man, I watched you chopping wood and I felt a tingling in my heart. I thought of becoming your wife. I pictured you ploughing our small parcel of land in warmer months, sweat dripping from every strand of hair onto your face. I imagined you returning from the sea in winter with lots of fish. I would prepare meals for us from what we grew and the fish you caught.

'At night I lay in bed and dreamed of you holding me in your strong arms. I'd close my eyes and breathe in your scent. That strong smell of wood smoke and seaweed. Oh, the thought of being with you. To feel your body pressing against mine, the taste of sea salt on your face, your beard rubbing against my neck, the warmth of your breath on my lips.

'But while my heart was on fire, yours grew cold, and instead made room for another woman. She emerged like a mermaid and threw all my hopes and dreams into the stormy sea.

'When the battle broke out and you joined the men to fight for our land, all I wanted was for you to come back safe, to live, even if you would be sharing your life with someone else. But the battle was worse than I could ever have imagined; so many of our people were slaughtered. I don't even know what happened to dear Papa; he never came back.

'When those evil men tortured and killed our mothers, my whole world collapsed. It was a nightmare I couldn't wake up from. Oh, how many times I wished I had been killed too.'

She speaks softly, her eyes wet with tears. I squeeze her hand and stroke her soft hair.

'I'm so sorry,' is all I can say.

She takes a deep breath and continues: 'When those violent men entered my body, I closed my eyes and imagined giving myself to you. I pictured you amid all the bloodshed. I thought to myself, *If he can throw his body in front of their swords to defend Gotland, I can brave the dreadful men who are invading me.* It makes me ill to imagine how many women and girls they claimed.

'I don't even know which one of them fathered the bastard I lost. It's for the best that the child died, so it didn't have to live a life of shame. I don't even know how I survived. Those dear nuns took care of me in my darkest hours. And then, when I had regained some of my strength, your dear uncle brought me here and helped me and your Mårmår to feel safe again. He provided us with shelter and love. I owe him my life. Who would have thought that your uncle would be the one to look after us? A merchant caring for simple peasants like us.

'And now here we are, you and me—together. I have been waiting for you, Valentin. I have counted so many days, weeks and months waiting for you to return. Please tell me that you are here to stay. We can start all over again. Let us claim Gotland back—our island home is calling us. I know you've given your heart to Gretel, but she is gone now. Let her go. She isn't coming back. Let us do what the spirits wanted us to do from the moment we were born. Open up your heart and let me in, that's all I ask of you.' She holds my gaze. Her blue eyes set my heart on fire.

'Maybe another life, my love,' Geirdís whispers under her breath. Her eyes are barely open, her face is calm. 'Maybe another time.'

I rest my head on Stjärna's. I inhale her scent: she smells of rosemary and wood smoke.

'Stay with me,' says Stjärna.

I want to say something, but I can't. I want to hold her in my arms and tell her how I have been searching for her, longing for this moment, all my life.

I want to tell her everything, but the words won't come.

Instead, I reach into my pocket and find the chain with the sun wheel pendant. I fasten it around her neck, kiss her hair, then pull away from her warm hands and leave.

☾

All the lights are out when I arrive back at the hotel. The receptionist has left a few tealights burning in the foyer. The smell of roast meat from the dining room is lingering in the air.

I go to my room and crawl under my doona, shutting myself off from the world. I bury my face in my pillow and, sometime between the tears, I fall asleep.

When I open my eyes, I can see daylight creeping into the winter sky. I look around the room looking for Stjärna, but there is no sign of her. *She was here a heartbeat ago*, I tell myself. I gaze out the window. Snow has covered the trees; the nature strip outside the hotel is blanketed in white.

I look at my hands. I can still feel Stjärna's warm hands clasping mine. Through the night I felt the rhythm of her heart, and she whispered to me for hours, describing everything that had happened to her, to us.

I sit up in bed and look at the Gotland ferry sitting silently in the harbour. My flight for Stockholm leaves at 9.40 am; I still have time.

I decide to go for one last walk around town. Every day and every night I have walked the same path to Stora Torget to see St Karin's. I have seen it in the early morning light and at midday. I've photographed it at sunset and watched it be enveloped by the dark. I can't enter the church on my own—the gate stays locked in winter—but I lean my forehead against the iron and hold on to the bars, imagining Gretel's worried face as she climbs the stairs after spending the night with Valentin. I am even sure that I once heard Stjärna weeping upstairs and Geirdís's appeals to Thor for strength and the monks' prayers to God, each taking comfort in their own faith.

My final stop is Lilla Strandporten. Standing in front of this old gate is comforting and heartbreaking at the same time. I touch the arch, and we whisper to one another. I say that I wish she could hold me, and she says she wishes she could too, but she would crumble if she moved. I don't want her to crumble—she must stand tall: she needs to tell the story. There is always a compromise.

AUTHOR'S NOTE

FORTY NIGHTS IS A work of fiction. Whilst the characters in the novel are purely fictional, their experiences have been a recurring theme throughout history. Humans have lived through conflict, invasion and loss of culture and homeland for centuries. This book only scratches the surface; the real human tragedies are far greater than what this novel could ever capture.

All the major events in *Forty Nights* are reported in numerous reference books and sources. In setting the scenes in Iran, I have drawn from my personal knowledge. I have relied on many yarning sessions with my wonderful Somali friends who enlightened me on the experience of their people in war-torn Somalia.

To get the best understanding of life and major historical events in medieval Gotland, I consulted Professor Tore Gannholm, historian and author based in Visby. He generously provided me with academic references on the history of Gotlanders and information on life, language and trade in medieval Gotland.

I also received tremendous support from staff at Almedalen Library in Visby, Gotland and the National Library of Sweden in Stockholm who sent me numerous scanned articles and images and referred me to key historical records and references. I would like to particularly acknowledge the following sources which enhanced my knowledge of the history of the Gotlanders: *Ortnamn på Gotland*, Ingemar Olsson, 1923; *Guta Saga: The tales of the Gutes*, Maria Herlin Karnell, 2012; *An Isle of Sagas*, John Nihlén, 1931; *Medieval Manner of Dress: Documents, images and surviving examples of northern Europe, emphasising Gotland in the Baltic Sea*, Else Marie Gutarp, 2001; *Guta Lag and Guta Saga: The law and history of the Gotlanders*, Christine Peel, 2015

My trip to Gotland in February of 2018, which included personal guided tours of many historical sites in particular St Karin's Church and the Gotland Museum, complemented my research and consolidated my understanding of the history of this magical island.

I do not claim to be a researcher or a historian; however, I have done my very best to be as accurate as possible about the historical events across the lands featured in this novel. It has been my intention to honour the lives impacted by the cruelty of time and to remind us all of many voices lost in history. If I have failed my task in anyway, I seek forgiveness from the spirits who have been here before and those who are here today.

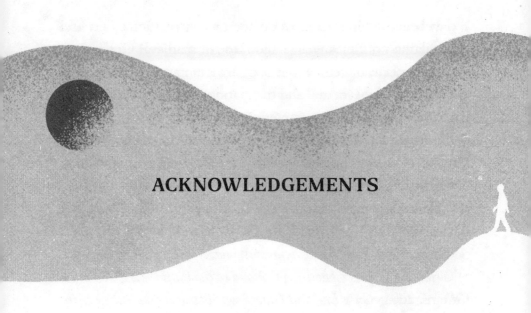

ACKNOWLEDGEMENTS

I AM DEEPLY HUMBLED to receive such overwhelming support from so many people near and far. When I started writing, never in my wildest imagination did I believe that I would publish this book one day.

My deepest gratitude to Aunty Di Kerr for welcoming me to Wurundjeri Country where we first met and yarned about my story. Norm Stanley, Nikki McKenzie and Corina Eccles, thank you for welcoming me to Wadawurrung Country and for sharing your stories with me.

My warmest *esso* to my Torres Strait Islander sister, Terori for all the *yarn-ups* and for giving me the gift of understanding water ceremony. My beautiful Aunty Jean, your gorgeous turtle painting has been my guiding spirit all through my writing journey.

My beloved Maman, you have been my inspiration all my life. In the darkest of times, your passion for literature was unwavering, as was your love and encouragement. Your memory is failing but I know that your heart will always remember me. How I wish you could be here to celebrate the publication of this book with me.

Emily Bitto, my beautiful mentor and dear friend, I am grateful for your generous support and coaching over the past few years. Thank you for guiding me to finesse the art of *showing not telling* and for being there for me all the way.

Big thank you to Sam Cooney for the pre-submission edits of my manuscript and for your passionate interest in my work.

Thank you to my agent, Grace Heifetz of Left Bank Literary for embracing my manuscript and presenting it enthusiastically to the publishing world; *for finding it a home.*

My lovely publisher Robert Watkins, thank you for receiving my dream of publishing this novel with your heart. Thank you for treating it with such care, respect and passion, and for ensuring that my voice was not lost in the publication process.

To the wonderful Ali Lavau, thank you for your impeccable copyedit and for your lovely feedback on my manuscript. You are simply the best!

George Saad, what can I say? Your design has left me breathless. Because of your magic touch, the book is now complete. I will cherish your art forever.

The lovely Ultimo team, from the bottom of my heart I thank each and every one of you for accepting me so warmly into your creative world. James Kellow, thank you for your kind and gentle approach. Brigid Mullane, thank you for your diligent management of the editing process. To Emily Cook and Katherine Rajwar, thank you for all your hard work behind the scenes to introduce me and *Forty Nights* to the literary world.

I thank all my dearest friends and family members from all corners of the globe who believed in me and cheered me on as I poured my heart in this story. In particular, my wonderful friend, Lillian, thank you for believing in me right from the start, for all the yarning, for the appraisal of my earlier drafts and for encouraging me all the way.

My very special thanks to my dearest friend and cultural sister, Habsa. Thank you for trusting me and for enriching my world views.

Last but most certainly not least, my lovely Rita. Thank you for putting your faith in me, for pushing me along when I lost hope; for your patience when I hid in the deep corners of my cave searching for answers, and for smiling when I danced with joy to silly things.

Nyatne (Thank you in Wadawurrung language).